T0357413

Love
&
RESISTANCE

KARA H.L. CHEN

Love & Resistance

Quill Tree Books
An Imprint of HarperCollinsPublishers

Library of Congress Cataloging-in-Publication Data

Names: Chen, Kara H. L., author.
Title: Love & resistance / Kara H.L. Chen.
Other titles: Love and resistance
Description: First edition. | New York : Quill Tree Books, [2023] |
    Audience: Ages 13 up. | Audience: Grades 10-12. | Summary:
    Seventeen-year-old Taiwanese American Olivia joins forces with a secret
    society of students intent on ending the school's culture around
    bullying--all while making friends and falling in love along the way.
Identifiers: LCCN 2022052158 | ISBN 9780063237834 (hardcover)
Subjects: CYAC: Bullies and bullying--Fiction. | Interpersonal
    relations--Fiction. | High schools--Fiction. | Schools--Fiction. |
    Taiwanese Americans--Fiction. | LCGFT: Romance fiction. | Novels.
Classification: LCC PZ7.1.C49733 Lo 2023 | DDC [Fic]--dc23
LC record available at https://lccn.loc.gov/2022052158

Typography by Laura Mock
23 24 25 26 27 LBC 5 4 3 2 1
First Edition

For

my parents, who made me   *and*   my husband, George, who
who I am   showed me the world. You
                                                       make everything possible.

Love
&
RESISTANCE

One

WELCOME TO PAINSTOWN

SURVIVING HIGH SCHOOL is all about strategy.

Your goal this day, as it is every day, is endurance. To do that, you must become invisible. Do not go to the cafeteria. Do not go to the science wing, where social media supernova Mitzi Clarke has a Monopoly-type reign over the real estate.

No.

If you are on the fringes, like me, you go to the bathroom first. You stay there until the pre-homeroom bell, and then you walk to your locker (briskly, but not running, as running will bring you attention, and attention is bad). Grab your books, then slide into your homeroom without making eye contact. The last is very important. Go from class to class, do not volunteer unless called on, and wait for the sweet final bell. Then you start all over again.

I know this because my mom's in the military. I've gone to four different schools in four different states. Trust me: in order to avoid long days of torment, you've got to be tactical. I've never been popular, but I've never had food chucked at me, either. I'm good at being stealthy. At one of my schools, I'm not even sure anyone knew my name; I was just The New Girl. I consider that one of my biggest successes. (Sometimes they called me The Asian Girl, which was obviously horrible, but c'est la vie.)

School number four, the predictably named Plainstown High School of Plainstown, Ohio, was . . . well, you know. Plain. I was both new and a junior, which was a terrible combination. Even worse, Plainstown had a closed lunch period, which meant that I was basically trapped on a battlefield, armed with nothing but overly preserved meats and small containers of nearly expired milk.

Sigh.

Getting through lunch now would take savvy, sophistication, brains. It was not for the amateur, or the weak. Luckily, I was neither.

The first objective: examine the terrain. Plainstown's lunchroom also doubled as its small assembly room, so it was filled with those long faux-wood lunch tables with the parallel fixed benches. Excellent.

The key to this sort of setup is the end seats. Never, ever sit in the center if you are trying to be invisible. First, you'll have to do that awkward leg swing over the fixed bench and will inevitably trip and land on your face. Second, you will be surrounded by people, most likely popular people, who will immediately notice you. That's no good. The most successful outsiders are those who can keep their exposed sides minimized and protected, kind of like countries in the middle of a land war.

Look here—you can see some kids have already caught on. I recognized a red-haired guy from my English class, an overly passionate defender of poetry, eating by himself at one of the ends. A few tables over, a quiet guy from my French class also secured an edge.

And then: problem. The rest of the safe spaces were occupied, which meant I would have to ask someone to scoot over so I could sit down. Crap.

Lightning decision: Who to ask? I scanned the seats: Poet Guy, French Guy, giggling BFFs (no), lovey couple (*no*)—gah, this was taking too long. Poet Guy or French Guy? French Guy didn't speak much, so he was less likely to tell me off.

Fine. Bonjour, mon nouveau ami.

I took my tray (school purchased lunch, perfectly average) and made my approach.

"Do you mind if I—?" I said.

French Guy was clearly startled that someone was speaking to him. He scooted to the left (no protest, good choice, Olivia!).

And then we proceeded to eat our lunch in silence, side by side.

By the end of the week, I no longer had to ask. French Guy (who I learned in class was named Monsieur Griffin, first name unknown) would silently scoot, we would silently eat our delicious school lunches, and then, at the bell, we would silently get up and go to our separate lockers.

I began to notice stuff about French Guy, since, well, I was smushed up against him for half an hour per day. One: he always wore a tiny pin on his backpack, a shiny red circle. I was dying to ask what it was for, but that would mean, you know, actually conversing, so no. Two: Monsieur Griffin was quiet, but he was expressive. Like when he saw Mitzi Clarke cut in line during lunch, he unleashed the most eloquent eye roll I had ever seen. He also had expressions for *Seriously?* (when the cafeteria posted a list of terrible cheese puns on Mac N' Cheese Day; he gave me a little smile when he caught me making a face at "Have a gouda day!"). A subtle smirk when he was amused (when I got overly excited about my french fries two days ago), and a blank expression for when he was trying to be invisible.

The last I couldn't quite get. Monsieur Griffin was handsome—not in a flashy kind of way, but he had a certain je ne sais quoi. He wasn't tall, but he was far from the shortest in the class; he was smart, but not a show-off; he wasn't exceptionally athletic, but he wasn't completely uncoordinated, either. He liked to wear these dark red Chucks and indie band T-shirts, which was interesting, but not particularly unusual.

I didn't understand what set him apart from everyone else, but it was clear he welcomed the distance. Some girls in class tried to speak to him, only to be politely, but firmly, rebuffed. In fact, the only person he seemed to converse with—and I use the term loosely, as scooting over on a cafeteria bench once a day was not really conversing—was me.

It kind of became my personal challenge, to make Monsieur Griffin communicate with me, even if it was non-verbal. It violated my rules against personal interaction, but I couldn't help myself.

I should have stuck to the rules.

Two

LE CRAP

MONSIEUR GRIFFIN AND I continued our little silent film relationship over the next week. On Tuesday, in French class, we were taught the vast and important difference between j'ai chaud ("I am hot") and je suis chaud ("I am in heat"). I reflexively glanced at Monsieur Griffin, only to find him also suppressing a laugh. I stared down at my notebook.

Two days of silent cafeteria scooting later and it was french fry day again.

I had taken my usual spot next to Monsieur Griffin, looking at my delicious fried potatoes with something that closely resembled—but was not quite—happiness, when he laughed next to me. It was a quiet sound, a small exhale, but it was unmistakable.

I looked at him; I couldn't help it. He shook his head,

grinning openly now, then wordlessly passed me his paper tray of fries.

I told myself that a hot guy giving me extra taters was not the best thing that had happened to me in a long while, even though it sort of was.

The combination of cute boy and fried starches was too much. I immediately retreated like a hermit crab into my shell and did not talk to or look at him until the next week.

We continued in our usual manner until:

- the following Wednesday, when we both laughed at the absurd sight of our French teacher in a giant plush Eiffel Tower hat. Monsieur Griffin now sat next to me in French class, sliding gracefully into the seat to my left a few minutes before the bell.
- two days after that, when we both grumbled after our teacher announced a pop quiz.
- the next week, when I passed him a pen after his ran out of ink.

Two days later, our French teacher asked me to conjugate the verb "boire."

"Je boire—" I had watched a TV special on the Battle of Kunyang last night instead of prepping for class. I now realized my night off was going to bite me in the derrière. Think, Olivia. Boire = to drink. Je = I. Je boire. I to drink? Wait, that can't be right.

Tiny head shake from Monsieur Griffin.

"Je mean—um, I mean . . ." I said.

Cue cough from him. He discreetly tilted his textbook and pointed at the word.

"Je bois," I said, and Mademoiselle Kowalczyk turned back to the board. I mouthed "Merci" to him.

Pas de probleme, he wrote, then turned the paper my way. Not a problem.

But it was. It was. Because then came mid-October.

Mademoiselle Kowalczyk announced a project: we were to pair up and present a report on a historical event in French history.

Group work. The bane of any wannabe invisible girl's existence.

"This assignment," Mademoiselle Kowalczyk said, "is to be done in pairs . . ."

Which will be assigned. Which will be assigned. Which will be assigned.

"Which you can choose! You have five minutes."

Ohhhhh crap.

There was no good way to play this. Avoiding eye contact and waiting for someone to approach me risked not getting picked by anyone and being publicly assigned a partner by the teacher. This was equivalent to dropping my trousers and writing *loser* on my own bottom.

Which left two choices: a) picking people in my immediate vicinity, or b) choosing someone I had previously identified as also being on the fringes.

Options: beautiful blonde girl who always spoke perfect French, complete with perfect accent. I hadn't seen her hanging around Mitzi, but her high ponytail marked her as a potentially aggressive popular type who could eat me for breakfast. No thanks. Second choice: a ghost groupie who followed Mitzi and her people. She was pale, she was silent, she looked like a hostage. No, thank you. Third: Monsieur Griffin.

I *know*. I hear you. Monsieur Griffin, Monsieur Griffin. Ask him! C'est simple, right? But I have to confess I was slightly off my game. Because asking him was . . . risky. Risky in the sense that I cared if his answer was oui or non.

In the middle of my mini existential crisis, I noticed Monsieur Griffin staring at me.

"Would you like to be partners?" It was one of the few times I'd heard him speak; his voice was quiet and amused.

I gave a small shrug, which was intended to be more of a light affirmation and less of a muscle spasm. Still casual, still salvageable. But then—as if I had a pollen-coated exclamation point wedged in my windpipe—a "sure!" flew out of my mouth.

Oh my God. Exclamation point.

But Monsieur Griffin just turned his desk towards mine.

It was odd to face him, since we were normally seated next to each other in the cafeteria and during class. He had a very subtle widow's peak, and a small mole on the side of his neck. Dark hair, which stuck up a bit on the right. Small Band-Aid wrapped around his left index finger.

The front of our French textbook had the question *Où allons-nous?* floating around the front. *Where are we going?* Monsieur Griffin had scribbled *Anywhere but here* in English on a small green piece of paper and taped it to the corner.

"Um," I said. "Any ideas about what we want to work on?"

"An exploration of the link between french fries and personal happiness?"

My laugh was a surprised blushing burst. I couldn't quite tell if Monsieur Griffin was smiling, but he did look pleased with himself.

I said, "I think this project is supposed to be historical. And about something related to France."

"Oh?"

"Yes."

"Historical," he said. "Something academic." Now I was positive he was holding in a laugh.

"Yes."

I felt a sharp bump to my chair. Mitzi Clarke was seated next to me and had pushed her chair into mine as she talked. She didn't apologize; she didn't even seem to notice.

Listen, I knew exactly who Mitzi Clarke was. My first order of business at any school was to find out about their social dynamics. Plainstown was super small, with only about fifty students per year. Mitzi and her top lieutenant, Adeline Jackson, formed a tight concentration of power at the top, with Mitzi at the pinnacle.

She bumped my chair again. She didn't notice, again. Irritation, spiky and hot, flared.

"So," Mitzi said to Adeline, "I think my mom has some old French souvenirs, from when she used to travel a lot. We can look after school."

"Your house?"

Mitzi shook her head. "No way. Mom's selling off more of our stuff. Everything's a mess. I'll bring the box to your place."

Mitzi scooted closer to Adeline and scraped against my chair. Again.

"Anyways," she said. "I'm working all weekend on the biology internship application. I don't care what Mr. Wagner says. I'm going to use my TikTok as an example of relevant work experience. I have a lot of responsibilities on there. Tons of multitasking, you know?"

Really. I had seen her website and social media sites. They were all about designer clothes, super-sparkly shoes, and the like. I wasn't exactly sure what that had to do with biology.

As I was thinking this, there may have been a small, tiny— remote—chance that my face did not remain as still as it should have. It wasn't a smirk, or the tossed grenade of a *whatever*. It was more like a very, very slight twitch.

But it was enough.

Mitzi turned towards me. She had perfectly highlighted brown hair and flat, reptilian blue eyes. As her gaze flitted over, then focused on me, I pictured a swinging bull's-eye over a fighter plane navigation system, the green light turning to red. The high-pitched whine of a target lock.

Oh no.

No no no no no.

"Did you make a face?" she said.

Options: Deny? Pretend I had accidentally swallowed some gum?

"No," I said.

"I think you did."

I shook my head.

"Do you think there's something funny about me trying to study bio?"

That seemed oddly aggressive. But then I remembered how our bio teacher, Mr. Wagner, once condescendingly dismissed one of Mitzi's answers in front of the whole class. Then, when Gilbert Paddack repeated the same thing, Mr. Wagner said it was great. Was it because she was a girl? Or an influencer?

Mitzi might have some well-justified reasons for her attitude, but that wasn't something I had time to think about. Mitzi was still staring at me, and I was trapped in the death zone.

"No." I quickly stuffed my papers into my backpack. The bell was supposed to ring. Why wasn't it ringing?

"I see" was what she said, but what I, and everyone else, clearly heard was: *Watch out*.

My carefully constructed life of invisibility was about to end.

Three

ISOLATIONISM, MY OLD FRIEND

I MIGHT HAVE survived. I may have spent the remainder of my days under the uncomfortable glare of Mitzi's impressively ferocious stink-eye, but I would have lived. I would have had to add a couple of U-turns to my class routes, taken a few more minutes in the bathroom, made a quicker exit here and there.

It should have been okay. At any other school, or with any other person, it would have been okay. But Mitzi Clarke was a supernova of influence and her power could not be denied. And that made all the difference.

A word about Mitzi.

You know the story: every school has a popular group, and every popular group has a ringleader. Sometimes it's the academics. Sometimes it's the athletes. Here, it was Mitzi Clarke and her BFF, Adeline Jackson.

Mitzi's mom was a former television and movie star actress,

and Mitzi had leveraged her mom's fame by starting her own hugely popular TikTok account, where she posted about fancy outfits and the latest fashion and makeup advice. She also posted videos of herself having cheerful lunches at school, waving to people in the halls, decorating for school dances with her friends. She had made her status as a popular high school student into an empire.

In addition to Adeline at the top of the hierarchy, there was a small knot of Mitzi's close followers—an outer ring of VIPs— who followed all her accounts and defended her against negative online comments. Those people sat at the popular table in the cafeteria, the one in the back that didn't get bothered by the foot traffic and food smells from the lunch lines. They parked in the closest parking lot to the school. Basically, they were the high school equivalent of countries with the Most Favored Nation status in the United Nations.

And then there was everyone else.

Normally, this would have been of only peripheral concern to me, as I preferred to keep my existence entirely separate from anything resembling human society. But the problem was when I made my petite erreur in French class, I lost the protection of my invisibility. I was on Mitzi's radar, and that was bad.

I didn't realize what a precarious position I was in at first, probably because Monsieur Griffin—first name Alexander, but he asked me to call him Griff—and I actually started talking during lunch.

I wasn't sure if our conversation would spill over outside of class. But it did, the next day.

Alexander—Griff—did his usual scoot in the cafeteria. His tray, I had noticed, was always filled with dishes that were similar—but not quite identical—to what the rest of us were eating. I was covertly studying his meal when he said, "Do you think Texas Straw Hat is a real dish or something they just make up back there?"

We both looked at my tray. Stale tortilla chips, topped by one round scoop of brown unidentifiable meat, limp lettuce strands, and pale pink tomato-like squares.

"I think they are not allowed to call them tacos for legal reasons." I was absurdly—on-the-edge-of-ridiculously—pleased when he laughed. Hold yourself together, Olivia!

But I couldn't quite manage it. It was an effervescent thing, the force of his attention.

"Have you thought of any new ideas for class?" he said.

I shook my head. "Have you?"

"The attempt by the French to take all the credit for fries?"

There's a moment when sarcastic people recognize each other. It's a rare but beautiful thing when this happens.

"The attempted coup of the french fry by Canadians with a lot of gravy?" I said.

Griff leaned back, delighted. "Poutine? Very impressive. We could bring samples to class."

"Yes. Nothing says extra credit like cheese curds and gravy."

"Exactly." Griff was apparently one of those people who liked to look at you directly when he talked. Unlike me, who liked to focus on the table or ketchup packets or sporks. "So, I might need your number."

"My . . . number?"

"To talk about the project."

He wanted my number? To . . . talk to me? About the project.

I slowly passed him my phone. He typed in *Griff,* deleted it, then typed in *Your Handsome French Partner.*

"Seriously?" I said.

Luckily, Griff didn't appear to notice that there were only two other entries in my phone, and both were for my mother.

"Your contact information should be accurate," he said. "Or else how are you going to remember me?"

"Yes, but which Handsome French Partner are you? I have so many."

"Touché. Also, ouch, Mademoiselle Chang."

I executed a perfect eye roll, and he laughed.

"All these weeks of silence, and I thought that you were just shy and modest," I said.

He leaned towards me and touched my arm with his fingertips. His eyes were dark green, with bursts of brown in their centers. "Nope."

Two thoughts pressed against me at the same time. One: despite Griff's self-imposed social isolation, he was clearly not a true outsider, like me. He was quiet but not awkward, softspoken but confident, a loner but not fearful. He was someone with nothing to prove. And that casual touch? Griff was no amateur in the act of flirting.

Second—and more important—he was interesting. I couldn't think of anything more dangerous.

* * *

I remained firmly committed to my invisibility tactics as we walked into French class. When Mitzi sighed loudly after I pronounced something incorrectly, I didn't react at all. I was impassiveness personified. I was impenetrable.

And when she tried to correct someone during the lesson (but totally gave him the wrong answer), I didn't even look in her direction. I could do this all day, all year. It might cause permanent damage to the muscles of my face, but it was totally worth it.

I did some research into what happened when others crossed Mitzi. She was apparently a fan of the carrot and stick; her supporters were exclusively invited to lavish parties thrown by Adeline (or, rather, Adeline's wealthy parents). But people who crossed Mitzi were a victim of some mysterious shaming mechanism that I didn't yet understand.

I didn't need to know the details. Lake View Middle School had already given me a college-level education in ostracism and aggression. That was before I had ruthlessly implemented my isolationist policies. I knew all about the abyss of social shame.

I was definitely too savvy for that to happen to me. Again.

Four

HOW TO HOIST YOURSELF
BY YOUR OWN PETARD

I CONTINUED MINDING my own business that afternoon. Our biology teacher, Mr. Wagner, had offered extra credit if we did an additional experiment after school. So now it was just me, my test tubes, and my beautiful ammonium carbonate.

I had just strapped on my ultra-stylish safety glasses when into the room walked one Mr. Alexander Griffin.

We stared at each other, then he smiled and dropped into the chair next to me. "So it's true: clear plastic does match with everything," he said.

Oh my God. I ripped my goggles off. "What are you doing here?"

Tone—accidentally hostile. Foot, right in mouth.

Griff didn't appear to notice. "Extra credit? Lab?"

Mr. Wagner must have offered it to all of his classes. A group of three girls wandered in and took seats in the back.

"Do you mind if I join you?" Griff said.

Sure + nope = soap, which was the word I blurted out before I grabbed my book from my backpack. Thanks for trying, brain.

But Griff just pulled out his lab notebook and said, "So your face does move."

"What?"

"You. In French today. What was going on there?"

He noticed? "Nothing."

"Overly engrossed with verb conjugation?" he said. "Constipated?"

"No!"

"Perhaps your meals are too potato heavy?"

"OMG!" I said. "Stop."

He laughed, and the other students looked at him curiously. Griff was normally silent in his classes and in the halls, so a laugh from him was like seeing a unicorn prancing through the multipurpose room.

I passed him a pair of goggles. He pulled them over his head and said, "Who says you can't be both comfortable and fashionable?"

I pointed at the chunk of his hair sticking up. "Um, you have ..."

Griff pulled at it, making it even worse. "Hmm?" He tugged at some strands trapped behind his goggles; they waved up and spilled over his forehead. He pointed at my pair when I snickered. "Are you seriously going to say no to those?"

I picked mine up again. Fine. "Watch out, Paris and Milan," I said, and tugged them on. Then Mitzi, Adeline, and their groupie wandered in.

As they say in France, merde. A whole big stinky pile of merde.

The door was way too far away and I had already set up my stuff. Dive under the table? I think that was only for earthquakes. Run to the bathroom? Too late.

It was time for some emergency maneuvers. I bent my head so my hair would cover my face. (Yes, I know that my hair color is instantly recognizable. This was basically like trying to take cover behind a miniature schnauzer, but I was panicked and out of options.)

Griff looked at me curiously but didn't say a word.

Mitzi strode forward, not noticing the other people in the room. Of course.

"I'll use this footage for the internship application," Mitzi was saying to Adeline. "It'll show Mr. Wagner how I can blend my two interests."

Mitzi began setting up a tripod and a portable ring light, but the three girls in the back were in her way. She sighed.

"Are you going to be long?" she asked.

One of the girls looked up and bumped the beaker next to her hand. The liquid sloshed onto the countertop.

"What?" Behind her goggles, the girl's eyes were huge.

"How long are you going to be here?" Mitzi asked.

"We . . . ," said another girl. "Mr. Wagner said we have this room until three? For the extra credit lab?"

Mitzi checked her watch. "I have a shoot at three. We'll film around you. That's not a problem, right?"

Griff and I looked at each other, but the trio in the back didn't say anything.

Mitzi started setting up her equipment, then stopped. "I'm so sorry, but can I ask you to scoot over? I need this corner."

The trio paused, then silently packed up their things.

"Thank you so much!" Mitzi chirped.

It was hard—even for me—to remain stoic. I don't think that Mitzi was trying to be mean. She just thought she was entitled to do whatever she wanted. Unbelievable.

Indeed, Mitzi was cheerfully chatting to Adeline and her groupie. She had totally moved on.

Griff lobbed me an acid-tipped *Really?*, then lined up our test tubes. Perfect—the sooner I could get out of here, the better.

One of the girls came by, and I silently handed her a set of tubes from the equipment shelf. She smiled slightly, but I could tell she was upset.

Mitzi and Adeline kept talking, oblivious. We couldn't help but overhear them, since the room had gone dead silent.

"Mr. Wagner says I need to get my grade up before I can apply," Mitzi said to Adeline. "Which is totally unfair since I have to skip class for my gigs. And I don't know why it's so important anyways. I'm just going to submit this video—he'll come around. Wait, put the light away from the window."

Adeline dragged it towards the table and adjusted the tripod. "It can't hurt."

"I mean, everyone knows his class is the hardest. And he only gives out four A's."

"It's ridiculous." Adeline started filming with her phone, panning around the room.

The girls on the side started doing their lab, talking quietly. One of them crouched next to the table, to make sure that the liquids in the beakers were level. The other one added a few drops to a test tube, then meticulously recorded the results.

Mitzi looked over at the girls, then at me for a hard second. She turned towards Adeline and said in a low voice, "Of course they're all here. They always wreck the curve."

Hold up.

What?

Mitzi went back to fiddling with her tripod, oblivious. She seemed to think she had just tossed a snarky comment to Adeline, but she was louder than she thought. We all heard it.

I glanced at the others, who I vaguely recognized from some of my classes: Meera Banerjee, Krisha Chaudhary, Carole Bitao-Allen. Krisha was frozen, her dropper poised over the test tube.

They?

"They" meaning people who were serious about studying? Or "they" meaning *Asian* people?

I had never talked to Meera, Krisha, or Carole before, but in this beat of stunned surprise, we were in perfect understanding. We shared a universal *Did I just hear that?* look. Wrecking the curve? Because—what?—all Asians are supposed to be smart?

What. The. Hell.

My mom, herself subject to countless acts of assholic micro-aggressions, once had a talk with me, right before I entered high school. I had already been crushed by Lake View, had bled and been scarred, but I had come up with the perfection solution: isolation. When I told her my plan, Mom looked at me for a long moment.

"Don't ever think it's you," she said, finally. "When racism happens. It's their issue and not yours."

My mom was the daughter of immigrants who had come to this country with nothing and was currently a lawyer for the military. She never took crap from anyone. But when it came to me, she would sometimes look intensely sad, like the world was a minefield and she had no idea how to carry me across.

She just hadn't fully realized my genius. Sure, for most of human history, isolationist policies were arguably selfish and irresponsible. However, they could definitely work for me. Absolutely.

Years later, that one phrase kept haunting me, though: *when it happens*. When. And I did see it, again and again, tiny bombs detonating around me as I swerved through my schools. Small explosions of bullshit.

I was already more visible than I wanted to be. I should curl up like a pill bug and live the rest of my existence rolling through the halls and ducking into corners.

But.

I come from a long line of justice-minded people. My mom volunteered at a pro bono clinic on the weekends, using her law degree to defend others. Her father, my grandfather, would always stand up if he witnessed something unfair, like if someone got overcharged or was being picked on. Maybe because his own life had been so difficult and hardly anyone had helped him. He would always fight, and if the English words wouldn't quite come, he would continue hollering in Taiwanese. Even if they yelled at him or made fun of him, he would never stand down.

I also come from a line of people who sometimes get mad and do things before they fully think about the consequences. So that was unfortunate.

"What did you just say?" I asked. The words popped out, quick as a thought, quick as anger.

I knew the precise instant I reappeared on Mitzi's radar. She stopped. Stared. Like I was a dog who had pooped on her lawn and had dared to come back the next morning.

"What?" she said. "I wasn't talking to you."

I had been doing so well—going to so many schools with my head down, slipping in between classes like a tiny, sneakered ghost. But this look on Mitzi's face was too familiar. Smug. Dismissive. Like she knew she could get away with what she said, because that's what she had always done, gotten away with it.

"You said, '*they* always wreck the curve,'" I said. "What is that supposed to mean?"

"I don't know what you're talking about. Why are you freaking out?" But an ugly red splotch was starting to form on the side of Mitzi's neck and on her cheeks.

"Are you saying that because we're Asian?"

24

"No." She refused to look at me, though. Then she muttered to Adeline, "Everyone knows it's true."

Mom had also always drilled into me the concept of *mea culpa*, taking responsibility for one's mistakes. And the three steps to a proper apology: Acknowledge the wrong. Sincerely apologize. Take action to do better.

Mitzi was failing on all fronts.

The rage heated and blew open before I could stop it.

"Don't try to blame anyone else if your grades aren't high enough," I snapped. Adeline was still holding up her phone, but I could see her response perfectly: shock, outrage. Then canniness, studying me closely. But I couldn't stop talking. "Maybe if you and underling junior here didn't spend so much time on your little TikTok videos, then you might have a chance in this class."

Their groupie bumped into me, sharply, before I could say more. Logic, cold and horrifying, rushed back in.

Griff's expression was one I had never seen before. I would tentatively describe it as a cross between *So this is happening!* and *Oh, shit*.

Indeed, I almost saw the words as they flew out of my mouth, like slow-moving particles of my own petard.

And when they landed, when those words burst over Mitzi like a popper from a confetti cannon, she didn't respond. She didn't need to. She simply turned her blazing wrath on me and *thwunk*.

I was a dead girl.

Five

HELLO, PARIAHVILLE

ONCE YOU ARE marked for social death, there is very little you can do to reverse the process. You can only try to extend your time on earth.

I had the disease, and it was terminal. Suddenly, my comfortable life of invisibility ended.

It started small at first. Stares as I got off the bus. Whispers swelling behind me as I went to class. My personal space bubble increasing from six feet to about half a mile as people veered out of my way. Due to my tactical error (aka My Big Mouth), I went from blessed anonymity to back in the trenches. I began to employ full-on evasive maneuvers, sweating all the way.

I was the gopher that had stuck her head out of the hole when everyone else was hiding. Now I had a target on my head, and it was only a matter of time until it got bashed in.

My smartest move now would be to lie low for a long while, possibly until the end of time.

I started slipping to the bathroom in between classes and arriving at school right before the bell. I grimly rucked through the halls with all of my books in my backpack, avoiding any people. If this was urban warfare, this was me strapping on my helmet, ducking behind corners, and crouching behind dumpsters. Goal: don't be seen. No straight shots.

But it still wasn't enough.

My grandfather had been in the army before he left Taiwan, and had been a history and military buff his whole life. Before he died, he used to tell me stories every night before I went to sleep. Our favorite thing to do was to talk about war strategies, and how often the best way to win a war was to avoid it.

But sometimes, you can't. Sometimes it comes to you, whether you want it to or not. Sometimes you lose your temper and insult people instead of making the point you really wanted to make.

Sometimes you bring the war onto yourself.

It had felt so right to call out Mitzi. I didn't do it in the best way, *true*, but was it wrong to speak up?

Obviously, yes. Twelve-year-old me had tried it at Lake View Middle, and it had been an equally bad idea back then.

Lesson—totally not learned.

Mitzi didn't post an ad with my face on it and ask her followers to virtually launch themselves at me. No, that was too direct and easy. Rather, she let her friends know that she was having a rather unpleasant disagreement with yours truly. That I, *out of the blue!*, had freaked out and insulted her.

Mitzi didn't say more; she didn't have to.

If Mitzi was having a fight with me, then, by definition, everyone who talked to me would be, in a sense, crossing Mitzi. This was the George W. Bush doctrine of governance, where everyone was either for or against you. That stance wasn't quite ideal for American foreign policy, but in the tiny, closed jurisdiction of Plainstown High, it was shockingly effective.

I don't know how I had somehow forgotten about this basic theory of international—and teenage—relations. Maybe it was because I had no friends of my own. In any event, when this finally happened to me, I was completely unprepared, even though I shouldn't have been.

My afternoon started out deceptively well. I saw Mitzi by the lockers, and she was chatting with her friends, benignly. They always walked in the center of the hall, not bothering to check if they would bump into anyone; they knew people would move.

There wasn't anywhere to hide. The hallway was almost empty, and it would be obvious if I flat out ran away, even though that's what I wanted to do. I settled for the very effective method of hoping they wouldn't see me if I didn't look their way.

And then—miraculously—they passed. They didn't even seem to notice I was there.

Okay! This was going to be okay. I would file this under "PLEASE REMEMBER: DO NOT LOSE YOUR SHIT

NEXT TIME," then I would dive back into my gopher hole. Perfect plan.

I walked—some might say strolled, even—into sixth-period study hall. Things were great. Part One of Operation Survival was to Become Invisible. That was still on. Now it was time to push Part Two: Get the Hell Out of Dodge. I had a plan: make a checklist for my college application requirements, start drafting my personal statements, and research how to graduate early.

Plainstown High sucked in just about every way one could measure suckage, but at least this school sent a lot of students to Georgetown, which had one of the country's top programs in international relations. It would be the place where I could finally focus on studying what interested me most: governments. Power dynamics. But what I really wanted to know was this: Why did some countries—or people—have it better than others? And why were some—like my grandfather—forced to continually struggle?

College was going to be my salvation, a way out of the closed system of high school. I figured out long ago that our core problem was that we were all forced to be in the same classes, buildings, lunch periods. We were heated molecules of gas in a tiny sealed jar, with no option but to bounce off each other, sometimes violently. But if you opened the container, if you allowed those atoms to go into the open air, suddenly there was freedom.

I wanted to be that small escaping particle.

This is what I needed to do: apply early decision next fall, get my diploma, then au revoir. In about a year I would be in Washington, DC, away from all of this nonsense. I just needed to keep my head down and survive. That was all.

Turns out it was not so easy. Especially in study hall, which was basically like recess in supermax prison, overseen by a guard with an obsession with Pinterest.

Next to me, this kid from my AP Psych class was leaning back in his chair, staring at the ceiling. He was one of the few other Asian students at this school, and he never talked. Occasionally, he scowled at people. He was terrifying.

I had pulled out my notebook and was taking some notes when Adeline hissed my name. I—foolish me—looked over. Adeline flashed her phone screen, smirking. On it was a homemade video of me confronting Mitzi, only she had drawn horns on my head and flames in the background. It was playing in a horrifying loop.

That was bad enough, but it wasn't what I was focused on. I was looking at the two black flecks superimposed on my face, the thin lines added over the corner of my eyes, exaggerating the shape.

This was not whispers or shunning, which were annoyances to be endured. No. This was almost physical, like a person on a bicycle swiping at you with a knife. Slice and go. It took a few seconds for me to process my shock.

The only other Asian person in the room—the boy— glanced over at Adeline. Then he stopped and stared. Unlike me, he didn't have to stop and think; he sprang to his feet.

"What. The. Fuck. Is. That," he said.

"Mr. Choi!" Our study hall teacher didn't bother to stand. I guess taking a break from scanning Pinterest counted as taking things seriously around here. "Language!"

The boy pointed at Adeline, but she had already slipped her phone into her purse. "Did you see that racist shit, Ms. Holly? Isn't it your job to pay attention around here?"

"Mr. Choi. Office!"

He glared at Adeline and she recoiled. Then he gave me a short bro nod. Asian solidarity. I managed to give him an appropriate nod back before he slammed out the door.

This suppressed humiliation was all too familiar. I had learned, the hard way, that if someone wanted to target me, the most obvious, easiest, and most devastating thing to do was to shove aside my personhood and make me nothing but the shell of an *other*.

Adeline had been in the background when I had called out Mitzi. She had been studying me, trying to decipher what suddenly made me so confrontational. I now knew why. With her attack on my race, on *me*, Adeline shot her missile right into the only soft spot in my armor. And in this moment, I knew she realized it.

Later that afternoon, Adeline passed by my locker and waved the video in my face.

This time, I was ready; I knew what she was capable of. I knew the drill: keep a blank expression as a part of me died; slowly continue to put my books back into my locker, even as my face got hot with something that felt fucking close to shame.

The beautiful blonde girl from my French class came striding down the hall, unsmiling. There was something in her hand. As she came closer, she merged into the crowd of kids passing us. Adeline was too busy laughing to notice when the girl snapped a quick video of her, then palmed her phone. But I saw it.

"Gotcha," she said. Then she was gone, ponytail swinging.

That night, I got an email from an unknown address. There was only one line in the message: a link to an anonymous video, which had been released to various social media platforms. It showed Adeline taunting me, and then somehow—incredibly—showed the video itself, which hadn't been posted. Had someone hacked her phone? I tried to look up the email sender and see who was behind all of the accounts, but I couldn't figure it out.

The clip was already going viral. At first, Adeline tried to defend herself: Come on, seriously? I was kidding. She was the one who freaked out and insulted our TikTok accounts. Other comments started rolling in: Why is this a big deal? Don't we have bigger things to worry about? A bunch of people called her out for what she had done to my eyes, but then another group came back in the comments: The rice squad is strong tonight.

By midnight, all of Adeline's accounts went on hiatus.

I woke the next morning and was quiet at breakfast. I knew I had insulted Mitzi with my little jab at her TikTok empire, and really, I was sorry. I expected some pushback. But not this.

My mom knew better than to press, and she would never, ever say I told you so. But she had been right.

When it happens.

I had covered my eyes like a child playing hide-and-seek, who thought she was hidden from others as long as she couldn't see them. But they could see me; they could always see me.

"Is there something that you'd like to talk about?" Mom asked.

But I didn't have the words for her, a way to explain the churning mess of feelings. I knew, too, that she was always working, tirelessly treading so she could keep both our heads above water, especially after Dad left. I didn't want to be the added brick in her arms.

So I said I was fine, even though it was far from true.

At school, people whispered about Adeline, but no one wanted to talk to me directly. Which was ideal, as far as I was concerned.

In French class, I tried to make eye contact with the ponytail girl, but she pointedly did not look at or speak to anyone, including me. Same with the guy from my study hall. It was as if none of it had really happened.

This was all kind of inexplicable and weird, but that was Plainstown. I had noticed other strange things, like when Casey Ortega kept getting cornered at their locker (they having the misfortunate to be located alphabetically in between Joanna Orteau and Meredith Ortermeyer, the most ornery of Mitzi's VIPs), they received a mysterious note from the office telling them their locker was being relocated to a safer part of the school. When Aaron Kaminski was mocked by Brett Clifton for being scared of a spider in bio class, the next day Brett opened up his car door and hundreds of plastic tarantulas spilled out. They could hear Brett's screams all the way across the parking lot and in the hallways at school.

Whatever. I would take help wherever I could get it. No matter what happened from now on, I needed to take shelter in my gopher hole. Military strategists called this the art of non-engagement. It wasn't surrendering so much as wisely coming back to fight another day. Or never. That was also an excellent option.

But when Adeline was forced to shut down her accounts, even for a short while, it became an escalation of the worst kind. I just didn't know it at the time.

A few days later, I was in the lunch line when someone bumped my shoulder. It was Griff.

"Ms. Chang."

"Mr. Griffin."

"May I accompany you through the lunch line?"

"You may?"

Griff was suspiciously cheerful. "How disappointing they don't have Tuna Surprise today. It's Friday."

"Every day is a surprise. Is this real food? Is it not? It's a surprise!"

Griff gave his little huff of a laugh, then examined the menu. "Do you mind if I go first?"

I shook my head.

"Hi, John," Griff said to the man behind the counter. "How are we doing?"

"Same old. What's our project today, Griff?"

"We'll be having two: one for me and one for my friend,

Ms. Chang, please. Two taco shells, without meat. Two bowls of chili. Tomatoes from the salad, but no lettuce. And do you have cheese?"

"Yup. I can get some slices."

"Perfect. Thank you."

John disappeared to the back, and I said, "I thought you have to take what they give you."

"Oh, Livvy," Griff said. "We never *have* to take anything."

When I first met him, Griff seemed to exist in a separate social sphere, which was strictly occupied by a party of one. However, since we'd started talking, he'd begun to wear a different expression with me: an intoxicating mix of admiration and amusement. I didn't like to think about a) how much I had studied him in order to actually notice this, or b) how almost-like-happy this made me feel.

"Well, regardez, Mademoiselle Chang." Griff sat at our usual spot, then carefully smushed a part of his taco shell into his paper tray. He poured chili over it, then sprinkled tomatoes and cheese bits on the top. He then did the same with mine. "It's no Texas Straw Hat. But it's almost edible, I think."

It was more than that; it was close to—dare I say it—tasty. That was a word I never previously associated with school lunches.

"Impressive." I took a large bite.

Griff shrugged, but I could tell he was pleased with himself. "I've had to cook a lot of my own dinners."

"Same," I said, and Griff looked surprised. "But I would not have thought to add chili."

"Brilliance comes in many forms."

"So what are you calling this masterpiece?" I asked. "Griff Straw Hat?"

"Chilaco Delight?"

"Perfect."

On the other side of the room, Adeline and Mitzi were whispering together, and Mitzi kept squinting at me. That was not ideal. Adeline had been furious since her accounts had been shut down, but she now looked darkly thrilled that Mitzi was coming to her defense. You couldn't see the bond between Mitzi and Adeline tightening as they united against a common enemy, but it was there.

After I had called out Mitzi, a few people started acknowledging me in the halls. It was subtle—small nods here and there. The occasional tiny smile. I mostly ignored them, but Mitzi noticed. She was not happy about it.

This was bad. My grandfather had told me all about oppressive governments, how they closely monitored potential threats and signs of dissent. It made sense; if you have set up an inherently unfair system, the last thing you can allow is unrest. But I wasn't a threat. I was a hermit crab.

"Are you doing okay?" Griff asked. He carefully arranged bits of cheese on his chili, not looking at me.

There really was no okay, was there? Once the vase falls to the ground, there is only glue and scarring.

"I'm fine." It's what I told my mom after what I had endured at Lake View, it was what I said after Dad left, it was the burning lie I held on to after Grandfather died. It was the easiest thing for others to hear, so that's what I said.

But Griff didn't let it go. "Are you sure?"

I wished I could explain what I was feeling, but I couldn't spin emotions into syllables. When you walk through life wearing a target—your face—there are times when you forget you are different. But there are always reminders. Sometimes it's a too-long stare at the store. Sometimes it's someone talking to you a little too loudly because they don't think you speak English. In each case, it's the same hard shove: *You are not one of us.*

Griff snapped the rest of his taco shell into tiny pieces. "Welcome to Plainstown. Like all high schools, a bastion of kindness and humanity."

"It's not only here, unfortunately." I looked over the students chatting at the cafeteria tables; same setup, different faces. "But this place is worse than most."

It was true. At my other schools, there were cliques and random bullying. But Plainstown had an insidious hierarchy. Mitzi, Adeline, and the VIPs all parked in the "A" lot, the one closest to the school. At first I had assumed they got those spots because they arrived early. But it soon became clear that the other students deliberately left the lot empty for them. The VIPs would drift in late, since they didn't have to make the long trek from the back lots. During lunch, they never had to worry about people bumping into them or having their clothes smell like hot dog, since the popular table was in the back of the cafeteria. They walked in the halls without people getting in their way, and sat in the best seats during football games.

No one seemed to challenge it, or protest, even though it was clearly unfair.

Griff, for once, was serious. "Would you fix it if you could?"

"What?" I said. "Everything? All the cliques and the sheeple who allow everything to continue? Not possible. Clearly, the best option is to withdraw and disavow all of human society."

"Cynical."

"Realist. The only way things could get better is through homeschooling or graduating early."

Griff looked like he wanted to say more, a lot more. But instead he took a pinch of his jagged chips and sprinkled it over my meal. "But you wouldn't have Chilaco Delight at home. And you wouldn't be dazzled by your charming French partner every day."

"Oh, how tragic. That would be like not seeing the sun."

Note: it's extremely difficult to pull off banter when your face constantly betrays you. Was there an evolutionary purpose to blushing? Did early Homo sapiens defend themselves against predators by making their faces hot and red? Methinks not.

Griff pushed the tray towards me, his hand brushing mine. "Exactly."

I passed him a french fry, which I probably could have baked on my flaming cheeks. "That's for working Chilaco Delight back into the conversation."

He snatched it and popped it into his mouth. "You're

welcome." He placed one tiny tomato square on top of my Chilaco Delight.

Unfortunately—so unfortunately—I hadn't noticed Adeline and Mitzi behind us during this conversation. I didn't register Adeline laughing and tucking her phone into her pocket. I was turning, pulling the pieces together, when a sudden, cold wetness splashed on my back.

Adeline said, "Oops. Sorry."

The liquid stuck to my back, dripping on the floor in bright red punch–colored drops.

Mitzi was off to the side, I noticed, which would give her plausible deniability if things went south. The girl was a canny chess player, always planning ahead so she could get the result she wanted without having to do the dirty work herself.

Griff sprang up and lightly placed his hands on my shoulders. He turned the back of my shirt towards him.

There are people who expand when they get angry; they scream or throw things. Griff iced. He became quiet fury.

"Are you done with your lunch, Olivia?" he asked.

I nodded.

"Then we're leaving." He scooped up our books. The cafeteria was silent, but I could feel the eyes on the stain on my back.

I would not cry.

Griff led me to the door. He glanced over at me, but my chin was up, my gaze forward. Hold it together, Olivia. Ten more steps. Nine. Eight.

Mr. Roberts, the cafeteria monitor, was at the doorway, but

he did not try to stop us; he only gave me a sympathetic look and let us pass.

Griff strode down the hall, and I followed him. I was doing all I could to keep it together. If it was any other shirt, I probably wouldn't have cared. But this was one of my most precious ones: a tee my father had given to me before he left, when we still loved each other. And with this huge red stain, it was now ruined.

Griff stopped at his locker and yanked out a dark blue sweatshirt. When he turned back towards me, I—the girl who majored in Griff Expressions 101—did not recognize the concentrated rage in his face. It looked exactly like what I was feeling: the special shade of fury that springs from being helpless over and over again. It was something that I, alumnus of three other academic cesspits, was quite familiar with. But why was he so angry?

Griff gripped the fabric until he saw my face. His hand loosened, and before I knew what was happening, he had dried off the punch with some tissues, then bundled me up in his sweatshirt.

"You have short arms," he said mildly.

"Have you ever thought that your arms are too long?" I focused on everything else but my sullied tee: the warmth and fuzz of his clothes, the faint smell of soap.

Griff rolled up the sleeves, his fingers brushing against my wrist. "Has something like this happened to you before?"

Answering should have been easy; a yes, tipped over the edge of my tongue. Or a tiny nod. But that would have acknowledged those early dark years with the fist of rejection squeezing my chest, those Friday and Saturday nights with Mom, watching movies and trying to ignore my silent cell phone. It didn't fully cover the later times, when I realized how very easy it was to become invisible. For people to forget about me. I wasn't the girl who let herself dwell on those things. Not anymore. Survive, and get the hell out. That's all I needed to do.

Griff let the silence sit. I liked that about him—he didn't ask more questions or make a joke. He waited, then tugged my sleeve. "Come on."

"Where are we going?" I asked. But he just led me towards the library.

"Mr. Griffin." The librarian, Mr. Arya, smiled at him as we came in. Did Griff know everyone? "Are you staying here for lunch?"

Griff nodded, smiling faintly. "Do you mind?"

"Of course not. Pick a table."

"He told me students can't eat here," I hissed as we made our way to a back table in the deserted nonfiction section.

"He told me the same thing," Griff said, "the first time I asked."

Griff stopped at the computers, next to the guy from study hall. The boy gave me another silent bro nod, which meant we were practically Asian BFFs.

"Tell me." Griff's voice was low. "How bad is it? What are they planning?"

"Bad." The boy did not look at Griff directly. "Something's definitely up. But I'm not sure what."

I didn't have time to wonder how the two of them knew each other, or how the study hall guy had all of this information. As soon as he started talking, Griff looked at me.

"What?" My voice was annoyingly faint.

"Shit," Griff said. "Listen—"

The red-haired Poet Guy from AP English stepped forward. I hadn't noticed him since I was—well, freaking out.

"Griff," he said warningly.

What? They knew each other? I had never seen them speak, even though we were all in the same lunch period. Yet Poet Guy's tone was familiar, sharp. And Griff's expression—stubborn, defiant—was clearly a continuation of a conversation that had occurred many times before.

I would have dismissed all of this as a byproduct of my panicked brain, except I suddenly noticed one thing: a tiny round red pin on Poet Guy's backpack.

Just like the one Griff had.

I whirled around to the study hall guy. He had one as well, on his jacket. I noticed one other person here—the blonde ponytail girl from our French class. She also had a pin.

"What is this?" I stared at Griff. "What's going on?"

Griff was watching me with approval. "Mademoiselle Chang. Welcome to the Nerd Net."

Six

THE NERD NET

MY ELOQUENT RESPONSE: "The what?"

"No one calls us that but you, Griff," the study hall guy said.

"What?" Griff said. "It's alliterative. Plus, the term 'nerd' has a certain cachet."

It was as if the mere mention of the Nerd Net unlocked a frozen picture; suddenly, everyone sprang into motion.

"Heidi," the study hall guy said. "How do I get the thingy on the screen to go off?"

The blonde girl nudged him out of his chair. "How many times do I have to tell you? How many? Guess." She grabbed his mouse. "What did you—? Oh my God, Will, this isn't rocket science. It's Instagram. And why aren't you doing this on your phone?"

"Devil machines," Will said. "Why can't people write letters? On paper?"

"Because we don't live in the 1900s. We now have something called the 'computer.'"

"You laugh, Hexler, but we'll see who's gloating when your psych test comes. Do we have to go over how psychologists and psychics are different again?"

"Do you want pictures of you in ugly Christmas sweaters all over the internet? Keep on talking, Choi."

Will nudged Heidi over until they were sharing the seat, then jabbed at the screen. "It's totally ridiculous I can't retweet things on here."

"That's because it's *not Twitter*, Will," Heidi said. "Make a Story. And why are you still using Instagram anyways? OMG! Move to TikTok already!"

"It'll be a frozen day in neverland before I go on that hell site."

Heidi shoved her phone screen in his face. "You are so wrong. CatTok is the best thing in the world."

Will looked at me. "Some might say humanity's most impressive accomplishment is penicillin, or maybe the space shuttle. But no. It's CatTok." Heidi smacked his arm.

The red-haired Poet Guy came up to Griff. He was tall, and the fastest talker I had ever heard. "Are we—we're talking about this, right? Because you already, with the 'Welcome to the Nerd Net!' so obviously—? Because I have big news—bigger than you can guess about Project Trojan Horse. I mean, maybe you can guess—"

Griff tossed me an amused expression, topped with a sprinkle of exasperation. "Livvy, this is Peter."

"Hi?" I said.

"Hi, Livvy! Is that Griff's sweatshirt? Listen, Griff, with the thing, you know, the other that we—we did talk about it, didn't we? With the—?"

Will hissed, "Arya!" and everyone broke apart and fell silent. By the time Mr. Arya walked into the section, they were strangers again.

Mr. Arya came up to Heidi first. "Ms. Hexler. We received a new book on computer programming, one I think you may approve of. It's on loan from Trinity."

Heidi looked up from the book she was pretending to read. I wondered if Mr. Arya noticed that her pink and green notebooks were still next to Will, who had gone back to typing and cursing at the computer.

"Emerson?" she asked, and I could tell she was genuinely excited. "Emerson on PHP?"

"Better."

"There's no one better than Emerson."

"Oh ho! Who's the expert?" Mr. Arya whipped out a thin yellow book. "Emerson is better than . . . Williamson?"

Heidi gasped and snatched it from him, then launched out of her seat and gave him a big hug.

Mr. Arya was like a bookish Santa Claus. He gave some social psychology magazines to Will, a slim volume of Sylvia Plath poems to Peter, and a French history textbook to Griff. But at no time did any of the Nerd Net interact with each other, other than one affectionate smile from Will to Heidi (who was engrossed in her book and didn't notice).

45

"Mr. Arya, this is Olivia Chang," Griff said. "She's my partner on the French project."

"You told me there was no independent study during lunchtime," I said to Mr. Arya.

"There isn't." He had the nerve to wink at me.

"Mr. Arya only allows independent study to those who have proven respect for the library," Griff said after he left.

"Proven respect?"

"I came here every day after school for two months," Peter said. "Technically, over fifty consecutive business days, but I didn't have many extracurricular activities other than lit society, so."

"You came here every day because your phone battery sucks so you were always on the computers, messaging Carlie," Heidi said.

"His girlfriend," Griff said to me in a stage whisper. "From Napleville."

"HE LOVES CARLIE." Will made two finger hearts. He somehow made them look sarcastic, which took some skill.

Peter blushed.

"I asked Mr. Arya for interlibrary loans from Trinity College," Heidi said.

"What did you do?" I asked Griff.

"Picked up a dropped book and reshelved it, in accordance with the Dewey decimal system."

Will said, "Amateurs. I suggested a centralized display area for class supplemental reading."

46

"Yet he refuses to use TikTok." Heidi turned towards me. "Yay to having another girl in this group! We're going to be best friends."

"Uh-oh," Will said. "You're done for. Heidi's like a barnacle on a boat once she decides she likes you."

"True," Heidi said.

"Wait, are you the one who said something about Mitzi's 'little' TikTok empire?" Peter asked.

It wasn't my greatest moment. I nodded.

"That's not good," Peter said.

"I know."

"No," he said. "I mean, that's a totally condescending comment, but that's not what I'm talking about. Do you know what that account means to her?"

"What? You mean all the fluffy skirts and stuff?"

"It's not just fluffy skirts. That's kind of reductive, isn't it?"

It took me a second to process what he was saying. Was he calling me reductive? And condescending?

But Peter didn't seem to think what he had said was a big deal; he was still talking. "No, Mitzi needs the income for her family."

Wasn't her mom a rich actress or something? "I doubt that."

"It's true. And Mitzi built up her platforms from scratch. People underestimate her all the time. It's the one thing she will not tolerate."

"How do you know all of this?" I said. Who was he, Mitzi's secret BFF?

"Her brother goes to the tutoring center that I volunteer at after school." Peter glanced at Heidi. "He's a good kid. He talks about her a lot."

"But—" All the questions rushed out at once, making a clog of words in my mouth. Why was Peter on such a high horse? And what was even going on with this group? Why didn't they talk to each other in public?

But then the bell rang. The Nerd Net scattered, strangers again.

"Griff—"

"Later?" he said quickly as we walked into French class. Griff took his usual seat next to mine and placed Mr. Arya's book on my desk. Fair enough—there were tons of people here and it probably wasn't the best place to talk. But he wasn't going to tell me *anything*?

Heidi came in a minute later and took a seat in the back, not looking at us. Then Mitzi and Adeline sauntered in, talking loudly.

Their groupie, whose name I had learned was Dawn, trailed behind them. She tried to take a seat next to Heidi, only to be repelled by an undiluted glare of contempt. It was more than dislike; it was personal. What was going on there?

Mitzi focused her attention on me, then whispered to Dawn. She was wearing a fancy dress and carrying a Louis Vuitton purse. In high school. What was Peter talking about? Why would she need her TikTok income for her family? But Mitzi did mention her mom selling their stuff the other day. Like, their belongings? That didn't make any sense.

Peter was right, though, that I needed more information. After what happened yesterday, I had rapidly progressed to the next section of my operations manual: gathering intelligence. I had quickly peeked at some articles about Mitzi's mom, and I do remember one in particular. Mitzi's aunt was also an actress, and her mom and aunt had both been nominated for a major award many years ago. A reporter asked Mitzi's mom if she was rooting for her sister. Instead of saying yes, Mitzi's mom said, "We all know there is only one winner. Sometimes she'll get it. But today, I will." She ended up losing. She later blamed it on the writers, saying she had a poor script.

My father was like that, always thinking there were only winners and losers. Life was a thing to be won, and people were either victorious or they weren't. He had pretty much ignored us since he left, until recently, so it was clear which side he thought Mom and I were on.

The rest of our class slowly wandered in. But no one tried to talk to Mitzi, Adeline, or Dawn. Curious. Jennifer Hamlish didn't bother to hide her annoyance as Mitzi and Adeline took the prime spots at the back of the room.

Right before the bell rang, Mitzi scribbled on her paper in wide circles, then slapped her pen down on her desk. "Does anyone have an extra?"

At another school, some eager wannabe might take this opportunity to brownnose their way into Mitzi's good graces. A pen and a small compliment, some conversation. Anything to show loyalty to the Queen.

Only that's not what happened. Adeline started searching

through her tote. Dawn pretended to, but she snatched the pencil sticking out of her backpack and hid it in her purse.

No one else tried to look. They didn't even fake it. Some flicked side daggers of contempt at Mitzi when she turned the other way.

Interesting.

Adeline finally found a beat-up ballpoint and handed it over to Mitzi, triumphantly. Mitzi grabbed it without thanking her.

It wasn't only in French class. Everyone always seemed to steer clear of Mitzi, Adeline, and the VIPs; people either deliberately ignored them or tried to hide. There was no small talk or friendly waves. However, everyone still allowed them free rein in the cafeteria and the rest of the school. They hastily moved aside if the group was coming their way.

Somehow, people were compliant with the system, but it was clear they didn't like it. A minority group in power was able to influence the majority. There was a reason this social structure seemed familiar.

"I have an idea for our project," I said to Griff after class.

"You do? What is it?"

"Le Tiers État."

"The . . . Third Estate?" Griff looked intrigued. "The lower class in France?"

I nodded as Mitzi and Adeline strode out of the classroom. Everyone else pretended to fiddle with their lockers or turned away from them. The hall was eerily hushed until they were out of sight.

In the 1700s, French society was split into three parts: the

First Estate (members of the clergy), the Second Estate (nobles), and the Third (all of the others). Even though most of the population was in the Third Estate, they didn't have more say over important stuff, like voting.

But the Third Estate pretty much went along with everything until the end of the century, when the King of France called a meeting and asked for more taxes. Instead of saying yes, the Third Estate got together and created a new National Assembly. The following years were full of turmoil and violence, and fundamentally transformed France and its society.

In other words, the Third Estate was known for one infamous act in history: starting the French Revolution.

Seven

TEAROOM, TABLE FOR ONE

I ALREADY RECOGNIZED Peter from AP English; I had been audience to his several impassioned analyses of iambic pentameter. It wasn't only poetry that set him apart. He was just *a lot* about everything. I thought it was kind of charming, but almost everyone else was annoyed. One time, in English class, we were asked to give short presentations on medieval plays. Peter announced a full audiovisual extravaganza, including a costume, music from the time period, and selected clips from related documentaries. But around ten minutes in, when the class was still waiting for him to set up his equipment, they started to get impatient. (The only thing worse and more aggressive than high schoolers are restless and bored high schoolers. The lesson did not end well.)

Today, Peter was debating with our teacher about the importance of poetry and the arts during times of global conflict. He dug around in his backpack for a long while, searching for a reference book or something. He started emptying out all of his things until our teacher said, "Peter. Enough." Peter stopped abruptly, flushing. He didn't speak the rest of the period.

Heidi was in gym with me. I took a step in her direction, but she shook her head sharply and turned away. Will was in our class, too, but they never acknowledged each other.

However, during one of our thrilling badminton games, Heidi and Will were on opposing teams. One of Will's teammates began yelling at him. Heidi got control of the shuttlecock and, in a move so quick that I would have missed it if I wasn't watching, pretended to accidentally bump it with the side of her racquet. It sailed straight at Will and he smashed it over the net for the game-winning point.

But they never spoke to each other. In the locker room, Heidi made a point of dashing out without talking to me.

I saw Peter on the way to my next class. Two girls from AP English passed him, but when he tried to say hi, they stepped aside and quickly walked in the other direction. Peter flushed and bowed his head. Oh no. Rule one of survival was this: never let the enemy see your injuries. Peter must not have figured this out, or was incapable of keeping his feelings under the surface. Given his trembling composure, I suspected the latter.

I was still slightly annoyed with him for calling me condescending, but seriously, someone had to go help the guy. His face was practically a beacon, shining the words *target here*. I was about to give him some friendly advice when, down the hall, I noticed Will subtly swerve in his direction. He gave both of the girls a hard stare as he passed, and they cringed and scuttled away. But Will never spoke to Peter or made eye contact. They could have been strangers.

In all the weeks of our French class, I had never, ever seen Griff and Heidi look at each other. None of the other members of the Nerd Net sat together at lunch, even though we all had it during the same period. Peter and Will never talked in public, but I swear Will had just defended him.

What was all of this about? I didn't have time to think about it. Towards the end of the day, I headed for my last class, AP Psychology. That's when the whispers started. I heard it like a hiss, rising and cresting behind me.

Oh, God.

If you want to know if people are talking about you, there is one simple test that works every time. You pick one person—here a non-VIP—and you try to make eye contact with them. If the gossip is not about you, they will look at you—maybe with hostility, maybe with confusion—but they will do it.

I picked a random girl in the hallway and tried to catch her eye. She flushed, her gaze sliding over me and down to the floor.

Oh my God.

I remember when I first saw a picture of an iron maiden in one of my history books, the coffin-like structure, the spikes that would impale the person inside. I remember thinking: that is what bullying feels like. It is the shocking pierce through your body, the crush from all directions.

I'm sure I walked down the hall. I might have even held it together enough to look like I didn't care. That was only because I had years of practice.

I strolled (not ran) to the bathroom.

I slowly (casually) made my way to a stall, ignoring the girls at the sink who giggled when I walked in.

But as soon as I shut the door, I yanked out my phone. I could tell from everyone's reactions that Will was right; Mitzi and Adeline *had* been planning something. But what was it?

Was it the mysterious way Mitzi and Adeline kept everyone in line? Maybe a website or something? How had everyone at the school gotten the same link at once? I checked Mitzi's account, but her latest video was about some new lipstick.

Then I swiped to the bottom of the comments.

On the very last line was a small, innocent-looking post.

This is hilarious! Then a teal dress emoji. And a link.

The emoji was Mitzi's logo. I had seen it on stickers on the back of her friends' phones and on the occasional tote bag. I clicked the link, then I wished I hadn't.

I had heard of school gossip sites before, of course. At Porter High, there was a whole tearoom where all the gossip was spilled. People passed around the link for the site among themselves and posted horrible rumors, until the administration found out and shut everything down.

This was an anonymous TikTok account with only one post. An audio clip of what I had said to Griff, about all the people at this school being sheeple, started playing in a loop over a song.

Above it flashed the words, *O.C. thinks she's better than everyone else. But is she?* Flash to a compilation video of me, one with my pant leg higher than the other, one of me chewing with my mouth open. I hadn't even known they were filming me. The final words flashed: *Like this video if you think she's cool! But leave a comment if you think that she's not.*

I checked Adeline's account, her latest video. Frantically scrolled to the bottom. Same comment. Same teal dress emoji. Same link. I checked the VIPs'. Same.

They had put out a hit on me.

By the time I discovered the video, it had already been forwarded, reposted, and generally exploded over the internet.

I thought back to what had happened in the cafeteria—I was just about to ask Mitzi and Adeline what the hell they were doing when Adeline splashed the punch on my shirt. It wasn't just an act of bullying—it was also a distraction. So they could keep that clip and make this video.

I had been angry and had spoken without thinking. Sure, it wasn't ideal that I called the other students sheeple. Fine. But to spy on me, to weaponize my comments, and to create this? Was this, to Mitzi, an eye for an eye? Retaliation for what happened to Adeline? The trolls came for her friend, so now Mitzi wanted to sic them on me?

The fact that the video was on TikTok meant any person on earth could log in and comment. And I saw they had already started, one or two passing swipes from anonymous people— maybe outside of my school, or outside of my state. These people didn't know me but felt very comfortable snarking on everything about me: my hair, my clothes, my complexion. They would never say any of this to my face, but behind their keyboards, they could say anything. And they did.

Grandfather always told me that militaries were merely tools; they have been used to uphold democracy, but also as a force to oppress and kill. In high school, social media was our military, and anonymous commenters were the disorganized armies of hate.

Could a soldier point a gun at someone, could they squeeze the trigger, if they saw a real person at the other end? What about the people online? When they pushed the post button, did they not think their victims were human?

This was me, shoved onto the spikes of shame. This was the iron maiden door slamming shut, the pain. This was me bleeding out.

I flushed the toilet. Washed my hands, nonchalantly. Bared my teeth in a smile to the two twittering freshmen by the door. Walked into my classroom. Placed my books on my desk, lining them up precisely with the edge.

Chin up. Tears in. I knew the drill. But I was so. Damn. Tired. Of. The. Drill.

Will was slouched in his chair in the corner, silent as usual. As I walked in, I was surprised to see a flash of sympathy from him before he reverted to his usual aggressive hostility. A girl tried to sit in the seat next to him, but he scowled at her. She ran in the other direction.

I tried not to pay attention to the muted buzzing of cell phones, as people texted each other the link, which was so, so hilarious. Each one was a bomb in a box, waiting to be opened.

Everyone might not put in a comment themselves. But people would watch the video. They would look for more links in Mitzi's comment sections, more teal dresses of death. They would laugh at each one. They would think it's funny, because it's always funny, when it's not you.

After class, Mitzi glided past me in the hall. She flicked me one stare, like a dagger flipping end over end. It landed, point side in.

I thought of what Peter told me: *Everyone underestimates her. She won't tolerate it.* But that couldn't be the whole story. This couldn't only be about revenge. Are people so ruthless over an insult? Grandfather would say: *People are the most dangerous when they have something to protect.*

What did Mitzi have to protect? And why? One thing was clear: her power over this school was once again secure. People were no longer looking at me like I was a potential savior. I was just a pariah, again.

The most effective way to maintain your power is by decimating your rivals. Which just proved my father right: there were winners and there were losers. And there were those, as they say, who didn't even know how to play the game.

When I got to my locker, Griff was leaning next to it, his face grim.

"I'm fine," I snapped. I slammed my locker shut, and immediately wanted to open it and kick it shut again. This whole incident confirmed my deeply held, almost religious, belief that all people were inherently terrible, and human society only concentrated that evil and allowed it to flourish.

Griff put a hand on my arm. "Do you want a ride home?"

I knew he meant to be kind. So I said, "I'm okay," instead of "Leave me alone," though we both knew that's what I meant.

This was not my first rodeo. I knew how these things work. Griff would pretend to have—or might genuinely feel—some sympathy. But it would rapidly evaporate in the hot inferno of unrelenting social shunning. No one could withstand that heat. No one had even tried, at least not for me.

I walked home, past the staring kids in the parking lot, past the jerks on the sidewalk. I looked back. Griff was still in front of the school, watching as if he was making sure I was getting home safely.

I knew better than to hope it was true.

Eight

BONJOUR, TATER PHONE

THE SHIT CONTINUED all weekend.

My phone, which was usually an overpriced screen for YouTube and TikTok videos, suddenly became a tinderbox. It buzzed over and over again after an anonymous genius doxxed me and posted my number. It may not have been someone in Plainstown. It could have been. Or maybe it was just some random kid in the middle of nowhere, taking the time to ruin my life.

Mitzi—whether intentionally or not—had set up the dominos, and now they were falling.

I knew this life; I had lived a smaller version of this before. Different school, different state, same old crap. I just thought, naively, that I could survive the rest of my time at Plainstown and get to the finish line. Mom promised me we could stay here until graduation, so this was supposed to be my last stop before the freedom of college. All I had to do was endure. Make it until the end. But even that seemed unlikely.

I spent Sunday morning halfheartedly researching Mitzi's accounts, as if I had a chance of doing something, anything, to stop this mess.

Peter was right about her family needing money. Years ago, Mitzi's mom and her younger brother were in a car crash. Her brother broke his leg in several places and was lucky to be alive. There were some photos of Mitzi and him in a newspaper; young Mitzi looked fierce, protecting him from the paparazzi.

With a lot of physical therapy, he would likely recover and not have long-lasting injuries. But the medical bills and treatment must have been astronomically expensive. Couldn't her mom and her Hollywood money take care of it, though? Huh. Come to think of it, I hadn't seen her in the movies or on television for a long while. I checked her biography—she hadn't been hired for any projects in years.

This might explain Mitzi's TikTok empire. But why did she need to keep this system in place at school? Was it because her brand was based on being a popular student? Did she somehow see me as a threat to her image—and her income? I had assumed Mitzi was trying to boost her own popularity with her channel. But was it also about survival?

My mom came downstairs and I quickly put away my phone. Sundays were the one day when she could sleep in and take a break from her never-ending string of emails and legal briefs. I liked to make her a pot of coffee and some eggs, two things she never got to enjoy without an argument when Dad was around.

Mom looked at the plate I was carrying and the omelet smeared with mustard in the middle. Then to my dancing alpaca pajama pants, which I was still wearing, even though it was almost noon.

"What's wrong," she said.

It's true that I kind of went through a mustard period when things got bad at Lake View. And through a wearing-my-alpaca-pajamas-all-the-time phase after Dad left and Grandfather died. It had been a one-two punch in the span of three months, and I hadn't wanted to do anything—not wear real clothes or pretend to talk to people at school who eventually got annoyed by how sad I was, as if grief had an expiration date. Not anything. That was when I discovered the irresistible lure of aloneness.

"What do you mean?" I tried to sound casual. I knew Mom constantly worked for the both of us, and the last thing she needed was to worry about me. It was our unspoken agreement: we would both try as hard as we could just to get through.

"Olivia."

"It's nothing." But I kept picturing the poisonous comments flying through the air, piling up in my phone.

Mom shot me her *no bullshit* look.

"Fine." I aggressively spread more mustard over my eggs. "There's a small . . . conflict . . . with some people at school. I can handle it."

Mom didn't say anything at first, which I knew was a classic cross-examination technique to make witnesses sweat and break under pressure. "What kind of conflict?" she said.

How to describe Mitzi and Adeline? "A kind of protestor-and-oppressor situation?"

"And you're the protestor?" she asked.

I nodded.

"Good. Are you sure you can handle it?"

I knew it wasn't an idle question. I had seen other parents talking to their kids and knew that this question was sometimes a throwaway, an excuse for them to either take over the situation or to ignore the problem. Mom was different. She let me measure what was right for me: *Are you full? Are you too tired? Do you need a sweater?* She honored everything I said. I didn't know it at the time, but she was building me a compass, and allowing me to always reorient myself north.

So now, I didn't toss her the easy answer; I thought about it carefully. My life was not pleasant, but the harassment was certainly tolerable. "I'm all right."

She gave me another Mom Look. I knew she wanted to say a lot of things but was allowing me the space to make my own decisions. I loved her for it. I hugged her as she said, "I am always here for you, Olivia."

I nodded.

"But you must let me know if you need help. Promise?"

I nodded again, but I was totally lying.

The doorbell rang. Mom glanced at me—we never had visitors.

It was Griff. He smirked when he saw my pants.

"I was expecting French Revolution clothes," he said. "But perhaps alpacas are more cheerful?"

I looked at him blankly, then noticed his backpack and notebook. I'd completely forgotten that he was coming over for our French assignment.

"Le projet?" he said.

"*Yes.* Right." Mustard stains on my shirt? Check. Hair unbrushed? Check, check. Wonderful.

I led him inside, and my mom tried to pretend like she was not passing out from shock. Way to be cool, Mom. It's not like I've never had a boy over before. Okay, maybe I hadn't, but still. Fake it, Mom! *Fake it!*

"Well, hello," she said. Casually. Then she grinned.

Oh my God.

"We're going to work on our assignment in the dining room, *Mom*." I stared at her. "Don't you have work to do?"

"Nope!"

If you've ever wondered whether mothers are somehow telepathically connected to their children, the answer is no.

Lightning decision: stay in front of Griff in mustardy pajamas, or change clothes and leave him with Mom? I looked at her. I had rarely—correction: *never*—seen her so merry.

All bad options! All bad!

I dashed upstairs. Four seconds later, I came zooming back, only to find Mom and Griff cheerfully chatting.

"What?" I said.

"Your friend, Alexander," Mom said.

"Call me Griff, please."

"*Griff* is quite charming."

What. Was. Happening.

My mom kissed my cheek. "Have fun, dear. I'll be out in the garden."

I waited until she left before I hissed, "What is going on?"

"I see where you get your grit," he said. "Your mother is absolutely wonderful. And absolutely terrifying."

"Pretty much."

Griff looked curiously at the coffee table in the living room, which was covered with neat piles of all my schoolbooks and papers. I technically had a desk and bookshelves upstairs in my bedroom, but I never used them; I usually ate and studied in front of the television.

"You like to work downstairs?" he asked. When I nodded, he looked like he was going to say more, but then my phone buzzed. I flipped it over without looking at the screen. I knew they were only electronic messages on a small device that was not connected physically to me, but each one felt like a filthy swipe to my brain.

"Livvy."

I couldn't bear to see if Griff's expression was pity, so I didn't look at him at all.

"What's going on?" he said.

I shook my head.

"Could I see?" Had his voice been bossy or flip, I would have lied to him. For a second, I thought about it, saying everything was fine. But I was so damn tired—so many schools, so many years of trying to get by. I was sick of pretending.

I nudged the phone towards him.

Griff began to read the messages, scrolling through them without saying a word. He grabbed his phone and dialed.

"Heidi." Gone was the joking Griff, my companion in snark. "Can you work on something?" He was silent for a moment. "Ready?" He began to read every single phone number that had texted me. When he was done, he said quietly, "It's for Livvy."

Seconds later, I got a text from Heidi. It was a photo of a symbol: a large gray N and an orange N in superscript next to it. N^N.

"Griff? What's she doing? What's N to the power of N?"

Did N stand for nerds? Nerd to the power of N meant . . . infinite nerds? A parabola of nerds?

We saw Mom outside the open window, wearing her absurdly huge yellow sun hat.

Griff waited until she passed, then said, "Demain, s'il vous plaît?" *Tomorrow, please?* Then, in an undertone: "How long has this been going on?"

"Someone put my number in the comments section on Friday night," I said.

"What? Who did?"

I shrugged.

"Do you have it?" he said.

I passed him my phone again. He took a screenshot, forwarded it to himself, then sent another text.

Another message to me from Heidi: Hang in there, Livvy.

"I don't—" I said. "What's going on?"

Mom stomped into the kitchen, then came into the living room. She was carrying the ugliest tomatoes I had ever seen.

"Aren't they gorgeous?" she cooed.

Griff was also looking at them with admiration. "Did you grow those heirlooms, Ms. Chang? Are those Black Cherries?"

I literally saw my mother's opinion of him rise. "They are! They're Olivia's favorite."

"Tomato salad," I said, "with basil."

Griff held up a hand. "And corn?"

"Of course."

My mom looked back and forth between us. She started to smile. Oh no. I quickly unloaded the tomatoes in the kitchen, then shoved the empty basket towards her.

"We need more," I said. "Lots more."

"Do we?"

"From the garden, *Mom*. I'm making a large salad for dinner. A huge salad."

"Actually, would it be all right with you if I take Livvy to the library?" Griff said.

My mom's eyebrows rose at his use of "Livvy," and I could tell that she was trying to stop herself from breaking into a jig of joy. Time to go. I pushed Griff towards the door, grabbing my purse on the way out.

You are not supposed to judge a book by its cover, nor a boy by his car. But I kind of loved Griff's—an old dark blue Prius, no bumper stickers, immaculately clean.

Plainstown High was an affluent school, and most of its students drove those obnoxious high-end cars. But, like the clothes he chose to wear, Griff's car was practical in a sea of pretension, a statement by not being a statement. It was something, like him, that totally blended into the background. Curious.

Griff was a fast driver, confident. He was wearing his blue sweatshirt today, the one that I had reluctantly returned.

The first test, of course, was the music. First—what did Griff listen to? Billie Eilish? Respectable. I tried to discreetly peek at his playlist as he reversed the car and shot down the street.

"You can take a look, if you'd like," he said.

I picked up his phone. It felt strangely personal, but he didn't seem to mind. He had an interesting mix of indie and popular songs. I scrolled to one of my favorites.

Griff looked surprised. "You like Hinds?"

"Absolutely. Wait, have you heard of Cœur de pirate? I feel like she might be appropriate for our trip."

I pulled out my phone and he waved a hand. I plugged it in and tried to pretend that sharing my music in Griff's car was a perfectly ordinary occurrence. Even though I didn't share my playlists, with anyone. And Griff turning up the volume, smiling, was also not a big deal. At all.

I said, "Nerd Net. Explain, please."

"Patience, my french fry–loving friend. Can I explain it tomorrow, with the others?" He turned in to the mall parking lot.

"I thought we were going to the library?" I said. "Are we going to a French Revolution store instead?"

"What would that even be called?"

68

"Gâteaux and Guillotines?"

He laughed, and a small glow of satisfaction bloomed. I tried to crush it.

"You slice your own cakes, is that it?" he said.

There it was: the irresistible pull of banter. It was the most perilous thing. Parts of my mind were perking up, stretching towards him. I didn't care how muscular or athletic a guy was, or how much money he had. But a boy who could volley and lob *le sarcasme*? That was a problem.

Griff sobered as my phone buzzed, then buzzed again. He gently tugged me into a cell phone store.

"Any chance you want to get a new number?" he said. "Heidi's taking care of the people who texted you, but it may take a little bit of time."

I was momentarily speechless. In all of my other schools, in the thick of the terrible things, I had always done the same thing—curled into myself and soldiered on. I never had this: a small act of kindness.

Griff put a hand around my wrist and led me down the aisle. "Come on, Livvy. Let's pick out a stellar phone case. How about this one?" He walked over to one in the shape of a bottle of hot sauce.

Of all the ways I had pictured my weekend ending, I could never have imagined half an hour of goofing off with Griff in the phone store.

"Matching BFF cases?" He held up a pair that made a pink heart when placed together. "I'll take BE–FRI–, and you can take –ST–ENDS."

"Only if we can get matching sweatshirts. It would be so worth it, I promise."

"Done." He picked up another one. "Hold on, we have another winner. Dog doing the dab?"

"That's disturbing. Unicorn vomiting a rainbow?"

"That's not disturbing? How about this one: 'NOT TODAY, SATAN.'"

"I can flash it at school," I said. "Dirty look? NOT TODAY, SATAN."

"Wait, game over." Griff put his hand behind his back. "I found it."

"How can you top a dog doing the dab?"

Griff hunched over his find, then dashed to the cash register. He blocked my view as the woman rang it up.

"Could you please wrap it in tissue paper?" he said as I tried to duck under his arm. The woman laughed as he swatted away my money. "Under no circumstances can she pay for this."

I tossed a ten-dollar bill over Griff's shoulder. He plucked it from the counter. "Nice try, Chang."

The woman threw in an extra screen cleaner, smiling.

I tried to snatch the gift from Griff as we left, but he held it above his head.

"Not until you get home, Ms. Nosypants."

Griff stood off to the side while I registered my new number, the white bag swinging from his hands. Every now and then he would peek inside, innocently.

I normally would have been humiliated from having the conversations with the phone people about transferring my non-existent contact list, but Griff distracted me so much that I barely noticed.

I slowly unwrapped my gift after I got home. It was perfect. As I turned it over in my hands, I realized that I would not remember this day as the one where the trolls drove me from my own phone number, but rather as the day when I received my first potato and french fry–themed phone case.

Nine

A PARABOLA OF NERDS

ON MONDAY, MY new tater phone was a blessedly silent brick in my backpack. I didn't know what Heidi did yesterday, and Griff still refused to tell me. But I noticed one or two people frantically trying to turn off their phones, as the halls pinged with ringing and buzzing noises. In French class, Heidi looked smug.

I checked my phone: all the comments on the video, including the one with my number, had somehow been deleted.

But that didn't stop the tight feeling of being watched. People—maybe people here, people next to me right now—had seen this video. Maybe they laughed at it, at me.

I didn't know who they were; they could have been anyone. No one. Everyone.

I was quiet at lunch. Griff tried to joke around a bit, but even the little Eiffel Tower he made out of his french fries failed to make me feel better.

After school, he was waiting for me by my locker.

"Are you free?" he said.

"Now?"

He nodded.

I mentally checked my incredibly crowded schedule. Huh. Free, look at that.

"I could be." If I were the coy type, or had any degree of suaveness, really, I could have made the comment sound alluring. As it was, it sounded vaguely menacing. "I mean, sure. If you're asking. Which you may not be."

Stop talking.

"I've called a meeting at Heidi's," he said. "Would you like to come?"

Was the Pope Catholic? Were the Colonial Americans super attached to their tea?

I was about to say yes, when the rational part of my brain remembered this was going to be a group thing, which was not a good idea. At the last party I had gone to, many years ago, I spent the night in the corner pretending to send texts on my phone. They were all to myself. Did I want a repeat of that? No, thank you.

"I should probably get home," I said.

Griff looked at me closely, then said gently, "Heidi asked me to invite you."

"She did?"

"I can give you a ride. And you can pick the music. Maybe."

I thought of how Griff and Heidi helped me, how Will defended me. What was the Nerd Net? What was their purpose? This could be the best way to find out. Worst-case scenario: this thing is completely excruciating, and I walk home.

"Sure. I guess," I said offhandedly. Suavely.

I was admirably nonchalant when I realized that Griff had added some of my music to his playlist. "You have excellent taste in music, Mr. Griffin."

"So I've heard."

In Plainstown, there were large houses and mansions. Heidi's was on a different scale. She lived on the very edge of the city, almost in Napleville.

"Is she royalty?" I asked, in awe, as we drove up a very long cobblestoned driveway. I don't think *house* was the right word. Her manor—her estate?—was surrounded by an immaculate garden, complete with bronze statues. Someone had decorated one of the metal deer with a red scarf and furry aviator hat. "Do her parents govern small islands?"

"Her stepfather invented something computery," he said. "Then her mom invented something even more computery. Then they got married and gave birth to millions of computer chips and fat stock options."

"Did they invent *the computer*? Because that's the only thing that could explain this amount of money."

"This is nothing compared to their other houses."

"Plural?" I said. "House*s*?"

"What do they call a large group of houses?" Griff said.

"A herd of houses? A compound of houses? That's what they have."

Will opened the door with a low bow. "Welcome to Heidi's modest abode. She's downstairs."

Calling Heidi's basement a basement was like calling a yacht a rowboat. The word *basement* implies a dark room where you keep all of your moldy papers and boxes. This—this was something else. This was a war room.

In the middle was an enormous wooden conference table, surrounded by short beige leather chairs. Along the far wall was a small kitchenette and a line of pale-pink-and-beige couches.

On the other side of the table was a high-tech operations control center, composed of at least six different computers whose brands and configurations I didn't recognize. There was a long beige desk, underneath two enormous computer monitors, which were built into the wall. Two boards flanked the monitors; one was a whiteboard, covered in incomprehensible mathematical equations, and the other was a corkboard with brightly colored papers pinned to it.

And seated in a pink roller chair in the middle of the desk was Heidi, typing a furious staccato melody on a computer keyboard. I didn't recognize the configuration of the letters—they were all in different places.

"What—?" I said.

"It's the Dvorak layout," Heidi said. "So much faster than QWERTY."

"She's like Mozart on an ergonomic keyboard." Will bounded up the stairs as the doorbell rang.

"My stepfather believes in having environments conducive to academic excellence." Heidi was still typing. "And my mom likes beige and pink. As you can tell."

"Thank you," I blurted. "For blocking those comments—"

Heidi cackled. "Oh, that was fun. I should be thanking you."

Will and Peter rumbled down the stairs.

"I am telling you, Will, you can't imagine the grace of women's field hockey. The players are so athletic, for example certain players—" Peter's red hair was spikier than usual, sticking up in excited peaks.

"And . . . wait for it," Heidi said. "Three . . . two . . . one . . ."

"LIKE CARLIE," Will and Peter said together.

"She's very fit." Peter looked dreamy.

"Oh my God," said Will. "It's like you've never had a girlfriend before. Oh, wait. You haven't."

"Honestly, Will, how can you be so cynical about something so beautiful as love? Didn't George Eliot say, 'What greater thing is there for two human souls, than to feel that they are joined for life'? Don't you believe in happiness?" Peter's hair seemed to grow taller in outrage.

"There is no such thing as happiness, Petey," Heidi said. Big words flashed on the monitor above her head: *IT'S ALL MISERY.*

Will laughed as Heidi said, "That was for you, Choi."

I stared at him. I had never seen Will with any expression other than hostility.

Griff tried to hide his amusement. "So this is the Nerd Net."

Groups were not my thing. Groups meant more than one

person, which usually meant factions and exclusion and/or cruelty coming from more than one direction. In other words, groups meant drama, without the fun music and jazz hands.

But as I watched Griff and his friends, I didn't see the usual fault lines, the split sections, or one person off to the side, desperately trying not to look left out (that was usually me). Heidi pulled Peter and Will over to the computer and showed them something, which made all of them laugh.

"So—?" I had so many questions. "What do you do, exactly? Why don't you talk to each other at school?"

They glanced at each other.

"A few months ago," Griff said.

"At the end of last year . . . More specifically—" Peter said.

"Right after Griff moved here." Heidi made a few quick clicks with her mouse. "In the spring. WAIT. Got it. TikTok takes forever to respond to takedown requests, so I kind of took matters into my own hands."

An error message flashed on the screen above her, and she threw her arms up. Will gave her a quick high five. Incredible. He actually seemed like he did not deeply hate the planet and everyone on it.

"The anonymous TikTok account?" I said. "You got rid of the whole thing, not just the comments?"

"Oh, I got rid of it. I also left an itty-bitty present." Heidi refreshed the page, and it redirected to Mitzi's account, where all of her videos now continually played fart noises. "Juvenile, but still, so, so funny."

Will ruffled her hair. "Heidi's always the best at potty humor."

Heidi stuck out her tongue at him. "Anyways, what were we saying? Oh yeah, Nerd Net. It was spring, right after Griff moved here . . ."

"Thank you. THANK YOU." I stared in disbelief at the monitor.

Heidi swiveled around in her chair. "It's what we're here for."

"It's what we do," Will said.

"It is." Heidi made one more rotation, her legs kicking out. "Last spring, all of us were kind of in a bad place—"

Peter said, "—then one day we all happened to be in the library during lunch since lunch is always the worst. Honestly, there is no legitimate reason not to have open campus. And Will came in saying Mitzi was—"

"—a fucking racist," Will said.

"—that."

"She told my sister to take the China table at the International Fair because of 'our people.' Which is obviously horrible for so many reasons. Plus? We're Korean."

"And then we started talking and found out we all thought the school was sort of messed up, so Griff suggested we work together," Peter said. "Then I thought, you know, we should try to thwart them."

"Thwart them?" I tried to keep up.

"If someone's getting picked on, we try to help them anonymously or separate them from the bullies," Heidi said. "A few class transfers, faked doctor's notes to get some people out of gym, that kind of thing."

"After one of Mitzi's friends tried to cheat off me, I might have given her the wrong answers," Will said. "Then gave our teacher the exam she copied, plus an extra one with all of the right answers. Hypothetically."

"And you don't talk to each other at school, because—?" I asked.

"It's a lot easier to execute our . . . plans . . . if no one knows we're connected," Griff said. "There's no centralized enemy to rally against."

"We all have different skills, and are better together than alone, so no one would suspect all of us. But I liked the idea of something, you know, kind of subtly tying us together, so the pins, that was me." Peter gave a little bow.

"The pins were Peter." Will rolled his chair over to the conference table and dug around a corporate gift basket, which was sitting on top. He tossed Peter a mini bag of chips. Peter caught it with both hands, looked at it briefly, then passed it to Heidi.

"I kind of like the pins." Heidi opened the bag. "Nacho, nice! Thanks, Petey."

"No one notices the pins?" I asked.

"No one notices *us*," Peter said. "That's our job. To be invisible."

"But I don't think it's good enough," Griff said. "Not anymore."

Ten

THE SEEDS OF DISSENT

THERE WAS A beat of silence, then Peter spoke. "What do you mean?"

"The same things keep happening again and again," Griff said. "Aren't you sick of it? Look at what happened to Livvy. That's exactly how it started with my younger cousin. All because—"

"—we live in a cesspool of evil?" Will pulled some fake grass out of the basket and made it into a little pile.

Heidi laughed, but Peter didn't. "What are you talking about, Griff?" he said.

Griff was gazing at the corkboard on the wall, which had some colored Post-its tacked to it. Some had checkmarks; others had various initials. "We hoped that if we helped a few people, we could make things better. But everything's the same. We need to do more."

"He's not wrong," said Heidi.

Next to her, Will created a small structure made out of boxes of gummies and chocolates. He fluffed the fake grass around it like a lawn.

"But what else can we do?" Peter was starting to flush, the color splotching across his face. "There are only a few of us, and we are talking about a social system with claws."

Griff leaned forward. "The same thing happened to Brynn. And the whole time, *no one helped her*. Not one person."

Too late? What happened to his cousin?

"We have to make things different here," he said.

"How?" Will dug around the basket some more, and triumphantly pulled out a pink stress ball. He tossed it to Heidi. "Plainstown is like every other town in America. This shit goes on all the time."

"But Plainstown has us," Griff said. "We have to be able to do *something*."

Will finally stopped fiddling with the things on the table. "How about shutting them down? Heidi could lock Mitzi and Adeline out of their accounts."

Heidi collapsed onto the couch and started tossing the ball. "They'd just start new ones. Then they would become more popular because they could spin themselves as victims."

Griff stood up and swiped it out of the air. Heidi pouted.

"We've been playing catch-up," he said. "We clean up after they do something. But I want to stop it *before*." Griff scooped everything on the table back into the basket, then pushed it under the sink.

"Hey!" Will said. "I didn't get my snack!"

Griff grabbed a small red box and tossed it to Will with an underhanded snap.

He caught it deftly. "*Raisins?* That's just hateful. It's like saying you want to put a pox on my family."

Peter didn't laugh. "We have been doing good things. Look at all we set up during the summer and what we've done since school started."

"I know, Peter." Griff's voice was gentle. "But everything is basically the same."

"How about we let everyone see the truth?" Will sprawled next to Heidi on the couch and she tucked herself into him, her head on his shoulder. "Post videos to the internet of Mitzi being her usual terrible self."

"No, she's too sneaky for that. She always works through other people, like Adeline. Or Dawn." Heidi spat out the last name with a curious amount of scorn.

That was true—Adeline was always the executioner of Mitzi's plans. She was the one who flashed the video, who spilled the punch on me, who captured the audio clip. She was always fetching things for Mitzi or setting up equipment for her.

"You need to play the long game," Heidi said. "You need to put a plan into motion before she realizes that something is up."

"So we get her expelled." Will wasn't kidding. "And she doesn't figure it out until they kick her ass out."

"I don't think compromising our moral framework is the answer, William," Peter said.

"You need numbers," I said quietly.

Will, Heidi, Peter, and Griff turned towards me.

"What?" Griff said.

I wasn't a talker. I certainly wasn't one in front of a group. But here's the thing about being a survivalist for years—no, scratch that. Here's the thing about being a survivalist for *your whole life*: you see things. You scrutinize the people around you, how they interact, how they form groups. You study the people who are in power and analyze how they got to the top and how they stay there. You become a social scientist in a cinder block lab.

All of this is in a giant database in your brain, and, after a while, you begin to notice patterns. You notice one overwhelming error in the system. Plainstown was the ideal place to figure it out. I couldn't at my other schools; Porter was too large, and Lake View had many groups of cruel people, not one concentrated cesspool of misery. Morris was relatively tolerable.

But Plainstown. Unlike my other schools, there was a centralized duo controlling everyone else. Mitzi and her followers took the best seats, the closest parking spots, with careless entitlement, as everyone else sat in oppressed silence.

My grandfather had taught me about different military strategies, but always made sure I understood that militaries could be used by governments that were terrible to their people. Mitzi and Adeline had gathered power but twisted it to only favor their friends. They used it to socially shame those who disagreed with them or exclude those they deemed to be not worthy.

"It's . . ." They were all looking at me. They might not care about my little theories. Certainly, the people at my other schools had glazed over when younger me started sharing the pieces of history that I loved.

But Peter looked intrigued, and so did Griff. Heidi sat up, and Will seemed to be paying attention, for once.

"So." I waited for a second, to see if they wanted me to stop talking. But no one said a word. "You have a simple setup here. Basically two leaders with a group of unified supporters. And a larger population of followers who don't challenge the system."

"All right, new girl," Will said. "This is interesting. Continue."

Griff smiled at me encouragingly, and I headed towards Heidi's whiteboard. Heidi nodded at my unspoken question. "Go for it."

I drew a slightly wobbly pyramid on the board, under Heidi's indecipherable math equations. I divided it into sections.

"The food pyramid?" Will said. "Let me guess. This is about how heavy dairy foods are going to make a comeback?"

Heidi elbowed him.

Peter was texting again. "Wait, we're redoing the food pyramid? Is that our plan?" His phone pinged, and he smiled.

"TURN OFF YOUR RINGER, PETER," Will said.

"This," I said, "is the social system of our school." I carefully labeled each part. *MITZI & ADELINE* were at the top. The slice underneath were the VIPs. Then I subdivided the much larger base of the triangle: *NERDS, GAMERS, ANIME/ MANGA PEOPLE, EMOS, FLOATERS, ETC.*

Peter made a face. "Are you going to classify people like that?"

A small wisp of embarrassment prickled. Why would he say that? Groups existed for a reason. At every one of my schools, there had been some form of each of these cliques.

"You don't think these are right?" I tried not to sound hostile, especially since I still didn't know Peter that well.

"No."

Everyone else was waiting. Even though I thought Peter was being a little much, as usual, I wasn't about to argue with him in front of the others. I crossed out what I wrote and replaced it with *EVERYONE ELSE*.

"And?" said Will.

I outlined the bottom of the triangle with my marker. "All schools are not like this. But here, you have a classic power structure. It's the same one that was in France before the National Assembly was formed, the same type of hierarchy in monarchies and dictatorships. These are the popular people." I pointed to the Mitzi & Adeline triangle and the slice below it. "And these are *all of the other students*."

"So?"

"So what I could never figure out was this," I said. "How do the few control the majority?"

Peter answered without looking up from his phone. "You're asking a fundamental question about the nature of government, but—in short—people choose representatives because at a certain point a larger population makes direct democracy too unwieldy to be effective." His phone pinged, and he chuckled. "Carlie does love cats."

"But this isn't a government, and Mitzi and Adeline aren't elected," I said. "So why does everyone follow them?"

I felt the force of their focus. Griff's face was grim, and Heidi looked as she had at the computer, as if she were carefully untangling the threads of a knotty logic problem.

Will said, "Well, it's easy to figure out Mitzi and Adeline's friends. People want to be included. Adeline throws all those huge parties every weekend, and the only way to get invited is if you are in. They also get all of those privileges at school."

"And for everyone else, it's fear." I could tell that Griff was turning the prism of this idea over, rotating it until it caught light. "The people on the outside don't challenge the system because they are terrified. Self-preservation keeps them in place." Something flashed across his face, a twisting tendril of bitterness.

"Actually," I said, "*why* is not exactly it."

The correct question was one I had wondered about over the years, had asked myself in anger, despair, hope, and curiosity. It was the flaw in the system.

"So?" Will said. "What is?"

They were all focused my way, again, and there was a not insignificant part of me that wanted to just dash up the stairs and run home. But as I looked at the humming computers, the carefully lined up Post-its, the whiteboard and the corkboard, I had a moment of certainty. This was the place where I could find some answers.

"It's this," I said. "What happens when the oppressed band together and overthrow those in power?"

Peter was staring at me. "Colony collapse disorder. The worker bees suddenly disappear . . . and the hive collapses."

"You'd have an uprising," Griff said, and started to smile. "You'd have a revolution."

Eleven

HOW TO OVERTHROW A HIERARCHY

I QUICKLY SAT down on the edge of the couch and watched the others explode into debate. Peter immediately rejected the idea, but Griff was more excited than I had ever seen him. Heidi was frozen in shock, and Will tried to get her attention.

The stakes *were* high: Mitzi—and Adeline—had the power to crush a person's social standing at school and in the vast, dark world of the internet. If the group did this—if they tried this and failed—it would surely mean the end for them, socially.

It was true that Plainstown High had a population unlike any of the others. At my other schools, the people followed a relatively benign leadership, or were largely able to ignore the popular group and live separate lives. People coexisted in a type of commonwealth situation, or in independent fiefdoms.

In Plainstown, the system of privilege had been set up and ruthlessly enforced, but the population was not entirely compliant. The students had more than an undercurrent of bitterness; it was a river.

I checked Mitzi's older posts and looked at some of the other hits that she had put out. In almost all the cases, it was someone who'd challenged her publicly, or someone who had gotten some social power. Mitzi stomped them all out with rumors—whether true or not—or shame.

But her victims pelted scorn behind her back. There were also small acts of defiance from people outside the Nerd Net, like the drama club humming "Evil Woman" from *Xanadu* as Mitzi passed. Or the anonymous Instagram that posted all the unsuccessful letters that Mitzi had sent to local medical centers, when she was trying to get an internship.

The kids at this school feared Mitzi. But they did not respect her. The gap between the two was all the difference in the world.

During the Revolutionary War, the colonies were cleaved from Great Britain by the axe of that resentment. War does not always happen because of one savage act of oppression; sometimes it is the accumulation of a thousand small indignities. It could be taxes on stamps or sugar. Or it could be the postings on social media shaming you every time you disagreed with those in power. Or the fact that you couldn't park your car or walk in the halls without being subject to some sort of tacit ordering based on your social class.

It wasn't only in America. And it wasn't just this time period. In other places, throughout history, people of certain races or nationalities or religions couldn't access particular jobs or positions of power. Privileged people sat in their comfortable lives and didn't feel the need to think of others.

Until the others made themselves heard.

On the couch, Heidi and Will were locked in a fierce unspoken debate. Peter looked anxious, twirling his phone in his hands.

"It's the American Revolution," I said. "It's the French Revolution. It's almost every political upheaval throughout history, throughout the world. It almost always comes down to the rebels having power or numbers. You don't have the power. But if you get the numbers, you can get the power."

"Livvy is right." Griff paced in front of the computers. "We've been trying to help people one by one. But has that actually done anything? Remember what you told me about Sarah Sloane? That was, what? Two years ago?"

Everyone abruptly stilled. Peter stopped looking at his phone. Heidi turned away.

Peter told me, "Sarah was a rival influencer. She started a small business selling these organic handmade soaps with little trinkets in the middle? So when you finished you could collect these little figurines? Anyways, she was doing well and had gotten a lot of press. But then some of Mitzi's sponsors left her and started going to Sarah's channel."

Heidi was still silent.

"Then—coincidentally—someone started a rumor that Sarah's soap had all of these chemicals in it or something," Will said. "She started getting reviews from one or two anonymous people complaining of rashes. Sarah paid a ton of money to get lab tests, to prove that she only used natural ingredients. But she still lost a lot of advertisers."

"That's what they did to her." Griff's voice was quiet.

Heidi was pale, and Griff squeezed her shoulder.

"When do we say *enough*?" Griff said. "I saw that video of Livvy, and it was like watching what happened to my cousin happen all over again. But this time I—*we*—can stop it."

Heidi was fingering the Nerd Net pin on her collar, her face heartbroken. Will gently pulled her hand away from it.

"We've always thought that we could make things better by helping the victims. But what if Livvy is right?" Griff said. "What if the best solution is to *get rid of the entire system*?"

A chorus of protest.

"Impossible." For a second, Will looked like he usually did at school: furious, cold. "Every high school in the history of high schools has cliques. Which group controls the hierarchy might be different, but there's almost always some kind of power structure. Every outcast is bullied by the people at the top. Different faces, same situation. And people always let it happen. Always."

"It's not that simple." Peter said. "And you can't group people together like that."

Was he talking to me, too? Was this about how I had called the people in this school sheeple? It was probably a rude way of saying it, but it didn't make it untrue.

"Besides, we've seen what Mitzi and Adeline can do." Peter twirled his phone in his hands again. "If we were caught, wouldn't it be over, for all of us?"

"Plainstown is different," I said.

Heidi said, "How?"

"You have a small student population. With, what? Two hundred people total? That makes everyone easy to mobilize. One person doesn't act out now because they're afraid of punishment. But if you could get everyone to band together—not only the seniors, but all the classes—it would give you power and protection. Mitzi wouldn't retaliate. She couldn't. Not against everyone."

"Less risk to the individual," Griff said slowly. "Livvy is right. Our problem has always been that people are afraid of standing up to them. But it's a completely different calculus if everyone does it together."

Will looked skeptical. "But how are we going to do that before Mitzi takes us down?"

"Your group is already decentralized and anonymous," I said. "You were right. Mitzi would never suspect you. You've already gotten away with it so far. You could do it."

"*We* could do it," Griff said.

"*You all* would have to be incredibly careful. If you got discovered before everyone else is on board, Mitzi could easily ruin you."

"Us." Griff bumped my shoulder. "You're in this, Livvy."

I shook my head as Will said, "But why risk ourselves when we are perfectly fine now? What could we possibly gain?"

"Are we fine?" Griff's tone was sharp. "Yes, we've helped a few people. But we're still anonymous. We've still never directly

challenged her. We are only fine because we're basically rene-
gades in hiding."

Heidi had remained silent through this whole discussion, her
head on Will's shoulder. But now she untangled herself from
him and sat up. "Griff is right. The question is not how we are
surviving. The question is how we are *living*. Remember what
Homer said."

"Now you bring up Homer?" Will said. "You hate when I
bring up Homer."

"Homer is my boy."

"In English for the rest of us?" Griff asked.

"'Better to live or die, once and for all, than die by inches,'"
Will said quietly. "That's what he said."

"Do we *really* believe that?" Heidi said. "Now is the time
to stand by it, Will. We're fighting them, but they are still the
same as ever. Griff is right. We need to attack the system."

The system was the silence that happened after my middle
school bullies slanted their eyes at me or mocked me for the
lunches I brought to school. It was the fear that prevented
sympathy from becoming actual words of comfort. It was
the terror keeping everyone locked into place, in their social
classes.

Above Heidi's head was a flashing monitor showing the
deleted anonymous TikTok account. I could feel the cold shock
of the drink on my now-ruined T-shirt. Could picture the
silent walk across the cafeteria, where Griff was the only one to
stand up for me.

"So what are we going to do?" Griff said. "Are we going to let things continue? Or are we going to fight?"

"Freedom to the Republic of Plainstown?" Will still looked skeptical. "Is that what you're saying?"

"Yes."

Peter finally stopped texting. "Are we doing this? Because it was not quite clear—I mean, no one voted. Shouldn't we vote?"

"Oh, we're doing this," Heidi said.

Will looked at her, then sighed. "Fine."

Griff said, "Livvy? You're already in. She dragged you in."

All of those years, all of those schools. Lake View Middle was the worst for me, but even after I implemented my isolationist policies, I could still see shades of the same system over and over again. The unpopular—whoever they happened to be—were tormented by those at the top.

What would have happened if those schools had a group like this? Plainstown had a resentful population, but so did some of my other schools. What they didn't have was an organized and intelligent set of rebels who would be willing to do what it takes to break the hierarchy. To overthrow the system.

What would happen if I didn't do anything? More humiliation, compounded by my own unwillingness to stand up for myself. More harassment, getting worse and worse until it became unbearable. I had been on this train before, and I knew it only had one stop. Even if I could graduate early, the torment would be for a year, with no hope of a future move.

Was I going to let things continue?

Or was it finally time—*finally*—for a change?

"Advisory capacity only," I said. "Strictly behind the scenes."

"Sure." Griff started to look cheerful again, which made me concerned. "Absolutely. A mere observer, really—with one minor field trip."

"Field trip?"

"We need to pick up some items. I just had a little idea," he said, innocently. "Totally behind the scenes."

"You promise?"

I wasn't sure if his smile was angelic or crafty, but this was certain: everything was going to change. I just didn't know if it would be good or catastrophic.

Twelve

THE REVOLUTION BEGINS

HOW DOES ONE stage a coup d'etat?

World history is very instructive on this point: you gather a revolutionary mass and force the offending party out. And the key to starting a rebel alliance is to find some rebels.

The previous efforts by the Nerd Net had focused on helping the victims. This time, we concentrated on taking down the system itself, which continued to exist because everyone feared Mitzi and Adeline.

It was not a trivial concern. What happened to Sarah Sloane—and what happened to me—was not only about punishment. It was a warning to all about the consequences of challenging them.

To break the regime, we needed to shatter this illusion of control. There were three zones where Mitzi and her VIPs flaunted their status: the parking lot, the morning hallways, and the cafeteria.

The parking lot was first. Economics tells us that which is the most scarce is the most valuable. For high school students, this translated into the teenage holy grail: the parking lot. At Plainstown High, the student lot was split into three sections: the tiny "A" lot closest to the school, the larger "B" lot next to it, and the smaller "C" lot down the street. One could roughly measure your social standing by how long it took you to get to the front door in the morning.

This was the long way of explaining how I found myself in my living room one evening, dressed in all black, waiting for the Nerd Net to pick me up.

My mom, who was working at the dining room table, scanned my outfit. "Do I need to be concerned? Is this a felony-type situation or a superhero thing?"

"Um." When in doubt, evoke the Constitution. "I plead the Fifth?"

Mom shot me her scary cross-examination look, and I tried to flood my mind with thoughts of perfectly innocent things, like puppies and rainbows. Clouds.

She said finally, "I'm not bailing you out of jail, you know. No cakes with nail files in them or anything."

There was a knock at the door. Griff snickered when he saw my clothes.

"What exactly do you think we're going to be doing?" he asked.

"Yes, do tell," Mom called from the dining room. "You're going where, exactly?"

I had never lied to my mom before, but I had also never potentially committed trespass, either. I hoped that telling the truth now would count for something. "We're going to the old hotel construction site on St. Andrew's?" You know, practically like going to Starbucks. At nine o'clock at night.

Mom left her seat and walked towards us. Bad sign.

"So," she said. "You've always made good choices, Olivia. Right?"

I knew this mom trick. She used to do this to me when I was younger: "Olivia, I know you always listen to your teachers. I'm so proud of you!" I would listen to my teachers before I realized that I had been totally manipulated.

"Yes?" I said.

She blasted another extra-long Mom Look. "Homework is done?"

I nodded.

"Fine. Back at a reasonable time, please. Mr. Griffin, I am also holding you responsible for this evening."

I gave her a hug, and Griff waved, weakly. Then we both sprinted out of the house.

"She's so, so terrifying," Griff said.

"She's all about free choice. And I'm compulsively conscientious, so. Speaking of, tell me again why we can't buy some traffic cones? As your advisor, I strongly advise purchasing those instead."

"Noted. But where's the fun in that? Besides, Peter called the construction company. They were happy to get rid of the sawhorses. They also offered a broken excavator, if, you know, we want to do any heavy lifting."

"We have permission?" You've got to be kidding me. "Then why are we doing this so late?"

"Heidi had a computer class after school, and Will had to help his mom move some stuff." Griff made a hard effort to stop smiling, but totally failed. "Sorry, I probably should have told you before you picked out your outfit."

Unbelievable.

I climbed into the car, with dignity. "Black is the classic color for stealth revolutionary operations, you know."

Griff coughed. "So I've heard."

Peter, Will, and Heidi were in the back seat and they were sharing a bag of chips.

"Well, she likes cats," Heidi was saying. "And she likes music. Maybe you can get her tickets to *Cats* the musical?"

Peter grabbed his phone. "That's a great idea! I think she would love it."

"You should also definitely write something for her. People love poetry from their partners."

"Oh, do they?" Will said. "Noted. Wait, do limericks count or is it only the fancy poetry?"

"One-year anniversary present," whispered Griff loudly. "FOR CARLIE."

"He's only been planning this since last spring," Will said. "We've also heard about this for THE PAST SIX MONTHS."

"That's sweet," I said.

"See?" Peter made a face at Will.

"The fact that Peter is the only one of you in an actual relationship might make him the most qualified to speak about love and romance," Heidi said.

Peter beamed. "Thank you, Heidi."

"I got your back, Petey." They high-fived.

"Ouch," Will said. "I feel like we were dissed. Griff, were we just dissed?"

Traffic was light in Plainstown, especially given the hour. Griff had borrowed his father's SUV, a high-end, gas-guzzling monstrosity. He parked it next to a large empty lot, which had been "under construction" since the early Obama administration. The developers finally gave up and now it was a large field surrounded by a fence and some old sawhorses. Some beautiful, free sawhorses.

"Tell me again why your dad needs a car this large?" I said.

"Why does the Pope need more followers?" said Griff. "Just because." He looked out the window. "He goes skiing a lot on the weekends. With his friends."

I noticed he didn't say "we." These are the sort of things that those of us with absentee parents pick up on. I heard all that was unsaid in those sentences: that his father, in the only time he would be free to hang out with his family, chose instead to leave them at home while he skied with friends. Some dads ski. Mine split and started another family in Minnesota. It all sucked.

Griff was silent. The one iron rule I had was this: I did not talk about my dad. But there was something in the tightness of his face that was too heartbreakingly familiar.

"Well, mine's also a jerk," I said cheerfully, and was relieved to see him smile.

"A jerk, or an actual asshole?" Will said. "You know there's a difference."

"How?" Heidi hit him on the arm. "You are totally making that up."

"There is. On the assholic scale, it starts with *pain in the ass*, then increases to *jerk*, followed by *kind of an asshole,* then the topper—*total actual asshole*."

I said, "Mine started a new family and forgot about us. But I guess he did give me a car when I turned sixteen?"

"So . . . actual asshole, then?" Will said.

"Yup."

"A guilt trip car?" Griff looked intrigued. "The one you don't drive?"

"The very same."

"Ah. Was the car a few years too late?"

Car, birthday cards, phone calls. It was all the same. All a few years too late. "Pretty much." I was planning on hocking the car for college money later. But until that golden day, I kind of liked the idea of it sitting unused and ignored in my garage. Stubborn and petty? Why yes.

"Wait, so you walk to school when you have a working car in your garage? On principle?" Will was incredulous.

Will might be shocked, but I somehow felt that Griff would understand. If his father was like mine—and I truly hoped his was not as bad—this car, this unasked-for object in my life, couldn't make up for all of the times that my dad didn't pick up the phone. Or when he switched his number and vanished. In fact, it was a fucking insult.

"I knew I liked you, Livvy," Will said. "That's fantastic."

"It sounds like something you would do," Heidi said to Griff, and he shrugged.

Griff stepped close to me after we got out of the car. I wondered if he had the same swirl of emotions about his own dad, if he could name it. But he was gazing at me like he was saving what he had just heard and was going to carefully fold it into his pocket. Like these little throwaway pieces were something valuable.

He tugged on my hat. I had worn a black one with a little pom-pom on the top.

"Is this a part of your stealth disguise?" he asked.

"It's to keep my head warm," I said. "Plus, the disguise was a good idea. I'm only here as a mere observer, so I should keep my identity concealed."

He pulled it again, smiling, and I tried to pretend that it did not make me all sorts of french fry happy, but it kind of did.

Heidi bounded out of the car, Will close behind her. The hotel site was abandoned, so they raced across the empty lot. Will suddenly stole her scarf, and she chased him.

I was still amazed at how different everyone was. At school, Will looked like he would drill a fist into anyone who looked at him sideways, and Heidi was the aloof princess, gliding through the halls. But here, they were both relaxed. Goofy.

Griff was normally indifferent to everyone at school, except for me. But here, he laughed as Heidi grabbed her scarf back and Will sprinted after her.

Heidi skidded by Peter and ducked behind him.

"Petey!" she bellowed. "Save me!"

Will pulled Peter into a fake headlock. Peter tried to pull down the arm around his neck and throw Will over his shoulder, but he couldn't do it. Will laughed and had him try again. This time, Peter succeeded in flipping him to the ground. Peter whooped and Heidi doubled over, chortling, before they both helped Will up.

"Will convinced Peter to join his tae kwon do studio," Griff said. "After it got bad last year. He's getting quite good."

"What do you mean?" I asked. "What happened last year?"

"Peter used to walk a mile to school because they tormented him on the bus. Now Will gives him a ride."

The three of them started carrying the sawhorses back to the car. Heidi was still teasing Will for getting thrown, but he was looking proudly at Peter.

I didn't think it was tae kwon do that helped him, though Peter was surprisingly graceful. He was relaxed and confident with the Nerd Net in a way that he had never been at school. They were not acquaintances or frenemies, like I had at my other schools. They were the genuine friends who would teach a guy to defend himself when he was getting picked on.

I remember going to camp once, and walking behind these four laughing girls, each of them with matching backpacks carelessly hanging off their shoulders. Some people got to have that. But not everyone.

Griff picked up a sawhorse, and I scrambled to help him with it before he injured himself. "Isn't it a beauty?" he said. "I can't believe we're getting these for free!"

Beauty would not be the word I would have used. The sawhorses were made of two battered wood triangles, with an equally beat-up bar in between them. They looked like they were constructed before the color television was invented.

Griff carefully loaded it into the back of the car. "Freedom to the Republic of Plainstown?"

I thought about the hierarchies at Plainstown High, how they were different from anything I had previously seen. I had spent a lot of time tracking and cataloging who became victims at my other schools. Almost every single time, they were people who had very little social capital because there was something different about them. Maybe they didn't own the cool thing—the AirPods, the shoes, the It brand clothes. Or—in a time when social media was tops—maybe they weren't conventionally attractive. Sometimes it's that cruelly random. Most of the time, though, there was some core difference—race, financial situation, sexuality, how they dressed—that was ruthlessly mocked.

For me, I was the only one of two Asian Americans at Lake View. They didn't know what to make of me. I got karate noises wailed at me, because we were in seventh grade and I guess that's what passed as clever back then. I got asked why I wasn't good at math. They didn't bother to distinguish me from Rosie Vuong because it didn't matter that we were two different people, because they didn't see us as people, not really. I just wanted to be an ordinary student, to belong. But they never let me forget what I was.

There are only so many times you can put your hand on a hot stove before you stop. Better not to give them the chance to burn you. Look at my father: there were only so many times I could call him, so many times I could wait for him when he was supposed to show up, before I had to shut that shit down.

These were the rules of survival.

Peter came up to us, flushed and smiling. If there was anyone who didn't know the rules of survival, it was Peter. The guy didn't just wear his heart on his sleeve; it was like his entire being was made of heart. He was asking for someone to break it.

"Griff, Livvy—you know, I had an idea? Maybe we could make a metal sign for the sawhorses, so it looks official?" Peter said. "I think my dad might have some tools and paint in the garage. He went through a metalworking phase."

"Or we could print out signs." Will lobbed a glove at Peter. "On the computer."

"We can't be sloppy."

Heidi hooked her arm through Peter's. "We'll look up the design so it looks legit."

Peter tossed the glove back to Will, but he overshot and it landed in the snow. "We need to at least take it to a printing shop. No one's going to believe it if it's on a piece of computer paper."

"Yes, Peter," Will said. "We'll print it out at the shop."

"With color."

"With color, Peter."

Heidi gave Peter a little hug, then the three of them raced to see who could grab another sawhorse. Peter got there first, with Will close behind, laughing.

A small feeling flared; before I buried it, some might have called it longing.

After all the sawhorses had been gathered, I waited by the side of the car while Griff loaded the last one in the back. Peter came up to me.

Should I say hi first? Wait for him to say hi to me?

I didn't have to worry.

"Livvy—I can call you Livvy, right?"

"Um, sure."

"I think I saw you in my gym class the other day. Which is honestly the worst; I'm not sure why they had to pick *shuffleboard* of all sports. But you know, my grandparents love it, so I guess it has some value."

"Totally?"

"Anyways, I didn't want us to get off on the wrong foot. About what I said about your TikTok comment, before. It's not little at all, though, you know. Mitzi's account."

Peter was bringing this up again? I was sorry for what I had said to Mitzi. I had a big mouth. Enough already.

"Why are you defending her?" I said.

"I'm not. I'm just trying to show you—listen, what she and Adeline did was horrible. Completely. But she hasn't had it easy, either. Both can be true."

I snorted. "Whatever."

"What? You think she can't have a hard time because she's popular?"

"Yes, it must be so difficult to catalog all of those sparkly skirts and shoes. To manage all of those likes and comments, and expensive purses. The poor life of an influencer."

I knew I was being snippy, but I couldn't help it. People like Mitzi had been condescending towards me my whole life, thank you very much. The ones who never had to worry about bills and loneliness. Who never had to think about others. People like the popular ones at Lake View, who had made my life hell.

Peter, for once, didn't say anything. It seemed like he could see straight through my anger and recognize the ugly fuel behind it. I looked away.

"Just because someone has fancy shoes doesn't mean that they don't also have a right to be unhappy. To be acknowledged." His voice was light, and kinder than I would have expected, given that we were arguing. "And all influencers aren't superficial. Do you know Anna Becker?"

"No."

"She saw there weren't a lot of women going into aerospace engineering. So she made all of these videos about female scientists at NASA, so girls can see themselves in the field. She now has millions of followers. And a lot of girls are going into STEM because of her."

I hadn't known that. Fine, so she was one exception. But what about the rest?

"Just . . . think about it?" Peter seemed determined to make me consider what he was saying. I wondered if this was what he was like as a tutor. He didn't seem to be able to let things drop, ever. Maybe that was what you needed to do if you were a teacher.

And to be honest, it kind of worked. Even though I didn't want to, I couldn't quite stop wondering about Mitzi, even after I got home.

It was true that every time I saw her walking down the halls, she never looked happy or relaxed. Rather, she was eagle-eyed, vigilant. She always made sure she looked perfect. On social media, she kept close tabs on her competitors and those who criticized her.

And I had to admit she was clever. When one of her competitors started to get traction, Mitzi didn't automatically take her down. Rather, she paired up with her and another influencer to make a collective campaign, which highlighted their different strengths. They all got major advertising deals.

She also leveraged her brand as a popular person at school. She posted videos from the front row seats of the football games, showing her fans the before and after choreography from the cheerleaders. Or she posted montage videos of the student council putting up dance decorations. If Mitzi didn't take those front row seats to the football games, or if there was some video of her eating alone with people ignoring her, would she have as many followers? Didn't audiences want to see the perfect life, not the messy miserable ones that we lived every day?

But Mitzi was also shockingly ruthless about maintaining

her position. A sophomore, Cora Hadden, had once dared to post that one of Mitzi's sponsored perfumes was terrible (it was; it smelled like bee farts). Almost immediately, her own accounts got a pile-on of negative comments. She got the teal dress of death the next day. They accused her of stealing funds from her dance team. By the time she cleared her name, she had missed weeks of rehearsal and a major competition. It was as if Mitzi and Adeline analyzed their enemies to see exactly where their weak spots were, so they could inflict maximum suffering.

Mitzi might have her reasons for acting the way she did, but she also chose to hold on to her privileges by bullying the population into compliance. She put her accounts and revenue above everything else. Griff and the others joked about liberating the Republic of Plainstown, but it would be true freedom, for everyone, if we could break the hierarchy. Mitzi had set up a ruthless reign of tyranny unlike one I had ever seen before. She needed to be stopped.

I just hoped we could do it before she found and obliterated us.

Thirteen

PHASE ONE: OPERATION PARKING

THE NEXT MORNING, the first BMW—Adeline's—cruised into the parking lot, late as usual. You don't need to arrive on time when you're in the "A" lot.

That is, unless the entire "A" lot is blocked off with beautiful, free sawhorses. And a fake CLOSED sign (in color). Adeline's car stopped in front of the sign for almost a full minute, then zoomed off.

Griff and I were in his Prius, in the far corner of the "B" lot, sharing a bag of popcorn.

"Do you think she knows this lot is full?" Griff munched on a handful as Adeline screeched past us. "Oops. I guess she does now."

Will, sitting in the back seat, popped his head in between us. "Pass the corn, friends."

Peter leaned towards the window. "Beauty lies in anticipation. I hope this is not a bad idea."

One by one, the VIPs' cars stopped at the tiny "A" lot, and then sped away. Since the "B" lot was already occupied, that left only Siberia—the "C" lot down the street.

Griff brushed the salt off his fingers. "Go time, team."

"Livvy?" Will asked.

I shook my head. "I'll be in the front row. Observing."

He saluted. "Got it, boss."

Blocking the spots wasn't the true goal. Mitzi, Adeline, and the VIPs had largely usurped the best of everything without any meaningful challenge. It was time for that to end.

Griff and Will gave each other a quick high five and then slipped into the crowd pushing its way to class. The first bell rang, and everyone outside picked up the pace—not being in homeroom for the second bell meant detention and, more horrifyingly, your photo on the much-mocked Tardy Board in front of the school.

When Mitzi's boyfriend, Brett Clifton, sprinted past us, his shirt was untucked and he was sweating. Like the countless others who had been forced to park in the "C" lot before him, Brett had to dash across both the "C" and "B" lots—and the faculty parking lot—in order to get to the building. It was a long run he'd never had to make before. When he finally stumbled through the front door, his backpack was unzipped, and papers flew in the air behind him.

People stared at Brett as he raced towards homeroom, panting. For once—*miraculously*—they weren't looking at me.

The Nerd Net's blockade was discovered and removed the next day, but the damage was done: two members of the women's field hockey team arrived early and tried to park in the first row of the "A" lot. The VIPs eventually chased them out, but it was the first time in the history of the Mitzi Era that anyone had even attempted to breach the sacred front.

For the next few days, one parking spot in the "A" lot remained blocked. In the middle was a battered wooden sawhorse with a curious metal symbol affixed to it: N^N.

Fourteen

N^N

OVER THE NEXT few weeks, the N^N symbol started appearing everywhere. In bathrooms. In the library, tucked between the pages of books. In lockers, on small pieces of paper. No words attached. No explanation. Just a flare shot into the sky: the revolution has started.

Fifteen

HOW TO BRAND A REVOLUTION

ONE WOULD ASSUME a certain amount of glamour would come with leading a revolution. However, the reality was this: the five of us, next to Heidi's crystalline pool, spray-painting an enormous piece of turf. Luckily, her vast backyard was large enough for our project. Our project, or, you know, any airplanes that needed a spare runway.

"So, now we're going to horrify Mitzi and Adeline with ecologically friendly grass?" Will said. "That's our plan?"

"This stuff is not exactly cheap," Heidi grumbled. "Do I look like I am made of money?"

"Depends." Will tossed her a can of spray paint. "Are all of the bills that you sleep on at night comfortable or do they slightly chafe your delicate skin?"

"Only the Franklins have sharp corners. The Clevelands are like feathers."

"Clevelands?" Griff said. "I don't even know what those are."

"Keep painting!" Peter called. This idea was his, and it was an inspired one.

Will nudged the corner of the fake lawn with his shoe. "Tell me again why we can't just paint the field?"

Peter straightened the stencil he had taped to the turf. "Obviously, the point of this exercise is to make a social statement and not create an undue burden for the staff of our school, so we should maximize exposure and minimize risk."

"The custodians can pull it up and it won't do permanent damage to the field," Griff translated.

"My God," Will said. "A socially responsible prank?"

"I'm not a heathen, and it might do you good to start thinking of others, William. We don't want to make things worse for anyone else. Just better for everyone." Peter sprayed carefully, with small squirts.

Will was silent. "Fine."

Heidi shook her red paint with gusto. "The blood of the revolution!"

Will plucked it from her hands. "It's not a rattle, Hexler." Heidi snatched another can from the ground and did a little dance, shaking it in a syncopated rhythm.

"More tape on the stencil," Peter said. "We don't want it to be sloppy."

"Oh no." Will sprayed in a wide arc. "God forbid we be sloppy in our vandalism."

Griff handed me a canister. "I know you are here in a strictly advisory capacity. But I hear spray painting is surprisingly therapeutic."

Griff had texted my tater phone earlier in the day and invited me over. I had stared at the message, at the little French flag emoji, and thought about refusing. I knew Griff would not hold it against me. Our little sawhorse adventure had been fun, but the rational and prudent thing to do would be to get some distance. It would have been right in line with my time-tested philosophy of keeping away from anything resembling human society.

But here was the thing.

Here was the tiny, little thing.

In all my years of invisibility, in every one of the times at Lake View when I was staring angrily and helplessly at the bullies who had made my life miserable, I imagined in vivid detail how a revolution like this might play out. I thought about all the possible outcomes, brainstormed strategies and responses and counterstrategies. I dreamed of seeing a regime toppled. Of, yes, an underdog triumph.

And here, in Plainstown, it was *working*. Some people made fun of the N^N symbol, of course—scribbling graffiti on top, or making fake TikTok accounts about it, etc. But people were talking about it. Small NNs began to appear in the comment section of Mitzi's posts, on her livestreams. I saw it on the margin of homework pages, on cell phone screens.

I *could* retreat to my hermit shell. But I could also be a first-hand witness to see if my theory was *right*.

The social scientist in me could not resist. I texted back a yes. So now I was spray-painting turf, as one does. Naturally.

Griff plucked the paint can from my hands. "You know, it actually works better if you have a little fun with it." He sprayed the word *JOIE* in large letters.

"Don't get paint past the stencils," Peter hollered. Of course Peter had suggested stencils, which he had meticulously measured and cut out of large pieces of paper.

"What's French for party pooper?" Griff offered the can back to me.

"Le party de pooper?" I gingerly pressed the button and a surprisingly large amount of paint shot out. "Le fête de poo poo?"

"I HEARD THAT," Peter said.

Heidi called, "Un trouble-fête. Un rabat-joie."

"Wait, are you already fluent in French?" I shouldn't have been surprised; her French was always perfect in class.

"Ask her where she spends her summers," Will said.

"Right." Of course.

"Sorry. I mean, ask her where she spends the first half of her summers. The second half is in Spain."

"¡Sí!" Heidi made a flourish with her paint. "Es un país de belleza y maravilla."

"More on the upper part!" Peter said. "Uniform color!"

"He's actually off his phone," Will whispered to me in awe. "Is this what happens when he stops texting? He becomes a tyrant?"

"Sí," Heidi said.

"I CAN HEAR YOU." Peter put extra tape on the edge of the stencils, pressing down firmly.

"An all-caps dictator," Griff said. "THE WORST KIND."

Heidi recklessly sprayed paint all over her section of the turf and Peter yelped.

Will handed me a fresh can. "Use this responsibly. Not like that one over there."

Heidi called over a word in Spanish that needed no translation, and Will laughed.

At school, Will was often avoided by everyone because he had a habit of staring down anyone who dared to pick on him. Or who interacted with him in any way. Despite this—or maybe because of it—he made the most sense to me. The best defense is a good offense; sometimes that meant being on the verge of fighting everyone, and sometimes that meant withdrawing from everyone and refusing to play the game. There was a certain power in isolation. But seeing Will joke around now with Heidi made me happy.

"So Mitzi thought your sister was Chinese?" I asked.

There are shortcuts you can take with other Asians, because we often have to deal with the same kind of shit.

"Right?" he said. "Why do they always think we're Chinese? Chang—you're from Taiwan, right?"

"Which is different."

"Absolutely. My parents were born here. My mom watches *The Bachelorette* and my dad wants to build an Iron Throne in our backyard. Heidi speaks Korean almost as well as I do."

"We take class together," Heidi said, "on Sundays."

Will said, "So now she can insult me in many, many languages."

"He's better at the hangul. But now I know how to say 'your mother totally loves me' in both formal and informal speech."

"True," Will said as Heidi wandered off to get more paint. "If we were on a sinking cruise ship, my mother would absolutely save Heidi before she saved me."

"How long have you been dating?" I asked.

"Oh, no." Will watched Heidi as she walked; he always did. I wondered if he was even aware of it. "Heidi and I have something terrifyingly wonderful, Livvy. No reason to mess it up with dating."

Heidi returned, but she did not look at Griff or Peter; she was heading straight towards Will, smiling.

"Really."

Will cleared his throat. *"Anyhoo."* He looked at me seriously. "Do you want to talk about what happened in study hall?"

Adeline's video, the slanted eyes she had painted on me. The memory burned through me, grotesque.

Did I? Yes. Of course. No.

I was surprised Will was bringing it up. I had only talked about these things with my mom, and, honestly, not that much because I didn't want to worry her. So now when Will was opening this door, I didn't know if I wanted to—or even how to—step through. I had no siblings, never had any close friends who had gone through the same things I had. I never had close friends, period.

The top, easy note was anger. Of course, what Adeline had done was terrible. But what I really wanted to ask was: *Is this what it's like for all of us? Or is there something about me?*

I always thought it was just me.

There was a fierceness to Will's question, an understanding that I saw he was trying to pass to me, like a gift. But I had too much to untangle: fury, discomfort, shame, fear.

When I didn't respond, Will leaned in. "I saw your face when she showed you that thing. It was bullshit. Okay?"

I looked down at the grass, then nodded.

Will bumped his shoulder with mine as Heidi came up to us. He lifted the cans from her arms. "Save those muscles for raking in all of your money, Hexler."

"It's true, the big bills do give me arm cramps," she said. "Thank goodness your macho self is able to lift those huge cans for little ol' me."

Will gave me a look—*See? Friendship is way better than dating.* But he did not see the expression of pure affection on Heidi's face as she watched him passing out the paint.

Griff nudged me and whispered, "Also, if you join the Nerd Net, you get front row seats to that."

"How long have they—?" I asked.

"Since they met. Love works in mysterious and in very, very, very slow ways."

Peter shouted, "MORE PAINTING! LESS CHATTING!"

"He is not allowed to stop texting again, ever," Griff said. "Talk about la tyrannie."

"I HEAR YOU."

Exactly twenty-seven minutes later, we had a beautiful, portable, socially responsible piece of vandalism.

"Time for an adventure," Will said. "Peter, you're coming, right?"

Peter started rolling up our project. "I feel like my talents are not necessarily breaking and entering, but since this is my idea, I am invested and would like to make sure the placement is ideal. And honestly, you are not the most detail oriented, Will."

"So that's a yes from Peter. Heidi?"

"Oui," Heidi said. "But I'm driving. AND TURN OFF YOUR RINGER IN THE CAR, PETER."

Griff picked up the other end of the turf and he and Peter headed towards the driveway. "Let the games begin."

The next morning, you could hear the buzz before you walked to the bleachers. Griff and I stood to the side as the students filed past us, and tried not to smile.

"Look, Livvy. Is that not the most beautiful football field you've ever seen?" Griff reached for my hand, his fingers warmly threading through mine. I jumped slightly in surprise, but he was gazing into the distance angelically. "What? I am merely uniting us in this wondrous moment."

He smiled, and I could not help but wonder how this small contact—his palm against mine, his fingertips against my skin—could have such a staggering effect. But it kind of did.

"I see." I tried to look as if a hot guy holding my hand was something that happened to me every morning. Griff, too, was looking excessively casual, but his face was slightly flushed. "We both happened to be in the same place, at the same time."

"With hands in the same place."

"Exactly. I mean, we both could have been reaching for a . . . pretzel, and boom, our fingers got all tangled up. Who knows?" I was disproportionately pleased to hear his small huff of a laugh next to me. Then he laughed loudly, shaking his head.

"A pretzel?" he said. "Is that what you're going with, Livvy?"

"It's better than my first version of that joke, which involved a porcupine."

He laughed again.

We surveyed the football field, with two hands that were coincidentally wrapped around each other. It *was* beautiful. In the center, meticulously outlined in bloodred paint, was a familiar gray-and-orange symbol: N^N.

As the students filed into the bleachers, the whispers started, followed by some awestruck pointing and muffled laughter. It took a few minutes for the teachers to notice the fuss, then Coach Henson sprinted across the field and tried to roll up our artwork. But it was too late.

The message had been sent.

The next week was filled with rumors. People wondered: Who had done these pranks? Why? We began to see the Nerd Net symbol and the N^N hashtag on social media. It was the subject du jour in the cafeteria. I saw Mitzi looking at a N^N symbol taped to the school wall, with a detached puzzlement.

She had no idea what was coming.

Sixteen

RECONNAISSANCE

THAT AFTERNOON, I studied Mitzi and Adeline, much like the Colonists gathered intel on the British armies before the Revolutionary War. I had researched popular people before, of course. Thanks to Grandfather, I was no stranger to *The Art of War*, and Sun Tzu's advice to know thy enemy.

Mitzi had been fixated for weeks on how to get this biology internship. Every year, the top student in Mr. Wagner's biology classes was offered a spot with the Ohio Science Foundation, and would be given access to professionals in the subspecialty of the student's choice.

The current frontrunner was clearly Meera Banerjee. She not only had the top grade, but also did research with another lab last summer. She was definitely aiming to win. She was set on becoming an environmental scientist, with a focus on natural resources.

The winner of the internship could sometimes put in a good word for another student, if any of the labs or offices had extra work. Since Mitzi's grades weren't great, I knew that's how she was hoping to get into the Foundation. She was interested in medical research because she had spent so much time in the hospital with her brother. However, there was no way Meera was going to help her after what Mitzi had said about Asians wrecking the curve, and Mitzi knew it.

But there was one interesting wrinkle. Mr. Wagner had just posted the class rankings, and the number two student was—wait for it—Adeline Jackson. There wasn't enough time for Adeline to get the top spot, since Mr. Wagner was going to send his recommendation for the internship in the next two weeks. It was almost certainly going to go to Meera. Which meant that Mitzi was hosed.

This was a shitstorm of epic proportions. Murder was obviously off the table, but short of that, I had no idea what was going to happen.

Mitzi could try to pressure Meera to give up the spot with her usual shunning tactics, but I wasn't sure that was going to work. Meera was an athlete, a long-distance track runner, and I had seen her practice through rain and cold weather and injury. I didn't think that social discomfort would sway her.

Mitzi must have come to the same conclusion, because she then did something interesting. She befriended Sonya Kirby.

It started during class. Mitzi gave up her usual spot at Adeline's table and sat next to Sonya.

"Hi," she said. "I like your skirt."

Sonya blinked at her. So did her friend Calvin, who was sitting on the other side of her.

The next day, Mitzi sat next to Sonya again. "You're so good at lab."

"Thank you?" Sonya said.

On day three, Mitzi made more small talk with her. She chatted easily with Sonya about their shared love of foreign films and what they liked to do on the weekends. As she talked, I saw Sonya relax, smile more.

As I shamelessly eavesdropped on their conversation, a small part of me wondered what it would be like to be that comfortable speaking to people. I was always the person off to the side, mentally rehearsing what to say. I remember once, in fifth grade, I was waiting outside the library when this girl I had never seen before sat next to me.

"Hey," she said.

This set off a whole existential crisis in my brain. How could she just talk to a stranger and say hello? How was that possible? Wasn't she worried I wouldn't say hi back? How could she approach a new person and start a conversation? I'm not joking when I say that casual greeting caused a major tear in my universe/perception continuum. I simply couldn't understand it.

But when I looked over, the girl hadn't noticed a thing. She tucked her headphones into her ears and started chewing a fresh piece of gum. As her ride approached, she tossed me a "see ya."

See ya. Just like that.

Some people have the "hey" and "see ya" gene. Then there are the rest of us.

At the end of class, Mitzi said to Sonya, "Adeline is having a party this weekend." Adeline looked surprised, then nodded slowly. "You should come."

What? I was confused until I learned one piece of important information: Sonya Kirby's father worked for the state. More specifically, at the Ohio Department of Natural Resources.

Within a week, Meera Banerjee had been offered an after-school job at ODNR, and had withdrawn her application for the internship. Adeline easily vaulted to the top.

Calvin came up to Sonya after class. He now sat off to the side in lab, alone.

"Hey, Sonya," he said. "I just had an interview for the ODNR job. Do you know why Meera got it all of a sudden?"

"I don't know." Sonya fiddled with her papers.

Mitzi stared at Calvin, unblinking. "An interview isn't a guarantee."

"They told me it was only a formality, based on my grades and past experience." Calvin ignored Mitzi. "They said my offer was coming. Did they say anything to you?"

Mitzi shrugged. "The better person got it, I guess."

"I'm not talking to you." Calvin put a hand on Sonya's arm, lightly. "Sonya?"

But Sonya put away her textbook, not saying a word.

Calvin went still. Then came the terrible understanding. "Unbelievable. Adeline's now in the top spot for the internship, isn't she? What a coincidence."

"Looks like it," Mitzi said.

Calvin leaned in. "You don't care who you hurt, do you? As long as you get what you want."

Mitzi flushed, and for the first time, her pleasant school persona cracked. "No, I don't. And neither should you. If you don't look out for yourself, no one else will," she said, and strode out of the room.

Calvin whirled towards Adeline and Sonya. "Don't think she won't do the same to you. Don't think you're not disposable."

The last thing I saw was Calvin furiously packing up his bag, and Sonya tugging on his arm. Off to the side, Adeline was quiet, and pale.

It was the first time I had seen anything even close to a fissure in Mitzi's camp.

It was the perfect time to launch Phase Two.

Seventeen

PHASE TWO

WILL'S IDEA FOR Phase Two required a bit of technical savvy. That's where Heidi came in. We were in her basement, where all of the computers were humming softly. An enormous box filled with snack-sized bags of chips was in the center of the conference table.

Next to Heidi were a pile of open books, with indecipherable titles such as *OWASP, O Fun!* and *TCP/IP and OSI.* "My stepdad thought computers were more productive than ballet or music."

Will stood behind her, looking amused. "She's about to go into the zone. And everyone in Korean now—hana! Dul! Set!"

As soon as Will said "three," Heidi's gaze focused on the screen and she began to type rapidly, making a rhythm to a song only she could hear. Will snagged a bag of chips and began to munch.

Peter came skipping down the stairs.

"Hi, guys—sorry I'm late, but did you know Windsor is still closed? You probably did, but for some reason I didn't and I took it and then it was too late to turn—" He stopped and looked at Heidi. "Oh. Did anyone eat the Doritos yet?"

Griff tossed him a bag. Peter snatched it, then chuckled as his phone pinged. "Carlie—"

"PETER," Heidi said. "IF YOU DO NOT TURN OFF YOUR RINGER, I WILL POST A VIDEO OF YOU DOING THAT TIKTOK DANCE ALL OVER THE INTERNET."

Next to me, Will sighed. "What a gal."

"So do you think you'll be able to do it?" Peter said. "Everyone except—"

"Shh," Heidi hissed. "Concentrating here."

"I mean, it shouldn't be too, too hard, right?"

Heidi stopped typing and squinted at him.

"Oh, man." Griff tugged my arm. "You're going to want to step back."

I snatched a snack-sized bag of pretzels and retreated to a pink couch next to Heidi's desk. Griff dropped onto the cushion beside me and pleasantly smushed himself against my left side, even though there was plenty of room on the rest of the sofa.

"Oh?" Heidi said. "Not difficult? Did you hear what Will said? We want to send some secret, anonymous, self-destructing message to the entire population of Plainstown High—"

"Well—of course—" Peter stammered.

"But not to Mitzi, Adeline, and their friends?"

"Well—"

Heidi held up her hand. "Couch. No more speaking. OR TEXTING. And don't eat the nacho ones."

Will plopped down next to us. "It's actually not that hard," he whispered as Peter sat beside him. "Just a pain in the ass."

The four of us on the couch meant that I was practically in Griff's lap. He reached over and plucked a pretzel from my bag.

"Do you mind?" he asked, innocently. "Mine are all gone." I could see the small pulse on the side of his neck, smell a light scent of soap, which reminded me of his blue sweatshirt.

No. It turns out I did not mind at all, in fact.

I'd had crushes before, of course—Jake-the-swimmer, Luke-from-the-bookstore, Marco-with-the-dimples. Those mostly consisted of one-sided sighing and aspirational dreaming on my part. There was one mini-relationship at Morris High, with Henry-from-honors-history; that ended when I discovered that he was tangled in enough mini-relationships to form an entire knot of bullshit. There was another flirting-with-potential relationship at Porter, but then I'd moved.

But I never had this: a genuine onslaught of charm from a hot guy. I was at a total loss. Was this how he acted with everyone? But he didn't, not with Heidi or anyone else at school. Why me?

Will said, in a stage whisper, "He doesn't even like pretzels."

"I love them." Griff leaned his head on my shoulder, munching. "They are my new favorite snack."

"Just toss him a few," Heidi called over. "Pretend he's a little squirrel."

I concentrated on trying to breathe like a normal human

being and not like some ridiculous marathon runner. Hold it together, Livvy! Breathe in for three—that's about normal, right? Not too long and not too short? Maybe four.

I put a pretzel in my mouth, but then I was thinking about how it was too dry and how horrible it would be if I coughed or choked, and now this was getting absurd.

I stood up. "I'm going to the bathroom."

"Thank you for letting us know, Livvy," Will said. "I tied my shoes all by myself this morning."

When I returned, Griff turned the pretzel bag back towards me. I carefully pulled one out as I took my seat (not too close, not too far, ugh, stop freaking out, Olivia!). I managed to think clearly enough to say thank you *before* I started chewing, and that was pretty much the most complicated intellectual decision I made all afternoon.

"So, what's the story with Mitzi's mom?" I asked. I quickly abandoned any idea of appearing coherent and went with my solid Plan B: diverting attention away from myself. "She looks super familiar."

"It's sad." Heidi kept typing. "Have you seen her stuff? She was amazing in her heyday. But she had a big flop about ten years ago—"

"Oh, I remember that one," Peter said. "The monster thriller?"

Heidi nodded. "Then she disappeared. Which is totally ridiculous because male actors can have flops all the time, but they don't get punished for it. Or for getting old. Or for not looking perfect all the time."

Huh. I thought of Mitzi, and how she constantly fiddled with her hair and makeup or looked at herself in the mirror. I thought it was vanity. But was there more to it than that?

"Her husband—Mitzi's stepdad—bankrupted them with these bad investments. Then cheated on her, so she dumped him. But she couldn't get another acting job, after," Heidi said. "I guess she must be going for sponsorships now? She's been desperate to get back to Hollywood, but I think she's done."

I suddenly remembered where I had seen Mitzi's mom: on some tabloid, where someone had taken a picture of her, no makeup on, hair in a messy bun, exiting a grocery store. The following social media swarm crucified her.

What would it be like to be judged for the rest of your life based on a job you had a decade ago? Or based on what you used to look like? If Mitzi's mom got all that shit for being a regular person and going shopping, what would happen if she tried to get an ordinary job somewhere? There is honor in honest work, but things like honor and nuance don't quite exist in the tabloids or on the internet.

"What about her sister?" I asked. "Isn't she also an actress? Can't she help them out?"

"No way." Will stretched his legs out, wiggling his toes. "They hate each other. It's this famous feud. They competed for every role. If one sister got a movie, the other would try to get the next one with the same director. They were constantly up for the same awards."

"So what happened?"

"They were both amazing, for a long time. Like two pro

132

tennis players making each other better, only they loathed each other. Then Mitzi's mom had the flop. Her sister tried to reach out to her, but then one of her friends told a magazine that Mitzi's mom was extremely difficult to work with."

"Was she?"

Will shrugged. "Who knows? Does it matter? Ever since then, Mitzi's mom has always blamed her sister for the loss of her career."

"But it does matter. If she really was a pain, doesn't she have to take a bit of responsibility for that?"

"You would think."

Mitzi had said, *If you don't look out for yourself, no one else will.* That wasn't merely a cliché. Maybe it was their family history, two sisters who had stripped their ties with each other, peeling off layer by layer over the years until there was nothing left. Maybe this was the lesson shoved upon Mitzi from a young age.

Was this what was going on with Adeline, too? I hadn't paid much attention to her since she always seemed to do whatever Mitzi wanted. But Adeline had her own TikTok empire.

It was vastly different from Mitzi's. Adeline did film and television reviews and—surprise, surprise—her account was almost one hundred percent snark. Where Mitzi's account was refined and unapologetically commercial, Adeline's was grittier, more controversial.

I clicked on a video: it was her making fun of a young actor with crooked teeth, who had been cast in a terrible television show. The comments were predictable: Hilarious! So true! This is the content we're here for!

Griff leaned over me, curious. It was almost too much at once: the floating smell of soap, the warm press of his arm. He said, "She became super popular over the last year."

I tried to concentrate on what he was saying.

"Can you scroll to the beginning?" Griff said. "I'm curious."

He leaned in farther. I absolutely did not notice how his fingers were close to mine as he held up half of the phone. Or how he had to lean his head towards me so we could both see the screen.

Video. I was studying the videos.

At first, Adeline had done little reviews of movies and television shows; they were mostly positive. But then, a few years ago, she posted one video totally eviscerating a film. It got almost double the amount of likes. She posted a positive video. Half the amount of likes. Snarky video—huge number of views.

I swiped my phone, almost forgetting that Griff was next to me. You could almost see Adeline's evolution in real time: positive, negative, positive, negative, negative, negative. Hate makes for more compelling content, I guess. When Adeline had flashed that video of me in study hall, she thought it was hilarious. Did she realize there was a real person attached to her joke?

Then I saw one small clip, buried. It was almost five years old, but Adeline kept it up for some reason. She was tiny, baby-faced, and it looked like she had been crying. A flash of words across the screen: *Left again.* Then it ended.

I scrolled through the rest, but there was no follow-up. Only one long break after an extremely mean video, then a pivot to more neutral book reviews. Was she trying to switch lanes? But the new stuff didn't get any traction, so she soon went back to her usual. From then on, her videos got crueler and crueler as she ruthlessly collected more thumbs-up and comments.

Griff leaned back into the couch. "So that's how she got all of her followers."

I looked up one of the actors that she made fun of, but he had quit social media. Adeline's nickname about his teeth had gone viral, and I saw it on blogs, posts, snarky articles. Adeline never issued an apology, but it was around that time that she tried to change to more neutral content. But soon enough, she returned to her old ways.

Are any likes good, so long as they are likes? No matter who they hurt?

In the ruthless world of *us* versus *them*, Mitzi and Adeline always picked themselves. That was the poison their whole empire was feeding off of, the rotting root at its center.

Across the room, Heidi suddenly threw her arms up in the air, then pointed a finger at Will. He tossed her a bag of nacho Sun Chips, which she caught with one hand. She pushed her swivel chair in his direction and tipped the opened bag towards him as she glided by.

Will snagged a chip and popped it in his mouth. "It's done?"

She smiled. "It's done."

It was time for a change.

Eighteen

OPERATION FLASH MOB

OPERATION FLASH MOB started the next day. Heidi decided to use Click, an app with messages that would auto-delete one minute after they were opened. However, the Nerd Net had to do the first step the old-fashioned way—with papers that Griff slipped into all the lockers before school.

There were only three things on it: a ClickCode (which would allow people to receive our messages), the Nerd Net symbol, and the words *DO NOT SHARE*. (The all-caps were Peter's idea.) The entire school received it—that is, the entire school except for Mitzi, Adeline, and their friends.

At exactly 4:30 p.m., on Wednesday, November 30, the Nerd Net Click account activated. It only sent one message:

TOMORROW. WEAR GRAY AND ORANGE CLOTHES AND SOCKS.

In the background was the N^N logo.

Then we waited.

The next day, the school looked like it was going to a giant football rally. Some people were bold with their orange, wearing bright T-shirts or skirts. Some were more subtle, wearing orange scarves, headbands, or earrings. Ethan Earle, from the drama club, walked in wearing gray tube socks with the Nerd Net symbol written on the sides in orange permanent marker. He had pulled them over the cuffs of his jeans like homemade, patriotic soccer socks.

The gray and orange was a statement, yes, but Will thought it could also be a test, an experimental buoy to see if people were starting to believe in the movement. Each of us tracked a specific clique to see if they wore gray and orange clothes.

As expected, the drama club came out strong, with creative and fun choices.

"Almost one hundred percent participation," Peter said later as we tallied our informal poll numbers at Heidi's. "Though it was expected, we thought—I thought—well, it was quite exciting when they started to use the N^N symbol independently as a positive statement—" His phone pinged and he started typing.

Will shook his head. "Well, thank you, Peter, for those four seconds of uninterrupted time. Heidi? The jocks? Did they participate?"

"Forty percent, but some of the shirts were ambiguous. But field hockey was high, swim high, women's basketball high."

"And the honors crowd?"

"Nearly ninety percent."

Griff reached over and made a huge checkmark on the whiteboard. "Perfect. Music was seventy-five–eighty percent. French horns were one hundred percent, though."

"Oh, those horns," Will said affectionately. "Those non-conformists."

"I also tracked Frank Pang and his friends." Griff put a huge X on the board. Frank and his pals also liked to menace the school population, but in a more we-will-kill-you-if-you-bother-us kind of way. "Zero, which was not a surprise, but I doubt they will ever support Mitzi."

"If you mean they will never, ever support her, then yes," Will said, "that is correct."

Griff smiled. "Friends. Let the revolution continue."

Nineteen

ROU ZAO FAN

BY THE TIME Griff drove me home, it was dinnertime. I could hardly believe that Operation Flash Mob had gotten so much traction. I expected a little—maybe some—participation. But not that much.

Griff pulled up to my dark house. Mom was at the office late again, so I guess I was on my own.

To my surprise, Griff put the car into park. "Your mom's working?"

I nodded.

"Same." It was silent for a moment, so I grabbed my purse. But then he spoke. "You said you had to cook a lot of your own meals?"

He remembered that?

"So do I," he said. "What do you make?"

"What?" I felt like I was in an alternative universe. Didn't he want me to get out? But it didn't seem like it; he was leaning back, relaxed.

"For dinner? Spill."

"Carnitas? Random Taiwanese dishes?" I said. "Sometimes shrimp pasta?"

"Sauce from scratch or jar?"

"Scratch."

Griff smiled. "Sugar or no sugar?"

"Seriously? No sugar."

He sagged in his seat in relief, and I laughed.

"Television on or not on?" he said. "Of course on, right?"

I nodded. Because the silence was too terrible without it. If loneliness had a soundtrack, it would, for me, be the low cadence of reruns in the background of an empty house.

"You study downstairs," he said. "I saw the coffee table in your living room."

"It's . . . more comfortable."

But he knew exactly what I was saying. "I used to leave all the lights on when I was little and had to stay home by myself," he said. "Until my mom yelled at me about the electric bill."

I laughed, because the same had happened to me. The dark and the quiet were too much. I finally figured out that it was much better to scrunch up in front of the television.

"So the living room? For you, too?" I asked.

"Why even have an upstairs?"

It hadn't been that way when Grandfather was alive. When he had been here I would run around the entire house, read books in my room and snuggle with my stuffed animals. There was always the sound of plates being put away, or Chinese news, or the smell of something cooking.

After, I kept everything I needed on the coffee table. My afternoons and evenings were a small circuit from the kitchen to the bathroom to the television. I stayed downstairs until Mom came home.

Now, after the cheer of the Nerd Net meeting, the thought of going back to an empty living room was especially terrible. I wondered if Griff felt the same.

"Do you . . . ," I said. "Would you like to come over for dinner?"

Griff straightened. "Really?"

"I mean, you don't have to. If you need to get home."

"I don't." He turned off the car. "I would love nothing more."

Griff started exploring right away. He picked up and put down pictures, books, knickknacks. He also had a lot of questions.

"Who collects souvenir spoons?"

"My mom." The dining room wasn't in too bad of a shape since we never used it, but the living room was an absolute mess. Also, I wasn't sure what was in the fridge other than old kimchee, and celery that we kept buying even though neither one of us ate it. "What do you want for dinner?"

"Whatever you were planning on eating," he said. "I'm not picky."

I popped my head out of the kitchen. "Are you all going to judge my cooking?"

"How rude do you think I am? Silently judge, though, absolutely."

We were out of tomatoes, so pasta was out. What did we have? Ground pork. Ginger root that looked slightly wrinkled but was still good. Green onions.

Mom had started the rice cooker this morning, taping a little smiley face sticker to the front. If it was only me, I would cook a quick rou zao fan and be done with it. My mom must have thought the same, because I saw a bowl of dried shiitake mushrooms already soaking in water next to the sink. But the dish was very Taiwanese—would Griff want to eat it?

"Did someone like bunnies when she was little?" he called.

I ran to the living room. He had a picture in his hand, one of me as a little kid dressed up for Halloween. I had a few teeth missing and crooked pigtails. It was a few years before my dad would leave and my grandfather would move in; the photo caught a sweet spot of time on an ordinary Halloween, one where there was no arguing between my parents about how much candy I was allowed to eat, or whether I needed to wear an extra layer of clothes underneath my costume. It was one of the rare times where I was just excited and happy.

"Maybe," I said, and plucked the picture out of his hands.

He picked another one off the shelf. "Is this your grandfather?"

I nodded. It was one of my favorite pictures of him, where he was in front of a bookcase he had made in our hallway, right after he moved in with us. Earlier that summer, I had gone with him to the lumberyard and translated his shopping list. He had moved to the United States for its freedom and promise, borrowing money to come here and study history at a top university. But he could never quite grasp the complicated, idiosyncratic turns of English, especially when he was working two jobs to supplement his scholarship and feed his family.

After his master's degree didn't translate into a job, he tried to go to law school, but the standardized test was full of reading comprehension questions that were too subtle and tricky. He couldn't return home, not when he had borrowed money for his dream, not when the economy and finding a job were exponentially worse in his hometown, not when you didn't—at that time—have the freedom to speak your mind. So he spent the rest of his life in the United States, working at bodegas and grocery stores, cleaning restaurants, driving vans. But he never stopped yearning for the classroom, as if he could hear, through the ivory towers, the voices of civilizations past.

The day we had taken the picture, Grandfather had just finished filling the newly stained shelves. "Look," he said to me, squeezing my hand. "The whole world, right here."

I took the photo from Griff and put it back next to Grandfather's books, which neither Mom nor I could read. Griff pretended not to notice when I turned away, blinking. He instead touched another picture of Mom and me, alone, in front of Taipei 101.

"Have you been . . . ?" he asked.

I nodded.

Mom and I took a trip to Taiwan when I started at Porter

High, a few years after Grandfather died. I had been hopeful, thinking that I would finally be able to see my face in the streets and stores and restaurants. Maybe this would be the place where I would make sense. And it was something, looking out and seeing Taiwanese people everywhere and eating delicious food that mixed the familiar with the surprising. But neither Mom nor I spoke or read Mandarin Chinese, so there were a lot of conversations that we could only understand parts of. We didn't dress the same as everyone else; people wore American brands in Taiwan, but the accessories—and how the clothes were put together and combined—were subtly distinct. Everything was just a little bit different, especially us. We visited some of my mom's cousins, and sometimes they would stare at me a little after I talked, like I was too loud, too American. I spent a lot of time by myself, hiding with books in a spare bedroom.

Griff waited for me to say more, but when I didn't, he peered at a small blue paperweight sitting on the bookshelf. "Yours? Your mom's?"

"My dad's." It was one of the few things he had left behind. Neither my mom nor I could quite throw it away, so it just sat on the shelf.

Griff held it in his palm, his fingers curling over the glass. "My dad had this hideous painting at our old house, which he absolutely loved. After we moved, I told my mom that if she gave me twenty bucks, I would hide it in the attic of the new house."

"What did she say?"

"Nothing. But I found a twenty in my pocket."

"And where is it now?"

"Still up there. He's never home, so I don't think he even notices. Or cares, anymore."

Griff carefully put the paperweight back on the shelf. The emotions were wrapped around him, and I could almost see him pulling them tight so that nothing could escape. I couldn't help it; I moved towards him. Put a hand on his arm.

I felt like I was stepping on sky, and any slip could pull me into the void. But I kept walking because I recognized the dark place that Griff had gone to, and I couldn't bear for him to be alone.

"Do you . . . want to see him more?" I asked.

Griff could have lied or held in his feelings. But he let them loose, defiantly. I wasn't scared. All of it—the shamed longing, the fury, the loneliness—was as familiar to me as my own heart.

"Sometimes." He looked away. "But I don't want to want it."

I didn't say anything, but we both knew that I perfectly understood.

"So." Griff stepped closer to me, touching the side of my apron. "Dinner? How can I help? And do I get a matching one of these?"

"It's not that easy," I said. The press of his fingers was light. Neither of us took a step back. "You have to earn it."

"Challenge accepted." He smiled, and I finally moved, walking quickly towards the kitchen. "What are we eating?"

"Uh, we're a little low on supplies, so our options are

limited." I shoved some spices into a cabinet and covered the mushrooms with a plastic plate.

"No problem."

"So, I could make this pork thing? Like a Taiwanese dish? With rice? I mean, we can also order pizza. Or if you don't want to wait for pizza because it takes a long time, I totally understand if you need to get home."

My mouth was a firehose and I had no idea how to shut it off. OMG! Stop!

"I don't need to get home," Griff said. "And I would love nothing more than to learn how to cook this magical pork dish."

It was a bad tactical error mentioning the rou zao fan. There was no backing out now, no going back from showing him the dried mushrooms rehydrating on my countertop or the oyster sauce in my fridge. I remember at Lake View Middle, I had once brought someone over to our house, and Grandfather was going full-on Taiwanese with the cooking, with dried shrimps and pickled veggies in different bowls on the countertop. It was actually one of my favorite dishes, and I was all excited to have my new friend try it. But she took one sniff and blurted out that she had to go home. She never came over again.

I waited for Griff to back out. But he seemed unperturbed by the mushrooms and entirely familiar with the ginger root and oyster sauce. And when I scooped a bit of the rou zao fan over his bowl of rice, he took a bite and closed his eyes.

"I can move in, right? Your mom loves me. And we can eat this every day?"

"Sure."

But I couldn't think of anything more reckless. It was too easy to clean up the dishes with him and to spread out our homework on the table and to study with the lights and music on. It almost felt like something I could get used to, which was the worst thing I could imagine.

Twenty

OPERATION FLASH MOB, PART TWO

EXACTLY ONE WEEK later, the Nerd Net launched a second ClickComm:

TOMORROW. PAJAMA DAY, KIDS.

The next morning, the school became a giant slumber party. People came in onesies, robes, cow pajamas, cartoon pajamas and slippers. Marc Papadapolis came in a superhero costume, shouting, "It's what I wear to sleep!"

The school officials were puzzled but helpless since no one had bothered to put a ban on sleepwear in the school handbook (Peter checked, because of course Peter checked). The hallways, which were usually grim, oppressive corridors of fear, had a sudden festive vibe. Everyone was ready to party.

Griff and I lingered by the front hallway to get the best view of what was about to happen.

"Where's Waldo pants?" I said to him.

Griff shrugged. "It's a classic."

I scanned him suspiciously. "Waldo's not located somewhere . . . obscene . . . is he?"

He laughed.

Since last week, Griff had come over to study a few times or to have dinner. Sometimes he cooked, the fancy, use-all-the-pots-in-the-kitchen type of dishes that I was too lazy to make.

My mom definitely noticed the extra, delicious leftovers in our fridge.

"Seafood risotto?" she said. "Have we started making risotto?"

"Kind of?"

If by "we" she meant me and Griff, then yes, we have.

I tried to put the rest in my lunchbox, but she swatted my hand. "Nope, that's mine."

Now Griff said, "Did your mom like it?"

"She ran off with it and never looked back. Not even a shred of a thought for her precious daughter, who now is stuck with Tuna Surprise for lunch."

Griff looked ridiculously pleased. "They have the little crunchy chips in the cafeteria today. We can make Tuna Crunch."

At the end of the hall, Heidi wore a T-shirt with some inde-cipherable mathematical equation on it and a pair of pink satin pajama pants. A few lockers down, trying not to gaze longingly at her, was Will, in plaid flannel pants and a T-shirt showing Freud slipping on a banana peel. Peter, looking nervous, wore a Shakespeare sweatshirt and matching sweatpants. And matching socks. Where he'd managed to find Shakespeare socks was a mystery.

And me?

My favorite track pants and an alpaca-in-a-party-hat tee.

Griff tugged at the bottom of my shirt, his fingers lingering on the hem. "Why am I not surprised? Though I am sad I don't get to see my favorite pajama pants again."

"The first act in our new democratic state shall be to give alpacawear to everyone," I said. "And matching pom-pom hats."

Mitzi strode through the front doors, then halted at the sight of everyone in their nightwear. She grabbed Adeline, but she was equally confused.

Mitzi and Adeline were famous for their lavish parties at Adeline's mansion. Those invitations were not only coveted but a status symbol. Each gathering was meticulously documented and posted, blasting to the world about what fun they were having.

Fun that—of course—not everyone was invited to.

But this morning, the whole school was partying. Without them.

One of Mitzi's friends had already switched to her gym sweatpants and T-shirt. Dawn was wrapped in a long white sweater. Mitzi held out her hand, and Dawn looked incredulous. She waited until Dawn slowly unwrapped it, then snatched it and covered her own perfectly tailored tank and designer skirt. And I have to give Mitzi credit: she sold it. She walked down the hall as if it were a runway, the sweater floating behind her. But, for the first time, she was different from everyone else. And she was the only one not having a good time.

Someone brought in streamers and threw them down the hall, bright yellow splashes of color. Someone else passed out donuts and cups of cider.

Mitzi ignored everyone, but Adeline looked intensely uncomfortable. Behind them, Dawn followed in her own brightly colored tank and designer skirt, her face tight.

When the group passed Heidi in the hallway, I was surprised to see Dawn staring at her. Heidi's return expression was a missile of scorn. Dawn looked away, then rushed to catch up to Mitzi.

The rest of the day, Mitzi and her friends were easy to spot; they were the only ones who were well dressed, and cranky.

Mitzi tried to post a photo of herself in Dawn's sweater. But every time she tried to take a picture, someone in pajamas photobombed her. She finally gave up.

A few tables over, Griff passed me his fries. I reached for them reflexively, and realized with some surprise that, at some point, I had become used to his daily sharing of carbohydrates.

"It's time to launch Phase Three," he said.

Twenty-One

PHASE THREE

PLAINSTOWN HIGH WAS weird in many ways, but one of its strangest rituals was the lap before the morning bell. PHS was designed in a square shape, and everyone would walk the hallways before homeroom each morning, like the school was some kind of large strolling track. Always clockwise. Always from around 7:15 a.m., when people would start streaming in from the parking lots, to 7:45 a.m., the first bell.

But that wasn't the weirdest part. And I had been at four different schools and had seen a lot of weird. What was truly strange was that there was a system to the laps, a whole hierarchy compressed into the anything-but-leisurely strolls. People walked in friend clumps, picking up pals at their lockers, occasionally jettisoning one or two into their homerooms. It was like a traffic roundabout, but instead of cars, you had angsty adolescents.

Like everything else, where you walked was a direct indicator of who you were. The freshmen, as an entity, always walked in the outer portions of the hall. Mitzi, Adeline, and the VIPs were in the inner circle. Social outcasts or those without a group would not walk; they would sit in homeroom. (That was me.) The unspoken rule was this: if Mitzi or her people were coming your way, you moved. Those who defied the rules faced consequences. (Example: Ethan Earle from the drama club had once dramatically stood in front of the oncoming mass of VIPs and refused to retreat. The next day, social media was plastered with pictures of him as the back half of the milky white cow in a local production of *Into the Woods*.)

It was a nice early-morning assertion of dominance, you know, kind of like sea lions pushing intruders off their favorite rocks.

It was time to break the hold, and weaponize the undercurrent of resentment running through the halls of Plainstown High.

This was a student body waiting for a revolution. And we were going to give it to them.

Twenty-Two

RESISTANCE, ONE CLICKCOMM AT A TIME

ON DECEMBER 12, at exactly 5:17 p.m., the Nerd Network sent their third ClickComm to the oppressed masses:

IT IS TIME TO CHALLENGE THE ARBITRARY HIERARCHY OF THE HALLWAYS. BEGINNING AT 7:20 TOMORROW MORNING, WE WILL BE CHANGING THE DIRECTION OF TRAFFIC EVERY FIVE MINUTES. THE FIRST SWITCH WILL BE AT 7:20 TO THE COUNTERCLOCKWISE DIRECTION. REVERSE AT 7:25 TO CLOCKWISE. SWITCH BACK AND FORTH EVERY FIVE MINUTES. TIME IS DETERMINED BY THE SCHOOL CLOCKS.
LET THE REVOLUTION CONTINUE.

Twenty-Three

OPERATION HALLWAY

I WAS NOT an early riser, but the next morning, I was all ready to go by 6:45 a.m. My mom, astonished, handed me my backpack and a snack. She had gotten home late last night from the office, at almost 3:00 a.m. Papers on the dining room table and her buzzing iPhone made me think that she worked a little more after she got home. But here she was, with a little bag of Hello Panda cookies for me and a kiss out the door. I gave her a huge hug.

She slowly patted me on the back. "Have a nice day?"

"Possibly the best ever," I said cheerfully.

I had reached the end of the driveway when Griff's Prius pulled up. He rolled down the window. "Ride? And donut holes?"

I climbed in. "Why, Mr. Griffin. Fancy seeing you here." I

failed to suppress the almost-happy bubbles that were rising and fizzing through me. But I made a hard effort.

"I know these aren't french fries." He handed me the box of donut holes. "But I worry about your digestive health. So, donuts."

"Excellent."

Griff was wearing my favorite blue sweatshirt today, with the cuffs pushed up over his forearms.

It was too comfortable being in the car with him, listening to music. It was getting to be too familiar to study his profile as he drove, waiting to see the tiny bracket around his mouth when he smiled—truly smiled, as he had been doing with me lately. It had kind of been my sole purpose lately, to make him laugh. That was trouble. I was getting too used to him—too used to the rides and afternoons and dinners together.

"Now I know this is the subject of intense debate," Griff said. "It might even be too personal of a question. But I have to know: jelly donut holes. The devil or culinary genius?"

I fished around the box for one and popped it in my mouth.

"You might be perfect," he said. The smile he tossed as he drove was quick, certain. Genuine. It made the happy fizzies rise again, and I did not want that.

"Why"—oh, God, the verbal diarrhea was coming and I couldn't hold it in—"why would you say that?"

I clamped my mouth shut, horrified. You gotta keep that shit in! My only saving grace was that it sounded more combative than I'd intended. Or maybe that's exactly what I meant. I didn't want this, I hadn't asked for this *niceness*.

Griff gazed at me, then smoothly turned in to the parking lot. "You don't believe it?"

It wasn't that I'd *never* had compliments from boys before. I mean, Luke-from-the-bookstore liked my use of proper grammar. Bryan, the flirting-with-potential boy from Porter, smiled at me a lot, but we hadn't talked much before I'd moved. Okay, maybe that was it.

I said nothing, clutching the donut box as if it were a magical teleporter that could shoot me to the black hole in the center of our galaxy, which would then crush me into blissful death.

Griff turned the car off and gave me the full force of his attention. "Livvy."

I didn't want to get used to relying on him. I didn't want to look at him when something funny happened, as if it meant more if we shared it. I didn't want this longing for something that was surely going to end in disappointment.

"Olivia," he said.

Because it was much easier to accept that something was not yours when you never hoped for it in the first place. You know what else I remember about Luke-from-the-bookstore? The time he came up to me, giddy, because he had gone on a great first date with a girl he'd met the week before. He was so excited to tell me, his *buddy*. I remember overly loud congratulations hurling out of my mouth.

I remember Henry-from-honors-history and the moment I found out that our magical date on Friday had been followed by his date with Cathy Prichard on Saturday night, and Missy Wilcox the weekend after. For weeks, I had said no to his invitations, until he wore me down with his claims that I was the only girl for him. Sure. The only girl for him . . . that Friday.

Griff wanted to call me perfect? I had been down that charming road before, and I did not make the same mistakes twice. That's why I was so good at survival.

"Of course I can believe it," I said loftily. Carelessly. Smoothing over the horrifying vulnerability. "I'm perfectly perfect."

"You are, you know." His voice was quiet. "But I know you won't let yourself believe me. So I will present my arguments the way you social scientists prefer: one by one, and with evidence."

"Really." So this was what torture was: simultaneously longing to both flee and stay, with equal force.

"One. You try not to be seen, but you help others when you think no one is looking," he said.

"Oh?"

"You were the first one over when Penny McMahon dropped her tray in the cafeteria. And you let someone else go in front of you in line because he had a cast on his foot."

I didn't think anyone saw that.

"Two," he said. "I saw your face when Mitzi ruined your T-shirt. I know that upset you, but you never let them see it."

"So? That's what everyone does."

"Not everyone. Three: you notice what everyone else does and how they behave. But you can't believe that anyone would study you."

My new favorite word: *defenestration*. The act of throwing someone—here, myself—out of a window. My face was hot, and my body was having the same reaction it would have if a large predator stuck its sharp teeth right in my face. Flee.

Griff put a gentle hand on my arm. "Why is that?"

Because almost no one had. Certainly not my father, who had only burst through my childhood occasionally, in spiky penumbras of irritation or temper. My grandfather had been the one who always cooked my dinners in those early years, when my mother had to study or work late. He would always make my favorite noodle soup right when I needed it the most. If school was hard, he would suddenly have a new history book for us to study or a stuffed animal to hug.

And now that he was gone, who was left? Only Mom.

"Well, what about you?" I said. The question sounded accusatory, because it was. "You don't talk to anyone."

"I talk to you."

"Other than me. And the Nerd Net."

"Why would I?" he said. I couldn't tell if he was joking or not. "I have all I need."

"You don't want to speak to other people any more than I do."

"Maybe." Griff looked out the window, and I almost heard it, an undertone of loneliness in a frequency only I could hear.

In the stillness of the car, I dared to ask: "Why?" It was a question that went two ways: Why didn't he talk to other people? And—more critically—why was I one of the only people he did speak to?

Griff leaned towards me, reaching for a donut hole. And that's how a space can become something that is shared— because when you allow someone to get close enough, you can learn intimate things about each other, like how warm his skin feels when it is next to yours, or how his hair carries a faint curl of smell, of pine and sun.

"I do talk to other people," he said. "I'm just more selective about it now."

"Because?"

"Brynn." He said her name like it was the beginning and the end of the sentence, like it was the story in itself. "My cousin. She used to come over every day after school. Until one day, she didn't."

I knew better than to ask follow-up questions. I did what he had done for me so long ago; I waited; I listened.

"I finally found her at a park next to my house, crying," he said.

"What happened?"

"There was a group of people who pretended to be her friends. They lured her in, especially this one guy she liked."

"Oh no." This was not going to end well.

I could almost see Griff's icy fury, pressing against him. "She told him all of her insecurities, all the problems she was having at home, everything. That day they posted all of it to a school gossip website."

And this is why people are the worst.

"I confronted the asshole who did it to her, of course, and her friends. I thought—" He stopped. "I assumed my friends would be behind me. They weren't."

"I'm sorry." I tried to picture Griff standing up for his cousin at school, the betrayal of abandonment.

He shrugged. "He was the most popular guy in our school. They had to choose between themselves or me. Self-preservation, right?" There it was again: the thin wire of bitterness that sometimes shone beneath the surface. "It was fine."

It didn't sound fine. "What happened to Brynn?"

"She transferred schools. But she doesn't like the new one. I don't know if she has any friends. If she even wants any."

I could understand that, completely.

"You know what was horrible?" he asked.

I shook my head. It was like the words started spilling out and he didn't know how to stop them.

"It wasn't just that our friends let us down. It was that I had no idea what was happening. Brynn and I went to the same school and lived three streets apart. She was basically like my baby sister. I didn't have a clue."

"Did she tell you what was going on?" I asked.

Griff shook his head.

"Were you connected on social media? Have any of the same friends?"

A silent no. "Brynn's friend dragged her into a group of other freshmen. I didn't know them well. And she didn't have any idea that they weren't actually her friends. Until it was too late."

"So how could you have known?" I said. "She was hiding it from you."

"I should have been paying closer attention." Griff stared out the window again. I tugged his sleeve.

"Listen," I said. "My mom asks me about school all the time. Do you think I ever told her what was going on, when it was bad?"

Griff didn't answer.

I touched the back of his hand. "She found out about Lake View after one of her friends—the mom of one of my former friends—called her. It was the only way she knew anything."

"But she's your parent. That's different."

"Is it?" I said. "I was very, very good at hiding what was happening. Until it got so bad that I didn't care if she knew. Then the alpaca pants came out."

Griff smiled faintly. "I feel like I shouldn't ask about those."

"Point is," I said, "she wouldn't have known because I was actively hiding it. She didn't know because I didn't want her to know. If your cousin was like me, then you can't blame yourself. You didn't live with her. You didn't have access to her social media accounts. She wasn't in your grade."

Griff was quiet as we got out of the car and walked towards the school. I put my hand on his sleeve.

"I thought it was my fault for a long time," I said. "Every time someone did something awful."

"But it wasn't."

"And it's not yours."

Griff had no expression, which was almost worse; it was like he was sealing all the dark inside.

"You can't make it your fault," I said.

But I knew he could. That he did.

He finally spoke. "I keep thinking—were other people at

my old school pushed around and I somehow missed it? I had my own friends. My own world. And I never thought to look outside it. Could I have helped them, like I wish someone had helped Brynn?" Griff looked towards the front door, where everyone continued to stream in. "I'm no saint, Livvy. I don't even think I was that great of a person, before."

"But you're going to fix things here." I dared to put my fingertips on his arm, turn him towards me. "You're going to make sure it doesn't happen to anyone else."

Mom's rules of apology, part three: make it better.

Griff finally smiled. "*We're* going to?"

I rolled my eyes. "You, with brilliant assistance from me."

"You're in, Livvy," he said. "Don't try to pretend you're not."

Across the lot, Will gave a discreet thumbs-up. At the front door, Heidi winked at us, then slipped inside the building. Peter followed a few minutes later.

Operation Hallway had started.

Griff said, "Are you ready?"

"Oh yes. One might say I've been waiting for this my entire life."

As a mere advisor to the Nerd Net, I should have stayed in my usual spot (hiding in homeroom with a test prep book), but there were some things—sunrise over the Grand Canyon, solar eclipses, the northern lights—that you had to witness in person.

From 7:15 to 7:17, the hallways were more full than usual, as everyone strolled in the usual clockwise direction. Only the Nerd Net noticed the peeks at the clock starting at 7:19.

At 7:20, as if signaled by an actual bell, the entire mass stopped and turned around.

It was the most beautiful thing I had ever seen.

Mitzi and her friends, at first, were angry when the first group bumped into them.

"Excuse me!" Mitzi elbowed the person back.

But then the next group jostled against them, and the next, and the next. Mitzi, Adeline, and some of their friends stood, mouths agape, as the entire school population passed them, chatting and laughing. Mitzi took a tentative step and then snapped at Dawn to follow her. They tried to regain their footing, which worked for a whole two minutes, until the whole crowd reversed again, at 7:25.

We passed some of the VIPs, who tried to follow the crowd again. They began to walk in the inner circle but were bypassed by a rogue group of freshmen and the entirety of the girls' lacrosse team.

"Oh, Livvy," Griff said. "If only homeroom would never come."

We passed Heidi, who was pretending to fiddle with her locker. She was radiant with glee. She discreetly stuck her hand behind her back and I gave her a quick high five.

At 7:30, Mitzi got scary calm. She stood in the center of the hallway as people nervously streamed around her. Adeline and Dawn flanked her left and right sides, and she quickly deployed them.

"Find out what is happening," she snarled. "Now."

Adeline was clearly not thrilled with her tone, but she strode over to a group of girls standing by a water fountain. Dawn went down the hall, but then quickly vanished after she turned the corner. I didn't see her talk to anyone.

Griff placed a light hand on my arm as we strolled down the hallway, but I could feel Mitzi's dark gravity pulling tiny, vulnerable freshmen and sophomores towards her, sucking up information.

Then she saw me. I had been aggressively implementing all my invisibility tactics since the Nerd Net had started their good work. No eye contact. No sudden movements. (It was basically the same rules that you would use to survive a random bear encounter.)

But now Mitzi looked at me suspiciously. Did my face do something? Quick, Olivia, be neutral. Neutral.

But it was too late.

Mitzi's glance pinged between me and Griff, who had moved closer to me. Her look became incredulous, then accusatory. I looked away first, my hand reflexively curling over Griff's.

He looked down at our hands, bemused, as I tugged him into the nearest classroom.

"She knows," I hissed. "I think she knows."

"Impossible." But I saw it, the flash of doubt.

Mitzi refused to move from the center of the hall until the first bell rang. Later, a junior went on TikTok and posted a clip of her—mid-shove, hair slightly askew and messy—and pasted a caption above it. *Is this the face of Mirabelle Cosmetics?*

The next day, an offensive post from the junior was "unearthed" and "accidentally" reposted in the comments section of one of

Mitzi's videos. The teal dress of death. The junior first claimed it was a lie, but then more screenshots with more comments became public. The girl eventually dumped her phone and deleted all her accounts.

That was the first warning shot.

After the editor of the school paper made a snarky comment about how Mitzi was never in class, Adeline left an anonymous note for the journalism teacher, suggesting that the editor had fabricated her sources. It wasn't true, but her reputation was permanently damaged. And when a sophomore VIP gave a heart to a post that was pro–Nerd Net, Mitzi publicly excommunicated her by leaving her off the invite list for Adeline's next party and jettisoning her from the popular table. After that, anyone who made a reference to the Nerd Net or made negative comments about Mitzi was socially annihilated.

This was a classic way to crack down on dissent. In other countries, rebels who spoke out against the government were quickly removed from the community and isolated from any potential supporters. Here, they were sent to social jail.

But Mitzi's reign started to crack. People stopped trying to copy Mitzi's outfits. Mirabelle Cosmetics reduced their advertising, and then dropped her. Most seismically, Mitzi started to lose traction for the first time. She used to be able to post a picture, and within ten minutes it would automatically be flooded with hundreds of likes and positive comments. But after Operation Hallway, there was a series of photos she released that were met with silence.

The Nerd Net met at Heidi's house after school.

Will reached over her desk and picked up a pen with a big pink poof at the end. "It looks like things are catching on." He started dusting his face with it until Heidi snatched it away.

But Peter looked troubled. "I saw some people shoving some of the VIPs down the hallway."

"Isn't that what they do to everyone else, all the time?" Will said. "It's a little thing called 'what goes around comes around.'"

"It's not the same. That's promoting cruelty."

"We're not angels, Peter. And how do you think change is going to happen? Do you think they're suddenly going to just give up their privileges? Because that's totally happened in history—never."

Will wasn't wrong. Grandfather and I had studied so many regimes over the years, and in almost every case, power had to be wrested away, sometimes by force.

Peter leaned back into the couch, frowning. "That's not what we're about. And that's not going to fix anything. It's just going to make them angrier."

"Aren't they already our enemies, though?" I said.

"Enemies?" Peter said. "That's kind of strong, isn't it?"

"Well, they certainly aren't our friends. Mitzi and her little groupies."

Peter was normally cheerful and affable. But now he looked incredulous. "Groupies?"

"What?" I shrank a little at his tone, but I couldn't just let this go. He was making me sound like the terrible person, when I was just calling it like it was.

"You keep using these labels," he said. "But it's not that simple."

I'd had enough. "Why do you keep defending them?"

Peter flushed. "I just want you to see that people—even the VIPs—are complex. They aren't just followers. That's not their whole story."

"Come on." The salty heat of anger flared. "They trot along and follow whatever Mitzi and Adeline say. And does it matter *why* they do something? Isn't the bottom line that they let Mitzi and Adeline act like assholes? That they enable it?"

It didn't matter to me why people made fun of my grandfather's accent or stared at us because we were different. It only mattered to me that they did it.

I waited for Griff's support, but he was quiet. Contemplative.

"You don't agree?" I knew I sounded argumentative, but I couldn't quite hold back. It wasn't like I was trying to convince them that the skies were colored with crayon. I was just stating a basic human fact.

"I don't." The bluntness of it was like a gust, slamming closed any connection I might have—for a second only—imagined that we had. "Not entirely. But I'd like you to come with us somewhere. Over break."

"What?" Parts of me were already shutting down. This had been nice, but like all things, it had to come to an end. That was fine; I had already prepared for it.

"Come with us to Castle," Griff said.

"Where?" I had never heard of it.

"It's a lounge on the edge of town."

"They have open mic for high schoolers in the evenings," Peter said.

But I saw it in Peter's face, the lingering disappointment with what I had said. Everyone knew that disappointment was a polite version of rejection. The thin line between the two was the first lesson I had learned from my father.

I was halfway to the stairs, purse in hand. "I have to go."

"It's just poetry," Peter said.

Poems all about, what? How I was too—what had Peter called me before? Too condescending? Reductive? No, thank you.

Griff was on his feet. "I'll drive you."

"I'll walk."

"Then I'll walk with you."

"I'm fine," I said, but he was already grabbing his coat and following me out. I didn't look at Peter or Heidi or Will. I didn't want to make a big scene. Especially since I was sure that I wasn't going to be invited back.

Twenty-Four

WINTER BREAK, BROKEN

GRIFF FOLLOWED ME out.

It didn't matter. I knew exactly what was going to happen because this was exactly what had happened at my old schools, before I had implemented my isolationist policies. I opened my mouth and blurted out some things. People got uncomfortable. And then the invitations stopped coming.

It was the natural order of things, like the summer follows the spring, or the promises that my dad made were inevitably broken.

Griff put a gentle hand around my wrist. "Hey," he said. "Why are you in such a hurry?"

"I—" I said. "Do you believe what Peter was saying back there? So the VIPs are secretly, what? Kind-hearted saints or something?"

Griff tilted his head. "That wasn't what he was saying."

"That's what it sounded like to me."

I don't know why I was trying to pick a fight with Griff, one of the few people who had ever wanted to be my friend. But I had been at the bottom; I had been tormented while the Lake View sheeple stood and watched. No one helped me. They just let it happen.

"Peter is just saying sometimes it's not simple," Griff said.

"Do you think so? Really?"

Griff's hand was still around my wrist, his fingers in a loose circle. "I don't know."

I wouldn't know why he would, after what had happened to him at his last school.

"But," he said, "it might be something to consider. For both of us."

"Why do you want to spend time with me?" I should just know now. Get it over with. "If Peter's right, and I'm so condescending and reductive?"

"He didn't say you were condescending and reductive. He said your comments were," Griff said. "There's a difference."

Was there? I didn't think so.

"One is something that you've said. The other is who you are," Griff said. "He's not saying that you're a terrible person. He's just disagreeing with you."

That distinction had never occurred to me. Maybe because no one had ever made the effort—or had the patience—to point it out before.

Griff slid his hand around mine. "Come next week. Only once. We're on break, so we have plenty of time."

I remembered the other boys I had known, at my other schools. Luke-from-the-bookstore had invited me to a basketball game. I had been excited—I thought it might be my first actual date—but when I mentioned I didn't like basketball and wanted to do something else, he just took someone else. He didn't ask me again. And that was that.

"I'll pass," I said.

Griff didn't look mad, like I'd expected. And he didn't pull his hand from mine. "That's fine. But I might ask you again."

"I'll still say no."

"Okay."

But I knew it wasn't. It never was.

Winter break started out as usual. Mom was at work, and I was alone in the living room with all of my college research.

Griff texted me occasionally, small little messages. He didn't mention Castle, or poetry, again. And he didn't come over for dinner. Maybe he didn't want me to go with them anymore. That was totally not a big deal. At all.

Heidi was in some European country for break, and Will was in Seoul. My tater phone had been almost silent, so it was like old times, when I was invisible. Only this time I minded, just a little bit more.

I didn't know why Peter and Griff had been so insistent on me going to this open mic thing. Poetry? It was probably going to be some sad people mumbling sad things into a microphone. It sounded less like fun and more like torture.

And what? I was going to suddenly love the VIPs? Hardly.

Peter was so certain that Mitzi and Adeline had these complex, challenging lives, but I couldn't see how that could be true. They were both pretty, had tons of people who wanted to talk to them, and always looked perfect. Adeline was totally rich and didn't have to worry about things like scholarships or financial aid.

I mean, *maybe* Mitzi had some financial stuff going on at home. And a brother who was still recovering from a terrible accident. And she always had to live in her famous mom's shadow.

Fine. I would dig around a little more. To prove Peter wrong.

I scrolled through Mitzi's TikTok. There was the usual fashion stuff, makeup ads. I scrolled through the comments. People loved her, no surprise. Then I saw one little comment.

Jclarke: you should have picked the other dress.

Jclarke? Was that her mother? Why was she saying that on Mitzi's account?

I started to scroll through her other videos. Jclarke didn't comment on everything, but when she did, it was usually along the lines of You should have put your hair up with that high neckline. Or That necklace is too large for your frame. From a stranger, it would have been totally rude. From your mother—I couldn't imagine.

If she was saying that in public, what was she saying to Mitzi in private? I did a search for interviews with her mom. There was one small clip, a makeup tutorial from her early days. Mitzi's mom was supposedly helping a young actress with her makeup, but she kept making all these passive-aggressive comments about the size of her nose and the state of her complexion.

There was a voice off camera. "Isn't that a little much, Joanna?"

Mitzi's mom said, "If I don't tell her how to look better, who will? How can she fix it if she doesn't know? It's the only thing that matters in this business."

Wow. Was that what it was like in their world?

Suddenly, the doorbell rang. I ran to the front of the house to answer it.

It was Griff. And Peter.

I stared at them, as if aliens had suddenly beamed themselves onto my porch.

"Hi," Griff said. Like it was totally natural for him to be standing in front of my house, again.

Peter was peering at our front bushes. "I love all the Christmas lights—did you and your mom do those? Sometimes people wait until the last minute to put them up and I think it totally ruins the festivity of the season."

"Hi?" I said.

Griff was wearing a dark blue wool coat and a scarf with a subtle plaid pattern. His hair lifted up a little in the wind, and the shoulders of his coat were dotted with snow. "So . . . I just got back in town."

He left? Was that why he had barely texted and hadn't come by for dinner?

Stop thinking, Livvy.

174

"From seeing my cousin?" he said. "Didn't you get my message?"

"What message?" I tried not to—I hope I didn't—sound hostile. It wasn't like he owed me anything.

Griff tilted his phone towards me. There was an email, sent to me days ago, saying he was going out of town. I checked my phone. It had gone to my spam folder.

Email? Seriously?

"We went to see Brynn and my aunt and uncle. My parents decided at the last minute and we drove out the next morning. I always think that it feels weird to text that late." Griff stuffed his hands back into his pockets. "Plus, didn't you see my PDF? The scan of the risotto recipe?"

Oh.

Griff was looking at me like it had been a month, not a week, since we had last seen each other. I wondered if I was doing the same.

"So we were going to Castle and your house was on the way," he said. "No pressure—seriously—but if you'd like to join us, we'd love it."

He had invited me again, just like he said he would. And Peter didn't look mad, even though we had argued; he just looked like he wished I would come.

"Where's Castle?" I asked.

Griff told me. I knew he lived fairly close to me, but Castle was in the opposite direction. My house was absolutely not on the way.

"Only if you'd like to go," he said.

I curled my hands around my phone. Griff's messages made sense now—he had sent a picture of a phone case shaped like an alpaca, a cream puff the size of a person's head. I thought he was trying to tell me he no longer wanted to come over, that he wanted the safe distance of texting. We would be texting friends. But this whole time, maybe he had been wondering why I had never asked him about his family or his trip.

Why was human communication so complicated? Even if we spoke the same language?

I said, "Sure, I guess. For a little bit." Griff smiled and tugged me towards the car.

Peter beamed. "You'll see. That'll be all you need."

Twenty-Five

CASTLE

CASTLE WAS NICER than I thought it would be, with high ceilings and a spacious hipster warehouse vibe. They decorated for the night with white holiday lights and shiny red hearts strung from the iron rafters.

To my shock, I learned that Peter was a freaking celebrity in this place. As soon as he entered, a huge cheer went up and a billion people came up to him.

"Oh, wait until he gets onstage," Griff said. "It gets more unbelievable."

What was happening? I felt like I'd stepped into an alternate universe. People were milling about freely, comfortably, without any of the anxiety or exclusion that we had at school. There was a lot—a *lot*—of hugging and laughing.

Griff led me to a front table, where a beautiful girl was sitting. She exuded coolness—not the aggressive kind Mitzi and her followers had, but the inherent self-confidence that can't be faked. Her clothes were not like anyone else's, but were perfect for her: leather jacket, puffy blue tulle skirt, rainbow leggings. Flat boots, no heel. She was next to another girl who was also Black, and a guy with epic purple hair and horn-rimmed glasses.

Peter finally extracted himself from the crowd and ran to kiss the girl. For a long time.

"Carlie?" I said in a stage whisper.

Griff smothered a laugh.

Peter finally detached himself from her face, and they beamed at each other.

We did the usual introductions, and I couldn't believe the difference in Peter. At school, he always looked like he was trying to dash through a heavy hailstorm. But here, he was radiant, relaxed. His arm was around Carlie, who was cheerfully talking with Griff.

Then the lights dimmed, and the chatter dampened into a reverent hush.

The performances began. I had never been to a poetry slam before and had a vague idea that there was going to be a lot of rhyming stuff, or maybe some dry Shakespeare monologues. I couldn't have been more wrong.

This—this was words and rhythm and rawness; it was tears and grace and passion. This was rage: women calling out men for harassing them, a Japanese boy articulating his fury for having his masculinity stripped in the media. This was hysterical poetry, joking about first dates and being bad at sports.

But through it all, the poets were incredibly vulnerable. These were strangers talking about feeling alone. Feeling unattractive enough to get plastic surgery. Crying for a parent who didn't care. They splayed out their most painful and hidden parts, unfurling it onstage without apology.

It was the most magnificent, fearless thing I had ever seen.

These poets took the emotions I ruthlessly suppressed—the sad hope, the loneliness, the self-consciousness—and turned it into a battle cry.

I peeked at Griff. He was ignoring the brilliant performance onstage and the other people around us. He was only gazing at me.

There was a small, walled-off part of myself, which had not been let out since I had been tiny and trusting, that cracked open in that moment.

A girl I vaguely recognized walked onstage, and I forced myself to turn towards her. But it was impossible to ignore Griff next to me; he transformed the air between us into prickling sparks.

The girl said, "This is for my friend, who's a little too shy to perform today." The others gave her an encouraging shout of support. She opened her notebook. With a shaking voice, she started to speak of

need

everyone had it, like a shadow, but hers was a parasite. It wormed in through a childhood cut, devouring everything within her until nothing was left but *hunger*

it was insatiable, unsatisfied with its diet of likes and hearts, so she grabbed more more and more until

one day

she realized she would do anything to satisfy it//there was no cost too high//she would feed it even herself because

she loved it.

The girl bowed her head. I finally recognized her; she was one of Mitzi's VIPs. What? Who was she performing for? Then I saw a person on the side, still wrapped in her coat and scarf. A perfectly highlighted chunk of hair covered her face.

Adeline?

Was that poem by *Adeline*?

I didn't have time to process it, because Peter reached for Carlie's hand, and they moved towards the stage.

The audience was applauding before they'd even started. It was as if Peter shed his school persona the closer they got to the microphone; with each step, his shoulders pulled back, his chin went up, his back straightened. In the blazing overhead lights, his red hair was as bright as I had ever seen it. It was a flame.

Peter gave a brief grin. He was centered, commanding. He and Carlie glanced at each other. Then they launched.

It was *electric*. They were performing a poem about inter-racial dating; each line was precise, each movement perfectly synchronized. They would alternate lines, then merge into a fierce unison. The audience was standing before the halfway point, chanting and shouting. When Peter and Carlie got to the defiant finale, I almost couldn't hear it because of the cheering. I was on my feet.

Griff leaned over to whisper in my ear. "They were the North American Poetry Slam finalists last year."

I stared at them. That was Peter? Fast-talking, texting Peter? Peter who had been tormented at school for so long—this whole time, he had *this* in him? How had no one at school ever realized?

But wasn't that what Peter had been trying to tell me this whole time? Not only did he have this inside, but everyone did. Each person had their own poem, burning.

I wrapped Peter and Carlie in a hug when they stepped off-stage; I was not a hugger, but I couldn't help it.

Some people can say hey to strangers. Some people can force people to bend to their will. Then there are those who could do *this*.

"We're here twice a week," Peter said. "You can come any-time."

I thought of Adeline's friend and the poem she had read. No one talked about poetry night or Castle at school; it was like a sacred pact of privacy once you entered these walls. But I never would have guessed that Adeline or her friend would come here, much less perform.

I had assumed that Adeline was merely Mitzi's cold execu-tioner, and maybe she was. In her videos, she seemed genuinely thrilled when she released content she thought was clever and funny. Maybe it made her feel powerful to take people down. I had seen her face when she flashed her video at me in study hall. I'm not even sure if she cared that I was Asian. She had done it because she knew it would get the maximum rise from me.

But, somewhere, I wondered if there was a part of her that realized what she was doing. Was that why she allowed her poem to be performed so publicly? Why she acknowledged the parasite of need?

Peter hugged me. "Do you see now? What I was talking about?" He didn't rub it in, like my dad would have.

I nodded.

Griff said, "Do you know who's also good?"

My mind was still whirling, trying to reorganize the scrambled parts.

"Will."

My world flipped. "Will. William Choi? The William Choi that we know?"

Peter shrugged. "He has a lot of rage."

"He's amazing," Carlie said. "We're trying to get him to compete with us in the spring."

"I need a minute." I dramatically pressed a hand over my heart, and Griff laughed. "I need to adjust. The world is still round, right? Gravity still pulls down and not up?"

"We're also trying to get him to ask Heidi out," Griff said. "But one thing at a time, right?"

Carlie threw her hands up and shouted, "PLEASE LET THEM GO OUT ALREADY!!" People turned towards her, smiling, but she did not seem to notice or care. I wondered what that would be like.

Peter said, "I am not sure which one is going to happen first. But honestly, either would be what he needs."

"There's your next poem," I said. "Please Let Them Go Out Already."

Carlie laughed. "Congratulations on your poetry bug infection." She nudged me. "But you don't have to get onstage for it to affect you."

It was true. The poetry had worked its way into my brain, tearing everything apart and fusing it back together. As we were shuffling around in misery at school, who knew *this* was going on at the same time? That this existed?

"How do you . . ." I couldn't ask the rest; it was too vulnerable.

"Stage fright?" Carlie asked.

"No, I mean, how do you . . ." I paused. "It's just so *open*."

Peter and Carlie leaned into each other, and I was reminded of how they performed onstage, their graceful unison.

"It's a choice," Carlie said.

Peter kissed her cheek. "It's how you live your life."

I asked, "Why don't you perform at school? Or in AP?"

"In Plainstown?" Peter's voice was hard. "In front of those people who sit there year after year and judge me and everyone? No. This is mine. They will not take this from me, too."

"But there are those who might need it," Carlie said softly. "Who could be helped by it the way you were."

Their glances snagged on each other, spiky.

"No." He bowed his head. Carlie sighed and put a gentle hand on his hair.

"I get it," I said. "You don't owe them anything."

Peter looked at me, and we understood each other, the silent language of the tormented.

"They're not all bad," Carlie said.

"But some of them let it happen," Griff said. "Isn't that worse?" He was struggling, genuinely, to understand. What we had seen here was unquestionably inspiring. But it was also nothing like the cruelty and disregard we had seen outside Castle.

"It depends if you believe in transformation," Carlie said. "And hope."

Could people truly be different, on a fundamental level? The revolution was supposed to break Mitzi's power, but would it actually result in anything that would last?

And if it didn't, then was it even worth it?

I thought Griff would have a snarky comeback, but he was quiet, gazing at the empty stage.

I thought of Adeline's poem. She and her friend had slipped out at some point, but I couldn't stop thinking about them. Adeline's journey was not so simple. It didn't excuse the choices she made, how she would willingly be cruel to others for her own benefit. It didn't explain how a person could come to love and crave the dark, slippery negativity. But I had always wondered why someone could enable a person like Mitzi, how they could be complicit. I began to see the complexity of it.

"Hey, we're having a party at my place," Carlie said to me. "You're coming."

What? Oh no. Going to a poetry slam (large group of people, social interaction not strictly necessary) was a far cry from attending a party (lots of people, exponential awkwardness). I was about to tell Griff that I could call a car to get home by myself when I saw Dawn across the room. Had she seen us all talking to each other? Would she guess we were friends?

She started walking towards us.

Crap. Maybe it wouldn't look too suspicious that we were together, since Peter had just performed. Were any of the other VIPs with her?

"What?" Griff looked around. Then he saw her.

Peter clutched Carlie, then bellowed, "Well, nice to meet you! Come on, Carlie!" He dragged her away.

"What do you want?" Griff said to Dawn.

She scanned the room. "It was a great show tonight."

"What. Do. You. Want."

Today Dawn was dressed in oversized versions of the clothes I had seen on Mitzi's blog. None of her sweaters and shirts ever fit properly; she always seemed small and miserable, desperately trying not to drown in outfits that overwhelmed her.

"You have to watch out," she said in an undertone. "You've got to be more careful. All of you."

"Is that a threat?" I took a step towards her.

Dawn shook her head. "I just thought you'd want to know." She dashed off, leaving us staring after her, confused and vaguely alarmed.

Twenty-Six

PARTYING WITH THE POETS

I FOLLOWED GRIFF to his car. I wanted to go home, but Dawn had rattled me. I needed to find some answers, and the party might be the only place to get them.

On the way there, I checked Mitzi's TikTok account. She had posted a small and ominous video, which I played for Griff:

Finally, Li'l Mitzes, it has come to my attention that there are some out there who are willing to mock and bully others. Be careful! If you have any information about who might be behind recent events, please let me know.

Her post was followed by tons of comments, like OMG! I am so sorry this is happening to you! And Some people are the worst!

I said, "*She's* being bullied? Is she seriously trying to say that with a straight face?" But since we had started our operations, more students outside of the Nerd Net had left negative

186

comments on Mitzi's account. There had also been some more snark—both online and verbal—about how Mitzi was always skipping class and how she was going to fail out of high school. Was that because of us?

Mitzi was spinning the facts to make herself the victim. It was a clever use of media since the Nerd Net was, by nature, anonymous. We had no way to counter her version of events. And now she was becoming aggressive about getting more information about us.

"It won't take much," I said. "One person sends her a screenshot of our messages and she'll know the Nerd Net is behind everything."

"So Dawn was right?" Griff said.

I shook my head. "I don't know if she was threatening us or warning us."

"Dawn obviously suspects something. I wonder if she's talked to Heidi."

"Heidi? Why would she talk to Heidi?"

Griff didn't answer as he turned into Carlie's driveway. Napleville was only one town over, but the differences were stark. Stark as in it appeared that everyone was Heidi-level rich. Carlie's house required spotlights and lights along the driveway. You know, that kind of place.

Griff knocked on the door, then strode in. I trailed behind. The party scene was not my usual jam. By that I mean I would rather extract my own tooth without anesthesia than go to one.

Parties meant one of two things: either being ditched by the people I came with and hiding in the kitchen all night, or spending the whole time standing next to—but not talking to—a group of strangers, trying not to look self-conscious. In any scenario, it always ended with me trying to figure out how to get back home as soon as possible.

Griff saw me hanging back. "Hey." He placed a light hand on my sleeve. "We don't have to go in if you don't want to. I'm equally as happy to go to Donut 24."

A part of me wanted to book it. Au revoir. But what Dawn said was still worrying me. And the words I saw onstage were still exploding in my brain, the rhythms and ideas and passionate certainty. The intellectual in me wanted to speak to the poets, to deconstruct their work.

Griff said gently, "We can leave anytime you want to go."

We. We implied that I would not have to face the group alone. *We* meant the pair of friends who would go into a party together, check with each other, and make sure the other was not drowning in awkwardness. Did I believe Griff was that person?

With the other people I had known at my previous schools, it seemed like I was only invited to things because I happened to be there when they were being organized. I hadn't had this—a growing certainty that someone was genuinely looking out for me.

I nodded as Carlie waved us inside. Behind her, Peter was doing some kind of wild dance while a group of people cheered and laughed. He was completely without self-consciousness or fear, the kind of goofy that you could only be when you utterly trusted the people who surrounded you.

Carlie hugged me and pulled us towards the living room. I was bracing myself to be my usual persona, the self-conscious sipper of soda, standing in the corner. But she wouldn't let me. I was suddenly swirled in casually tossed introductions, in smiles and laughter.

"And this one woman—" one of the girls by the piano was saying, "was slowly chewing on this bowl of nuts and staring at me the whole time I was onstage. The whole time!"

The others were howling.

The girl mimed eating each nut one by one, her eyes wide open. Then she acted out trying to perform while becoming increasingly distracted.

"And I finish. She's still eating, not clapping, nothing."

The others lost it. "And then what?" one of them called.

The girl shrugged. "I walked offstage and gave her a refill. She said, 'You were not very good.' And she kept my nuts!"

Next to me, Griff laughed.

"Is everyone here from Napleville and Plainstown?" I whispered to Griff.

He shook his head. "Some from Hillview, some from Grande."

"Do any of them do theater?" I asked.

Carlie snorted, then nudged her friend off the piano bench. "Watch this." She broke out the opening chords of "Seasons of Love," and in unison, everyone sighed. "Pictures of kitties or old songs from *Rent*. It's all you need to win this crowd over."

Some of them went to poetry slam contests together. A lot of the Napleville people were also on their school's forensics team and competed in speech and debate. All of them were at Castle, every Sunday and every Thursday, attending the church of the spoken word.

As I watched them, I had the same feeling I had with the Nerd Net, trying to decipher the inaccessible alchemy that turns strangers into allies. Into ride-or-die friends. If I were a poet, this is what I would say: the mystery of how people become true friends was the code that I had been trying to crack my entire life. It was the puzzle logic could not unlock.

But as the night went on, Griff kept checking in. Peter kept introducing me to someone or the other, and Carlie made sure I was always included in the conversation with her friends.

I realized that I had gotten it completely backwards. I always looked at friend groups and wondered what was wrong with *me* because I could not fit in. As if friendship were a container I needed to squeeze myself into. But these last few weeks were showing me that you do not have to make everyone like you. You don't even have to make the majority of people like you. The thing you have to do—the only thing you need to do—is find the few, invaluable people who will click with you. Who will be your true friends. That is all.

I somehow found myself playing a hysterical game of charades and a truly filthy game of Cards Against Humanity. I was high-fived by a poet, a guy who had spoken movingly about what it was like to have his heart broken for the first time. I made jokes; people laughed. I asked them about writing and performing, and they all somehow understood that what I was really asking was what it was like to live without fear. And people spoke to me candidly, showing me the vulnerability I had never let myself express.

One person used to have a stutter and performing was an early speech therapy assignment. One told me that it took her three years to get onstage, and the first time she went, she threw up. They were strangers to me, but they were not, because I had heard their deepest stories; they had shared them with me and that would always tie us together. I didn't directly know what it was like to come out to my parents, but after this evening, I saw what that experience might be like. I had never stared at a bowl of food, terrified to eat it, but now, I could almost feel the agony myself.

This group was bound together by a web of steel cords; each cable was a story flung out and caught by the others. Each one of them had opened themselves up, and that was where the blade of hurt could have slipped in. But it was also where friends could enter and sit in the alone beside you.

But I had never had a web. A net. Until now.

Griff tugged me over and smoothly introduced me to someone, mentioning that we both liked history. I noticed he did that throughout the night; he gave a little conversational hook that shy strangers could hang on to. He remembered names and used them, like Mitzi did. He was chatty and friendly in a way he had never been at school. This was Popular Griff, and I had some questions.

I waited until we finally took a break from socializing and

found ourselves in the kitchen. A group welcomed him warmly, but I steered him towards an empty spot, near the chips (nacho, Heidi would have loved it).

"You weren't just popular," I said. "At your old school. I'll bet you were *really* popular."

He shrugged. "I was, until I wasn't."

"But here," I said, "you aren't a social outcast. You're a loner. There's a difference."

"There is."

"You're . . . choosing to be apart. You're opting out."

He shrugged again.

What would that be like? To not have a tiny, suppressed part of you that wanted to belong?

"Tell me what you're thinking," he said quietly.

I shook my head. "I'm . . . I'm just trying to process the idea of choice."

"Popularity isn't always what people think it is."

I normally would have scoffed at this. It would be easy for a popular person to say that, like it would be easy for a rich person to say that it was hard to have a lot of money. I mean—sure, it might be. But it was way more difficult not to have it.

But tonight's trip to Castle was still in my head, expanding. Even Adeline wasn't quite who I thought she was. It made me pause and listen to what Griff had to say.

"It's not all bad, being popular. I know you think it is. But it can be used to make a kinder system for everyone. Or, yes, it can make things worse," Griff said. "But what is popularity? Being part of a large group, always trying to get people to like you. It can mean that you are—somewhat—at the mercy of a group. Of what the collective thinks."

I thought of Mitzi, her videos. I had noticed they were exactly like every other fashion vlogger's fashion and beauty tips. I mean *exactly*. I had never seen Mitzi try on anything that wasn't previously internet-approved. If crop tops were in, she loved crop tops. If heavy eye shadow was in, she loved eye shadow. But in all those videos, and in all those hours of her trying to gaze engagingly at the camera, there was not one minute expressing what she truly thought, aside from whether or not something was cute. Not one.

If your income—if your very survival—depends on what everyone else thinks, how many risks can you take?

"Yes, I was popular." Griff's voice was quiet. "And my cousin twisted herself to get into the in crowd. She went from being an amazing field hockey player and cheerleader to becoming a follower. She stopped doing everything she loved and let them decide everything. Then they turned on her. Brynn made herself into someone else but didn't realize everything that followed wasn't real."

I thought of Dawn, in her too-big clothes, drifting behind Mitzi and Adeline.

"You and I both understand this hard truth: there is a cost to popularity," he said. "And when you're in, sometimes you don't realize that others have it harder than you. It's easy—too easy—not to notice. So yes, I opted out."

Griff's face sometimes had a shade of something dark underneath, an emotion I could never quite identify, until now. It was torment. What happened to his cousin was the blade constantly jammed into his side, slowly twisting.

"So the Nerd Net?" I asked.

He nodded. "After we moved, I disconnected from the system. And I now choose to help the people like Brynn."

For Griff, Brynn's nightmare had soaked through him, saturated and reshaped him into something fierce, purposeful. That was a different type of bravery.

"What you've been doing takes courage, too," I said quietly.

"Does it?"

"Griff. Of course it does."

He closed his eyes, briefly.

I touched his arm, and he reached over to wrap my hand in between both of his. He cradled it like it was something precious, shyly running a fingertip down my palm. I wanted to make a joke. Flee. But I didn't.

Someone tugged on my arm.

Carlie said, "Peter wants—whoops! Sorry! Um, Peter wants you two on our charades team."

Griff hadn't stopped looking at me. "Charades, Livvy?"

I nodded.

I said yes to a lot of things that night: to the party, to talking to people I didn't know. Yes to Griff, who pulled me into a random debate with the poets about whether digestive biscuits helped digestion. I did not run away and retreat to my hermit crab shell. And the result? I had fun. At a party. With people who could be my friends.

For the first time, I went to bed without that tight feeling of angst, the ruthlessly suppressed feeling of loneliness. I only had something that felt suspiciously like hope.

I didn't know that as I was peacefully sleeping, Mitzi was meticulously planning her counterattack.

Twenty-Seven

HAPPY FREAKING HOLIDAYS

TWO DAYS LATER, on Christmas Eve afternoon, Mitzi scheduled a series of live vlogs on her YouTube channel. The first ones were relatively innocent, talking about her favorite gifts for the season (the girl apparently loved anything overpriced and covered in sparkles).

We were in Heidi's basement, keeping tabs. Heidi was streaming it in the background on one of her many computer screens, and it was more than a little unsettling to see Mitzi's large pixelated face above us.

For the past week, Mitzi had been heavily advertising a Major Reveal! We needed to know if it was related to the Nerd Net. However, watching Mitzi endlessly open ridiculously expensive knickknacks was downright painful.

"One of her favorite things is a six-hundred-dollar bedazzled nail clipper?" Griff said.

"Don't look at me! I would never buy it." Heidi pointed her pink puffy pen at the screen. "I would get stock in the company, though. What a genius scam."

Will was watching the computer, looking horrified. "Facial pore steamer? Steaming your face seems like a bad idea."

"Hard agree," Heidi said. I noticed she was wearing a new necklace, an intricate silver one in the shape of the letter H. Will kept glancing at it, then at his new watch, with a mixture of awe and affection.

Mitzi did have a talent for presenting products—I noticed her corporate sponsors were prominently featured in the background or were explicitly discussed in her video. At one point, her semi-famous mom appeared on camera and extolled some makeup product.

As Mitzi brought out more products, the gifts started popping out. Griff gave Peter a book of poetry; Will got him a rack for his tae kwon do belts. Heidi got a DON'T MESS WITH ME mug from Griff and a Castle tee from Peter. Will gave out joke gifts, like a silver Mylar tracksuit to Griff, and a nose hair trimmer to Peter.

I brought a big purse today—somewhat self-consciously tucking small presents for the group inside. I didn't want to make anyone uncomfortable by giving gifts when they had none for me in return. But if they gave me something, I didn't want to be empty-handed either, right?

This whole almost-having-friends thing was super awkward.

But I shouldn't have worried. Peter came up to me and gave me a box elaborately wrapped with foil paper and curled ribbon. "Carlie loves holiday decorations—this is from both of us."

It was a beautiful copy of Walt Whitman's *Leaves of Grass*.

"Your mind will be blown," he said. "There is only before Whitman and after Whitman."

I couldn't help it: I hugged him tightly. Then I shyly handed him my gift, a framed copy of one of his poems.

"How did you get this? It's amazing!" Peter ran his fingers over the glass.

"I asked Carlie."

"She didn't even tell me! I love it!" He beamed, then dove for his phone.

I gave Heidi a Wonder Woman mouse pad, and Will a sweatshirt with a picture of a bell on the front and a SEND MONEY slogan on the back.

"A Pavlov joke?" Will said. "It's like you really know me."

Heidi handed me a small silver box. "This is from all of us, but Will and I both hate wrapping things, so."

I carefully opened it. Inside was a small, round red pin.

"Sorry, we would have given it to you ages ago, but they were on back order." Heidi hugged me. "Welcome to the Nerd Net, officially!"

"Use it responsibly!" Will said. "And try not to lose it in the washing machine, like Peter."

My last gift was from Griff. We exchanged boxes at the same time, grinning.

"Is this a matching tater phone cover?" he asked. "Because I've kind of been coveting yours."

He ripped his gift open, then laughed. I found him a "Creative Chef" cookbook, which described delicious recipes that could be made from combining ordinary ingredients—or slightly inedible items from the cafeteria.

I lifted up my box. I had gotten very few holiday presents over the years—some from my mom, of course, but that was usually it. My dad had ghosted me for so many years, until he had remarried, discovered remorse, and delivered the car over the summer. I had no siblings and no close friends.

I held the present, and looked at my book of poems, my pin.

I didn't notice the silence stretching until Peter finally spoke. "I know. It was the same for me."

Will said, "You're stuck with us now, Livvy."

I was about to pass the moment off as a joke, my usual deflect, but I thought about the poets at Castle, how they strode into the bright circle of light on the vast wooden stage.

"Thank you," I said. "I've . . . I've never had this before."

Griff scooted next to me and nudged my gift. "Open it."

It was the shirt Adeline had ruined. Only now the stain on the back was covered with beautiful, intricate ink drawings, bold colors, and swirling vines. It was gorgeous. And in the corner was a small Nerd Net symbol.

"One of my cousins is a bit of an artist," Griff said. "Your mom let me pick up the shirt."

Once again, he had performed this magical alchemy; he had taken something horrible and transformed it into something special. They all had.

Thank you was not enough, but that's what I said. The

others smiled, then they took turns pulling on Griff's new Mylar tracksuit over their clothes. Peter took a photo of himself and tried to text it to Carlie, but he was laughing too hard to type. He passed his phone to Griff, who gleefully added his own message and sent it off. Heidi tried to attack Will with the nose hair trimmer, but he covered his face with his hands, bellowing, "NO WAY, HEXLER!"

Those goofballs.

Suddenly, the tracksuit was on me, in all its silver, crinkled glory.

"Can you believe it was only five dollars?" Will exclaimed. "What a bargain!"

Griff helped me to roll up my sleeves. "We have a winner. Our next project in outer space has its first volunteer."

"I shall bring equality to the aliens!" I said. "Just don't let me near any microwave ovens on the rocket ship."

"You only need one more thing." Griff lifted the T-shirt from the box and pulled it over my head. Stepped close and fumbled with the pin before putting it on my collar, the backs of his fingers brushing against my skin.

If I were brave, I would say: *Don't. This isn't casual, not to me.* Instead, I said, "I will represent, in space."

Griff cleared his throat, then smoothed the bottom hem of my shirt. "Perfect."

We stood there for a moment, his fingers lightly on my hip.

On the screen behind him, Mitzi leaned into the camera.

"Li'l Mitzes," she said. "You might have heard that I've been the target of bullying for some time now."

Next to me, Will snorted. "OH. MY. GOD."

Heidi turned up the volume. "She is definitely getting nothing but coal from Santa tomorrow."

Griff and I both turned towards the livestream. He stepped closer to me, as if he could shield me. But Mitzi was impossible to ignore.

"You have probably seen posts referring to recent events." Mitzi's face filled the screen. "You might have even seen some unflattering things about me on the internet. Well, I needed to take a second to regroup, *naturally*, but I wanted to lay out what was happening for you today. A few weeks ago, a group of vicious, anonymous bullies began targeting me. They stole my parking spot at school, and then began to publicly humiliate me."

"They can't possibly believe this," Will said.

But they did. The comments kept popping up on the side of the screen, one after another: OMG, I had no idea! and You are so strong, bb!

Mitzi stared into the camera, unblinking. "Well, I have decided to stop being silent about this issue. I know many of you, Li'l Mitzes, might be in the same situation. I want you to know you are not alone. You can fight back." She held up a poster with our N^N symbol on it. "This symbol is used by the people who have been targeting me. If any of you know *anything* about this group, contact me immediately. Especially you local Mitzes in Plainstown."

The camera flashed to our symbol again, then Mitzi came back. "Together we can fight bullying."

The camera winked off. We were silent.

"Well, that's not great," Will said.

"It's a call to arms." I was stunned. "She's rallying her troops and setting up a surveillance network." It was what happened in many oppressive regimes; the government started using the people as its eyes, so it could spot and stamp out dissent. It was a brilliant move.

Heidi whirled towards her keyboard and began typing. "Mitzi clearly doesn't know who we are yet. And I don't think she knows we're using ClickComms. But it only takes one person to tell her what's going on. Then we're busted."

"We've got to hurry," Will said. "We have to break her hold on the school and get everyone to stop supporting her. Otherwise, she'll destroy us."

Twenty-Eight

WHEN SELFIES HAVE NO SELF

OVER THE REST of winter break, things on Mitzi's vlog and Insta were suspiciously silent, save for one small, ominous comment from an anonymous user in her Insta feed:

DM me. I have what you need.

It was sent right before New Year's Eve. But after that, silence.

We started the new semester nervously. Or at least I did, as I continued my usual evasive tactics at school. Griff seemed almost optimistic, and even made me some kind of cookbook-inspired veggie wrap during lunch.

But for me, the waiting was the bad part. It was a blade over my head, and I was just watching it swing.

I spent most of my time with my head down, minding my own business and trying to avoid Mitzi. But a few days after classes started up again, I couldn't avoid her.

I planned on getting cozy with my favorite book and spending some relaxing alone time in the library. Unfortunately, that was when Mitzi and her pals entered. As soon as I heard her voice cutting through the room, I quickly ducked behind a bookshelf.

Mitzi was with Adeline and Dawn, and they set up their papers at the table next to me. Crap. There was no way for me to escape without passing them. I was basically trapped in a canyon, albeit one lined with books about pets and turf management.

There was the sound of papers shuffling.

"You can start already," Mitzi said.

In the past, Adeline usually ignored Mitzi's rude tone. But now she stared at her, a little, before responding. "So, we were talking about glucose."

Since I had heard her poem at Castle, I couldn't quite stop thinking about Adeline and how she said she would do anything to feed the parasite of need. Anything? Like deal with Mitzi all the time?

"So, you can build it up or break it down." Adeline flipped a page. "See? It's this chemical thing."

"Wait, what? You're not making any sense." Mitzi was on her phone, texting.

"Cellular respiration?" Adeline's tone was cold, compressed.

"I missed the intro class because my mom dragged me to one of her gigs." Mitzi didn't look up. "What are you talking about?"

Adeline slammed the textbook shut. "I already know this stuff, you know. I don't need to be here."

Mitzi looked up, surprised. "What?"

"Never mind."

"I can ask Sonya for help," Mitzi said, "if you're so bothered."

Adeline recoiled. Calvin had told her, *Don't think you're not disposable.* And in this moment, I think Adeline realized it.

Adeline started again, but she slowed down. Made sure Mitzi wasn't offended. She must have known that Mitzi could push her off the mountain at any time, could leave her outside in the thornbushes. And yet, though her balance was precarious, Adeline didn't—couldn't—leave.

Mitzi tried to keep up. But even though she picked up a lot of things pretty quickly, there was too much material to cover. It sounded like Mitzi had missed way more than a week.

Adeline flipped the page of the textbook. "Let's go over glucose and pyruvate. ATP? Does any of this sound familiar?"

Mitzi seemed to realize she had gone too far. "Thanks for helping me, Adeline."

Adeline didn't answer.

"I mean it, I appreciate it," Mitzi said. "Sorry. I'm under a lot of pressure. We're not getting enough from my accounts and James needs more physical therapy."

Adeline thawed, slightly. "What about your mom's commercial? Did she get it?"

Mitzi shook her head. "The director said she was always

late to set and had a bad attitude. So he hired someone else. Of course, it was one of his friends."

That's when I figured it out: it was always someone else's fault. Mitzi didn't get the good grade because Asians wrecked the curve. Her mom lost her award because the writer was terrible. And her mom didn't get this commercial because her director only hired his friends.

Adeline said, "Well, what about the internship? I think I can get you in. If you do some extra labs and get your grade up, it'll be even better. You'll love it over there."

"I don't have time to love anything," Mitzi snapped. "I got into this huge fight with my mom about even staying in school. I had to quit volunteering at the hospital because she kept booking shoots for me after school. There's no way I have time to do extra credit."

But Mitzi found time to shoot the internship video—which wasn't required—while the rest of us were in lab. She had just chosen not to do the schoolwork.

"Your mom wants you to drop out of school?" Adeline was shocked. "Like permanently, or homeschooling? You're going to be able to graduate, right?"

Mitzi didn't answer, and Adeline looked sorry for her.

"Listen, I'll put a word in at the internship, but you have to tell me if you can't do it, for real." Adeline scribbled something on a piece of paper and handed it to Mitzi. "I'll be in huge trouble if I vouch for you and you don't show up."

"I will." Mitzi slipped it into her purse. "I promise. Oh shit.

I need to repost. It's been twenty minutes and my last one hasn't gotten enough likes."

Adeline grabbed her phone and started snapping a few test pictures. She tilted the screen towards Mitzi.

"No," Mitzi said. "The light's weird. And my eyes look squinty."

I felt the slightest sliver of sympathy for Mitzi, but honestly, I wanted them to leave so I could get out of here. My leg was falling asleep and I was starving. If Mitzi started taking more pictures, it could take years. They would find my decomposing corpse, teeth clenched around a half-eaten book about lawn maintenance.

"I thought it was fine," a girl said. She had a small voice, and I was not surprised to see that it was Dawn. I had almost forgotten she was there.

"That ridiculous NN is affecting my traffic. As soon as I find out—" Mitzi's voice became muffled.

Wait, what? I crept closer, cautiously.

"But I'm pretty sure it's—" Mitzi rummaged through her purse.

It's who? Did she know it was us? There was no way.

"But you don't know for sure," Dawn said.

"As soon as I do, that's it." Mitzi pulled out a thin scarf and wrapped it around her neck, patting the ends. "I just need to think of . . ." Her voice faded again.

Whew. She had no idea.

I glimpsed Dawn's face and was surprised to see she looked

desperate to escape. Not annoyed or impatient, but like she knew someone was about to detonate a bomb and she needed to get the hell out.

"Come here," Mitzi said to Adeline. She put on some new earrings, ones that I recognized from her blog. They were sponsored, and so was her scarf. Were most of her nicer clothes from advertisers? Was that how she had been able to afford looking so put together?

Mitzi held up a book. "Take one of me with this." There was a pause and a small snapping noise. Another pause. "No. My hair looks awful. Try another one."

This went on a few times.

"The last one doesn't look too bad," Dawn said.

Mitzi said, "You don't get it. Not bad is not enough." I suddenly remembered the first time I had seen Mitzi, after I first started school in Plainstown. She was by herself in the bathroom. I remember being shocked at how put together she was, how her shoes had the perfect heel, her skirt the perfect amount of fluff, her tank top the most popular label. My first thought was that I was going to be in big trouble, because I preferred my canvas sneakers and jeans.

But my second thought was that there was something unusual about this girl because she kept shading in her eyebrows with a pencil, wiping off minuscule imperfections, and then drawing them again. Even though the bell was about to ring, she kept trying for the perfect arch.

She caught me staring and snapped, "What are you looking at?" I had dashed out.

What would it be like to feel you couldn't walk out of your house without being picture perfect? To be a prisoner of everyone else's opinions? Mitzi's mom had been trapped and now her daughter was in the same sticky web. To the school—to the internet, the world—Mitzi would be Joanna Clarke's daughter, forever. Whether she liked it or not. Whether she was poor or not.

I thought Mitzi loved all the attention and adoration. And maybe she did. But right now, she didn't look like she was enjoying what she was doing. At all.

"Take another video," Mitzi said. "One of me studying. The last one got a spike in likes."

Dawn muttered, "Are you kidding me?"

"What did you say?" Mitzi stopped fake smiling.

Dawn's face spasmed, then flipped to a practiced blandness.

"My numbers are down," Mitzi said. "So stop complaining."

Dawn stayed silent as Mitzi's boyfriend, the ultra-popular Brett Clifton, walked in. Brett had his own little Instagram empire, where he mostly posted pictures of himself looking thoughtfully into the distance. The combination of them had increased both of their dynasties, much like the alliance between Henry V and Catherine of Valois was supposed to unite England and France.

"What are you doing here?" Brett bellowed. Mr. Arya glared at him.

Mitzi tossed her hair. "Getting some photos."

He reached for her bag. "Come on, we've got to go meet Tim."

"I'm not done yet."

Behind Brett, Dawn flinched at Mitzi's tone. But he didn't seem to notice it.

Mitzi said, "And I still need to study for bio. We have a huge test coming up."

"We're late." Brett closed her textbook and tossed it in the backpack. "Let's go."

The people next to them were trying not to stare. Others surreptitiously clicked photos. Mitzi plastered on a smile. "You're embarrassing me." Each word was ripped off and jagged. "I want to finish this first."

"Why are you studying? You need way more than one afternoon, babe."

Adeline looked as if she would give a thousand dollars to anyone who could extract her from the room, immediately. Dawn got very still, like she was mentally teleporting herself to another state.

"What did you say?" Mitzi was dangerously calm.

But Brett had already zipped up her bag and started to leave. I thought Mitzi was going to chew him out and knit a cardigan with his remains, but she clutched her phone and remained silent.

Brett lumbered out, and after a single, charged second, Mitzi followed him.

"Let's go," she said, and Dawn and Adeline both jumped. I was the only one who saw Dawn's face as she stared at Mitzi's back; it was crystallized bitterness.

Later that day, I clicked on Mitzi's account. The picture she wanted to post never appeared. And the next day, she failed her test.

Twenty-Nine

ONE HOUR WITH MY FAVORITE SPORT

THINGS WERE ON the cusp of success with the Nerd Net, and I had a vague hope that my personal existence might magically improve someday. However, when I walked into PE on Friday afternoon, I knew that today was not going to be that day.

The curtain between the main gym and basketball court was open, making one ginormous room of torture. That was the first clue that things were rapidly about to get ugly. The second one was that there were a lot of people waiting by the bleachers. A LOT.

I must have looked shocked, because a girl next to me said, "It's the combined class."

Which meant nothing to me.

"Practice for the tournament with Napleville?" she said.

The teachers were setting up nets. *Volleyball* nets. Combined class. I put all these observations together slowly, like a horrified general gradually realizing that the approaching troops were flying the wrong banner.

Oncoming horses → more troops for your enemy → hosed.

Napleville → Plainstown's main rival → volleyball nets → tons of people → hosed.

Oh my God.

Volleyball. The world's worst sport for a wannabe invisible girl. First, it was a team sport. Failure at volleyball wasn't only a failure for you; it was a failure for all your ridiculously aggressive teammates. Second, it required high amounts of coordination. Coordination was bad.

Listen, volleyball and I were not strangers. Morris Elementary: an afternoon in the nurse's office due to a ball in the face. Porter High: a personal high point when I missed a game-winning return by spectacularly tripping while trying to bump the ball. Contact with the volleyball is apparently an essential part of the sport. And, of course, the pinnacle at Lake View Middle School: standing on the court, trying not to cry, as the popular posse made sure every single other person was picked before I was.

I contemplated faking an illness. Across the room, Heidi discreetly pointed to her N^N pin, which was on the hem of her gym shirt, and flicked a tiny thumbs-up.

Peter was also in the combined class, his long, skinny legs pale against his blue nylon basketball shorts. He was uncharacteristically silent, which could only mean one thing: he was as terrified as I was.

The teachers had set up three separate nets, which meant

three different stations of pain. The varsity girls and guys were already stretching out, bouncing on their feet, and lightly tossing the battered balls into the air. One girl had knee pads, wrist guards, and a savage look in her eye. I stayed far away from her. I spotted a small cluster of VIPs and also edged away from them. Brett Clifton and his buddies had already claimed the second court, so that was also a no go.

I checked the clock: three minutes had passed. Fifty-seven minutes to go.

I felt a hard thump against my back.

"Sorry," Brett called.

Perhaps ducking out due to illness wouldn't be a fake excuse. I was debating what to do when Mitzi and Adeline strolled into the gym.

Things that could be worse in the next fifty-seven minutes:

- getting crushed by an asteroid during an extinction-level event
- being covered with nectar and then getting dropped into a giant nest of hornets
- having my old chums from Lake View make a surprise entrance to the gym, to the tune of "The Karate Rhapsody" (including the three-part a cappella harmony).

There was no shame in strategic retreat, right? But as I started heading towards our gym teacher, Mr. Bolton, Mitzi stared at me accusingly. She might not have hard evidence I was involved with the Nerd Net, but I was sure she had a strong feeling. She turned and smugly whispered something to Adeline.

Smug.

Like *Don't worry. I can make her run.*

Since Operation Hallway, I had doubled down on my usual defensive tactics at school while continuing my work behind the scenes. I made strategic retreats to the bathroom and took the safest routes to class. It wasn't quite invisibility, but it was close enough.

But now, I saw Mitzi's expression and wanted to claw it off. Because it said: *I wanted to make you scuttle, and you did. You are only safe at my whim.*

I thought that living my life of evasive maneuvers was keeping myself protected. Unharmed. But it was really letting everyone else control me.

Screw Mitzi. I pivoted and took my place on the court. It was only fifty-seven minutes, right? What could possibly happen in fifty-seven minutes?

A lot, it turns out.

It was as bad as you might have imagined. Both Mitzi and Adeline were on my team, something so statistically improbable that it would have been laughable if it hadn't been so miserable. At least Peter was on the other side of the net, so we could silently share our suffering.

I got volleyballs in the face. On the back of the head. On the back. I got screamed at, so loudly and with such detail that by minute forty I was at a place I had only been a few times before: on the verge of tears.

Heidi and Will were on another court and could only shoot me helpless looks. Peter, across the net from me, looked more and more distressed as class went on. He was having his own problems, since he was about as coordinated as I was.

"Yours!" one of the guys hollered at Peter, as someone from the other team drilled the ball over the net. Peter threw up his hands and blocked it, but it ricocheted to the floor, out of bounds. His teammates started screaming at him.

Peter was tall, but he seemed to scrunch down, getting smaller and smaller.

We started a new set. Behind me, Mitzi threw the ball up in a light, graceful toss, then smashed it over the net. A guy on the other team bumped it back, and it flew towards me. As I got into position, Mitzi screamed, "GET IT!!" and I missed. The ball bounced on the ground with a sickening spring, then rolled under the net.

Since the beginning of the game, Mitzi had seized control of our team. She started bossing the players around and assigned positions. She corrected people's stances and began a team chant, which was surprisingly catchy. I could see everyone starting to check with her before they moved, to wait until she shouted a command before diving for the ball.

It all would have been impressive except that the rest of her energy was spent tormenting me. And this last ball on the ground was the leather-lined nail in my social coffin.

"Pick it up," Mitzi snarled.

Everyone on our court was staring at me. I focused on the battered wood floor, the dark and uneven stain, the light-colored groove by my left shoe, which was in the shape of a crescent.

I had been in this position before, of course. Different school, same scenario. At my other schools, I would have held it in. I would have swallowed my jagged anger in order to preserve my invisibility. But at my other schools, I had been pushed more and more until, by the end, the rage I had to swallow was a knife.

I kept slicing myself to survive. Year after year after year. After a while, what if there was nothing left of me? What if I was so successful at making myself invisible that I made myself disappear?

A part of me—a large part, to be honest—just wanted to pick up the damn ball and get on with the game. But the rest of me—the part with, you know, dignity—could not humiliate myself. Not again. *Not again.*

"No," I said.

"What?" Mitzi turned towards me. "What did you say?"

The small, objective part of my brain that was still working realized that I had just wedged myself into an impasse. I couldn't pick up the ball without enduring major shame. And Mitzi couldn't back down without losing her grip on whatever authority she had left.

Mitzi had an obsession with ruling this school, because she believed that social power and social media power were all sides of the same coin. She saw how her mom had lost her influence when her high-end acting gigs disappeared. So Mitzi had carefully amassed power of her own. But she had to remain on top to preserve her brand.

This all might have been how it started, but at some point,

the influence had become a bright, winding narcotic, luring her farther and farther away from all of her landmarks. Now Mitzi was adrift, her only touchstone the ever-distant light of prestige, and fame.

But that meant that any challenge—even from someone like me—became a disproportionate threat.

"No," I said, louder.

The Plainstown gym, like every other high school gym across the United States of America, was kept at approximately 50 degrees Fahrenheit. I was trembling from the cold, the air cutting through my thin gym clothes. Across the net, Peter looked like he had just swallowed a live cockroach and it was currently laying eggs in his throat.

"Pick. It. Up," Mitzi hissed.

I shook my head.

A fearful look flashed across her face, so quickly that I almost missed it. Everyone was still staring. I could tell that Mitzi was weighing her options, much like a general scanning the battle-field before the first shot is fired.

Here was the difference between us: she had everything to lose and I had nothing. She was England, and I was the Colonies.

She knew it, and I knew it. Mitzi was expecting deference, but with this last, egregious attempt at public humiliation, she had pulled me into war.

"Dawn," Mitzi said, finally. "Go get it."

Dawn radiated fury, but Mitzi missed it. Peter palmed the ball, and handed it to Dawn, who looked surprised, then grateful. She turned, and for a second, I wondered if she was going to chuck it at Mitzi's head. But then Mitzi glared at her, and Dawn carefully handed it over.

Across the net, Peter and I locked eyes; his were disbelieving. Then he grinned. I smiled back, then we both began to play until the clock ran out.

Thirty

N/N

THAT AFTERNOON, MY phone pinged. Griff.

Is your mom working tonight?

Then: a taco emoji.

Um, yes?

Did he want to make tacos for dinner? I didn't think I had the right meat or toppings. Was he going to bring over the ingredients?

Two seconds later, my doorbell rang. Griff's nose was pink with cold, and the sudden adorableness of him, with his messy hair and thick scarf and wool winter coat, was shocking.

"Tacos?" he said. "All the poets and the Nerd Net are going to Carlie's." But I didn't think he was here to ask me to a party; he was scanning me like he was checking for injuries. "I heard about what happened."

Griff left immediately after school to help his mom get her car fixed. Had he come all the way over here to check on me? He could have just sent a message.

But if he had sent a text, he would not be here, in front of me, his hands curled over my upper arms.

"You want to talk about it?" he asked.

I shook my head. Griff was here. At my house. Checking on me.

"Okay." Griff pulled my coat off the coatrack, but then dropped it. He helped me to put it on, and was Mr. Alexander Griffin *blushing*?

I couldn't look at him as I looped my scarf around my neck. Griff straightened it a little, then shyly pulled my hair free. He ran a light hand over the strands, and this was the second bit of happiness I would let myself keep: the tremor of feeling between us. We were both on a wire, but Griff was not looking at the ground. He was only gazing at me.

"Tacos?" he said.

I nodded. I said yes.

When we got to Carlie's house, there was a full spread in the living room: a silver platter of soft and crunchy tortilla shells, bowls of steaming, delicious seasoned pork and beef, and endless white bowls full of toppings and chips.

I said, "Whoa. Are we all famished, is that it?"

"Courtesy of my parents." Heidi poured a huge pile of chips onto her plate. "They are happy that I finally have friends, so they had some catering delivered here. They felt guilty for going to a conference tonight."

"So that's what tacos are supposed to look like," Griff said to me. "I'm going to take a picture and send it to the cafeteria."

"Heidi's parents can give me their guilt guacamole anytime." Will plucked a chip from Heidi's plate and munched happily. "And their remorseful rice and beans, delicious!"

"Tell me again what the hell is going on at Plainstown," one of poets said, scooping a large helping of meat onto his plate. "Joanna Clarke's kid goes there, right? Mitzi?"

Will said, "Joanna Clarke's kid is a walking nightmare. I wish *TMZ* would cover that story." He held out his plate, and the poet slapped a tortilla on it.

"She's got good shoe game," one of the girls said. Someone next to her made a face. "What? I heard she's evil, but she does have great footwear. Have you seen her videos?" I recognized her as one of the poets from the first night, the one who had accidentally thrown up during her debut performance. I noticed she owned an impressive collection of heels herself, all tall and sparkly. I—to be honest—had kind of dismissed her as a popular type, until I saw her performance and realized what it had taken for her to do it.

She seemed different to me when her poem was over. When she had gotten offstage, I finally recognized her fear and determination. I saw *her*. And that's when I realized she hadn't changed. I had.

A boy slid next to the girl and bumped her shoulder. She

squealed and gave him a big hug. It was Ethan Earle, from our drama club.

"What are we talking about?" he said. "I feel like we might be discussing how awesome I am."

The girl beamed. "Of course."

I had seen Ethan around school. He was always surrounded by friends, usually from drama club. I didn't think of myself as someone with a lot of envy, but I was wildly jealous of Ethan—of anyone—who had his careless confidence. When he talked, it was obvious that he wasn't analyzing if he annoyed the other person, or if what he said would be taken the wrong way. He was only having a good time.

Naturally, I was terrified of him.

But I was learning—slowly—that people were not their clothes or physical attractiveness or confidence. They were just people. All of us, trying our best.

"Do you—don't you go to our school?" I asked Ethan. My tone was vaguely belligerent, but, still, I was talking to someone I didn't know. Which counted for something, right? "Do you also perform at Castle?"

He smiled at me, and the moment smoothed into something ordinary. I don't think he noticed my self-consciousness. Or he was kind enough not to point it out.

"Ryan dragged me there once," he said. "And that was it. Now we go every Sunday."

The boy next to him looked at him affectionately. "He's really good."

"True."

"So, what's this N^N?" the girl asked. "We've been hearing about it at our school. Some kind of counterculture thing?"

I had to give the others credit: none of them betrayed a thing, not a peek at each other, not a blink, nothing. Carlie subtly nudged Peter, but no one else seemed to notice.

"Why didn't someone start that in Napleville?" the girl said. "The oppressed uniting to overthrow their oppressors? I am all over that."

A guy sat next to her and handed her a drink. "Someone tried, remember? But then Neil Michaelson said N^N stood for Nerds and Nincompoops and it died a quick death. Go, Napleville."

"Right."

"I wish I had thought of it!" Ethan said. I remembered he had tried to defy Mitzi in the hallways and had been shamed for his rebellion. "The whole drama club is sick of her. We are so on board."

"There's no clue who's behind it?" I recognized the boy, a poet from Grande who had spoken of his first heartbreak. "Come on, there's got to be some hints about who's doing it."

Heidi shrugged. "They're pretty good at hiding their tracks."

"Is it working?" the poet asked.

Peter said, "It's a fascinating sociological study about the effectiveness of groupthink and how it can be harnessed for good purposes and not evil."

"You all have a super-small school," a girl from Grande said. "We have mean people, but they are kind of spread out."

"Yes," Will said. "In Plainstown there is no escape. EVER."

"Plainstown has tiny music and drama departments. This is what happens when you don't invest in the arts." Ethan lifted his glass. "Everyone turns into assholes."

All the poets cheered and clinked their cups together.

"Well, I want to meet this guy," one of them called. "He's my hero."

I knew Heidi was dying to challenge his assumption that it was a man and not a woman behind the movement, but she thankfully stayed silent. Will taking her by the shoulders and steering her towards the kitchen probably also helped.

"We'll let you know if we find out anything," Griff said. We were sitting next to each other on the floor, by the wall. He casually stretched his arm behind my back. If I leaned a little, it would be around me.

Griff glanced at me, then began chatting and joking around with the poets. He was offering me a choice, without expectation. I couldn't figure out what was so different, why the humming happiness I felt was so bright. Then I realized it was because the tight coil of doubt I usually had—the dark warning bell that rang with Henry-from-honors-history and Luke-from-the-bookstore—was gone. There was only Griff.

I leaned back, a little.

Griff's smile was instant, radiant. It was only when his arm tightened around me that I noticed it was shaking, ever so slightly.

"Why, Mr. Griffin. Were you nervous?"

"You kept me hanging for a second there, Ms. Chang."

I tried not to overthink how nice it was to have the weight

of Griff's arm around me, how he was close enough that I could tell exactly when he was taking a breath and when he laughed. When he was looking at me.

A few of the poets began practicing their pieces and getting input from the others. They would begin a poem, then stop, adjust. Redo it again. I hadn't realized that every gesture, every crescendo, was carefully and thoughtfully choreographed.

But there was an interesting gap between workshopping and the final act. Here, things were rehearsed, and each poem had a veneer of performance about it, a slight barrier to it being authentic. But that was gone by the time the pieces were in front of an audience. When those poets hit the stage, they were somehow living within each minute, even as their poetry unfolded.

I asked Peter and Carlie about it.

Carlie looked back and forth between me and Griff, and tried, highly unsuccessfully, to stifle her glee. "That's the goal. It's all about story and connection. You want to create a bond with each member of the audience, and the way to do it is through being honest in the moment."

"You need to believe it and live it," Peter said. "Audiences can absolutely tell if you don't. You rehearse and then you have to leave it all behind. P.S.—this is beyond adorable, you two."

My face heated—ridiculous blush! Get ahold of yourself, Livvy! But for once, I didn't want to get ahold of myself. I wanted to dive into the warmth. I wanted it to saturate every cell.

Griff leaned in, his mouth close to my ear. "Are we adorable?"

225

"I definitely am," I said, but my every molecule was redefining the term *freak out*. I would have been embarrassed, but Griff looked equally as jittery. Because of me.

A superhot, preppy guy walked into the middle of the room. I tried to pay attention to him instead of the warm press of Griff's leg against mine, tried to hold in the tsunami of happiness. But I couldn't quite manage it.

Griff absently played with my hair, smiling. "Are you paying attention?"

I tried to swat him, but he caught my hand, and intertwined our fingers together. He folded his arm, holding our hands close to his heart.

Honestly. I had no chance against him.

Griff faced the poet, and so did I, yanking all my focus back to the makeshift stage.

The guy had a strikingly handsome face and the casual grace of an athlete; I wondered what he was possibly going to perform about. But then he began to speak of his childhood, of being tormented by others due to a back brace that he had to wear when he was a boy. He told of shedding his plastic shell like a chrysalis, only to realize it wasn't so easily removed or forgotten. *They don't see it anymore*, he said, *But I do//I always do.*

Griff was motionless next to me. I loved that he gave each performance one hundred percent of his focus. But we would check in after each poem, volleying a silent rating. If I thought it was hard to resist Griff before, it was nothing compared to now, when he was flush with something that looked suspiciously like happiness.

Peter and Carlie were up next. They weren't practicing. They were taking prisoners. The first word was a rope thrown around the audience, then they yanked it tight. It was impossible to turn away.

Peter spoke fiercely of what it was like to have days wrapped in cruelty, where every space you thought was safe could turn into a trap. Carlie told of a society that stripped her of expectations, that constantly said she was *less* because she was Black. Peter and Carlie would bind their stories together with a word spoken in unison, then split apart, like water around a boulder. At the end, they said

together: *What do we owe such a world?*

Alternating: *kindness*, scorn, *violence*, empathy, ***nothing***.

Together: **hope**.

Next to me, Griff was still, thoughtful.

Peter and Carlie's performance was only three minutes long, but in that time, I lived their experiences. It was the exact opposite of Mitzi's vlog. She was a performer, a seller of things, a huckster. The authenticity was never there—it was an act, and everyone knew it was an act. It made me wonder what she truly believed. She had a stage—a vast platform—but she never revealed anything about her true self. Maybe she was afraid to.

If you let everyone else decide what you like, at what point are you no longer able to figure it out for yourself? If you don't know what you believe in, how do you know who you are?

The poets were able to connect with people in a different way than Mitzi; her audience envied her, was made to feel bad because they didn't have her looks or money or material things.

She created a wormhole, sucking everyone into her warped view of the world and spitting them out twisted, self-loathing, unhappy.

But the poets were a mirror, a way for the audience to see a part of themselves in another person. They encouraged people to challenge what they assumed to be true, to go deeper and feel an experience outside of their own. Was this the key to breaking Mitzi's hold on Plainstown? I thought about it as the party ended and all the poets trickled out.

Soon there was no one left but the Nerd Net and Carlie. Griff tugged me over to a couch and, to the untrained eye, it might have looked like we were cozying up to each other. Snuggling, even.

"What's Griff's face doing?" Heidi said. "I don't think I've ever seen this before."

Griff ducked, burying his head in my shoulder. "Hush."

"Get the camera, Will!" Heidi called. "Our baby has a girlfriend!"

I looked off to the side with as much dignity as I could muster. "SO, THE NERD NET. Aren't we talking about the Nerd Net?"

"Sure." Will held up his phone and snapped a picture. "Absolutely."

Carlie laughed. "OMG, you are both the worst." She nudged Peter. "Do something."

Peter was no better than Heidi or Will; I was surprised that he wasn't doing a happy dance. But at least he tried to help us out. "We're *totally* not going to talk about this, even though love really is the greatest thing." Carlie poked him and he yelped. "But! Moving on—"

"*Thank you,*" we chorused.

"You have been getting some press." Carlie became serious. "If they've heard about the Nerd Net in Napleville and Grande, it is starting to get big. You need to start being careful."

All my happy fizzies rapidly evaporated. I remembered Dawn's warning. What was Mitzi planning? After today's volleyball incident, I was even more nervous. But other than her video, the rest of Mitzi's social media accounts were suspiciously silent. A stone of foreboding pressed against me.

Griff handed me a glass of sparkling cider, his fingers brushing the back of my hand.

"To volleyball, and our dear friend Livvy."

"To Griff's girlfriend, Livvy!" Heidi and Will dissolved into snickers.

"To Homer," I said loudly. "And the Nerd Net."

Heidi and Will cheered.

Peter said, "I couldn't wait to talk to you once everyone else left—I thought I was going to faint. I don't know what you were thinking, but honestly it was glorious."

"Freedom to the Republic of Plainstown," Will said. "Today a volleyball, tomorrow the world!"

"It's time for Phase Four." Heidi swiveled in a neat circle in one of Carlie's chairs. "What have we got?"

My apprehension vanished. The volleyball game had been

replaying in a torturous loop in my head, how Mitzi had pinned me, again and again, on the board of humiliation without care or regret. Without repercussion.

We previously had been focused on showing that it was possible to challenge Mitzi's hold on the school. But everything was the same. Mitzi and her friends still didn't have any idea what it was like for the rest of us, what we faced every day. Maybe it was time they did.

N^N had gotten some serious traction on social media, spawning hashtags and memes.

I made a mental tally of the groups at school: the nerds, the gamers, the anime/manga crowd, the musicians, drama people, floaters, lacrosse players. If they all stood by us, it would definitely be a majority.

Wasn't it time?

I thought of Mitzi commanding me to pick up that damn volleyball, the tight press of helplessness. The lack of *justice*.

"I have an idea," I said, and the others looked surprised. Even Griff looked intrigued.

Will tipped his glass towards me. "Let's hear it, Advisor Girl."

I thought of Mitzi's face in gym class. Rage, hot and spiky, ignited before I could stop it. Mitzi hadn't only been asserting her power and control. She wanted to humiliate me. "I think we should try one of the oldest and most effective forms of psychological torment."

"Torment?" Peter said.

"What we've been doing hasn't been working. Mitzi still

doesn't understand what they've been doing to us every day." Mitzi and her friends glided through the halls, wrapped in robes of smugness and privilege. Even after all our operations, it was still the same. "So, let's make them."

"Make them?" Peter sat up. "What do you mean?"

"Every day, Mitzi and Adeline sit at the popular table like they're better than everyone else. I think they should be the *only* ones there." A hard kernel of certainty wedged itself into my mind; this was the right thing.

Peter was shaking his head before I stopped talking. "No. That's never been what this has been about. We should focus on breaking the hierarchy, not harming others."

"What do you think is actually going to do that, Peter?" Will said. "Slaps on the wrist aren't going to get the job done."

Heidi looked pale. "I agree with Peter. This isn't who we are."

"This is the same thing as Operation Hallway," I said. "Mitzi and her people have never had to feel the impact of what they are doing. They should."

"But that wasn't our intention." Heidi glanced at Peter. "We never meant for them to be pushed in the halls or for others to target their accounts. But this—this would be deliberate. That's wrong."

"Is it?" I didn't see the difference. "Mitzi's been profiting from her privileges. The whole world thinks she's the queen of our school. But that's only because she steals the best of everything. She terrorizes everyone, so they let her get away with it. Maybe it's time everyone knows what this school truly thinks of her."

231

"What, you're going to shun them in the cafeteria, then post that on the internet?" Peter looked horrified. "You're going to shame her?"

"This isn't shame," I said. "It's the truth. Mitzi's been telling the world that everyone at this school loves her. We're just showing that it's false advertising. It's taking back all the advantages that she stole. And all the profits that she got from that lie."

"No," Peter said. "This whole project has only been about taking down the hierarchy. About showing people the system can be challenged. That's it. It wasn't about taking anyone down."

"That's what I'm talking about, Peter. Breaking the social order. And it is only fair. Self-defense is legal; you are allowed, under the law, to use a proportionate amount of force to defend yourself. We're attacked every day. Aren't we allowed to use the same tactics on her?"

Heidi was silent.

"This is just making her *understand*." My voice was loud, but I didn't care. "And why are we even talking about rightness? After what they've done to me? To all the people at school? You think they deserve some sort of latitude? They never gave us any." No one had ever given me leeway, not at Lake View, not here.

Will said, "We tried helping the victims, but it didn't work. We tried to shake up the status quo with those other operations, but everything is the same. I'm with Livvy—this is the only way to get through to them."

Heidi shook her head. "Griff? Do you agree?"

I didn't know what he would say. I could see him weighing the options, playing out each scenario to its end point. He finally said, "Things for my cousin didn't happen at once; it became worse and worse, then unbearable. Maybe we need to overthrow the system before it gets that bad."

"Exactly," I said.

But Griff still looked troubled. "But do you think everyone else will go along with this?"

"They did with the other operations. They'll do it here." I had seen it, in the halls. People looking more hopeful. I knew the excluded groups—the academics, the emos, the musicians, the drama group, everyone else—would join us. They had all been pressed under this hierarchy for too long.

Peter stood up. "You're setting her up, then humiliating her. I won't do it."

Heidi was also shaking her head. "Neither will I." She gave Griff a look, one I couldn't interpret. "You know why."

What did that mean? Next to me, Will was also puzzled.

"This is the only way," I said.

But Peter and Heidi didn't respond. Griff, Will, and I packed up our things in silence, then filed out. The last thing I saw was Heidi and Peter in Carlie's now-empty living room, small and alone.

Thirty-One

PHASE FOUR

GRIFF PICKED ME up early the next morning. He didn't joke around like he normally would; he just silently drove to Will's house, on the other side of town.

This was a familiar shade of what happened when my father used to live with us, the oppressive silence after he would slam out of the house, fuming. My mom and I would sit in the broken aftermath and try to pretend things were normal. They weren't.

It felt wrong to be doing this without Heidi and Peter; since we had left Carlie's, I had a twisting discomfort that had only gotten worse and worse. But we were doing the right thing. We were. Heidi and Peter would see.

Will climbed into the car, a small stack of papers in his hand.

Since Heidi wasn't going to help us, we couldn't use the official Nerd Net ClickComm account; she had already put it on hiatus, and none of us had the password. So we were going to go back to our roots and send out flyers with a ClickCode for a new account. Peter would have joked that we should have put a "we've moved!" picture at the top. But Peter wasn't here.

"Have you talked to her?" I asked Will.

He shook his head. "She won't answer my texts."

I almost understood why Peter wouldn't be a part of Operation Cafeteria. But why was Heidi so opposed?

"Do you think this is a good idea?" I asked.

"Yes," Will said. "Why do you think revolutions happen? Do you think the oppressed ask permission and the people in power just give it up? Sometimes you have to seize your freedom."

Did Mitzi even recognize what she was doing was wrong? She must. She knew exactly what she was doing when she tried to humiliate me in gym. Yes, she had a lot of pressure—financial, family, her future. But she made choices about how she wanted to deal with it, and those choices had consequences.

It was time that she faced them.

Thirty-Two

OPERATION CAFETERIA

AT 3:45 P.M., on Monday, January 9, the following message blasted through Plainstown, from the new Nerd Net Click-Comm account:

DEMOCRACY FOR ALL MEANS EQUALITY FOR ALL. IF YOU AGREE, HELP US TO TAKE DOWN THE LAST AND WORST SYMBOL OF SOCIAL INEQUALITY: THE CAFETERIA.

TOMORROW, EVERYONE SHUN THE POPULAR TABLE.

Thirty-Three

HOW TO BECOME A BOMB

GRIFF MET ME outside my AP American History class on Tuesday.

"Ready?" he asked.

I nodded.

Heidi was down the hall and turned away when she saw us. The doubt seized me then, as I remembered her expression when Will, Griff, and I left Carlie's house.

We also passed Dawn, who was crouched by her locker. She looked vaguely nauseous. Had she somehow found out what was about to happen? Had she warned Mitzi? She scrambled up when she saw me. But Griff was already pulling me towards our table.

We took our usual spots and waited. Will had the best location to record, so he already had his phone out in front of him. Griff would get the backup footage.

The video we planned to release would be simple: a small montage showing all the times that Mitzi had claimed to be a popular person, all the times she insinuated that everyone in Plainstown adored her. Then we would drop in a clip from today, with the caption: *This is what the school really thinks of her.* Spreading it would be easy: I would post a link at the bottom of the comments section of Mitzi and Adeline's latest videos, along with a fake teal dress emoji of death. What goes around comes around.

Mitzi had lied. I was revealing the truth. That was all.

Across the room, Peter was furiously texting, his lunch forgotten.

Mitzi and Adeline strolled in first and confidently took their seats in the center of their usual table.

This was the right plan. It was. They had inflicted so much hurt, so much pain. This was proportional self-defense. This was justice.

People started to trickle in, and at first it was not noticeable. Some smushed into seats at the other tables. The drama group, led by Ethan, came early and sat, picnic-style, on the stage. They were soon joined by a few orchestra and band folks. One clueless freshman tried to sit at the edge of the popular table, only to be grabbed and steered towards another area of the cafeteria.

Mitzi looked up. By this time, the entire length of her table was empty, except for her and her friends. In the lunch line, some of the students were giggling.

Mitzi's face flushed. And this is what separates the tyrannical rulers from the rest of the frightened masses: she then slowly stood up. A small part of me had to reluctantly admire her nerve.

Her posture was perfect. She lifted her chin, regally. "I got an anonymous warning about what was going to happen. It was even suggested that I not show up."

She didn't have to shout because the room had fallen into a terrified silence. Adeline was staring at her, shocked.

"Who is behind all of this?" Mitzi asked. "Tell me. Now."

She wasn't embarrassed or intimidated. Instead, she had grabbed the threat by the throat.

My plan had been to get footage of her being humbled. Instead, all I got was a demonstration of exactly how much power Mitzi wielded, over everyone.

A bubble of anxiety and fear began to swell in the room, starting next to the popular table and radiating out to the groups of kids still waiting for their food. Under the table, Griff reached for my hand.

Mitzi scanned the room. She made eye contact with the freshmen, who looked at the floor, and then at the honors crowd, who were hovering on the edges. The swim team. The drama club on the stage. No one could look at her terrible gaze.

"I know who you are." Mitzi didn't need to raise her voice. "Identify yourselves and I won't go after you."

Peter's phone pinged.

In the empty room, the sound was horrifyingly loud. He peeked at it, and that was the end. When he looked up, Mitzi was staring at him.

No.

I jumped up. I might be in a fight with Peter, but none of that mattered right now. He was part of the Nerd Net, yes, but in many ways he was the one who had it the worst before everyone joined together. He had been a social leper, rejected by everyone for talking too quickly and too loudly, for being too extra, Too Peter. Walking a mile to school was not the only thing Peter did to survive; last year, he also started carrying all his books in between classes because he could not bear to be tormented at his locker.

I was new to the Nerd Net, but even I knew our unspoken agreement was this: protect Peter.

Peter, across the room, radiated fear. Gone was the confident poet who could command crowds. In his place was the boy he used to be, who had been conditioned his entire life to shrink and be afraid.

Griff started to stand, but I pushed his shoulder down. Grandfather always told me there is a point when war becomes inevitable. This was it. Mitzi wasn't backing down, but it wasn't too late. We had gotten support from most of the groups during our other operations. It would be fine.

But I needed to act quickly. Mitzi looked like she was on the verge of launching herself at Peter, who was still clutching his phone. Shockingly, Adeline put a hand on Mitzi's arm, like she wanted to stop her. Why? Because she knew Peter from Castle? Mitzi ignored her and moved towards him.

I said loudly, "Maybe people are tired of sitting by you. Maybe they're sick of how you treat everyone at this school, period."

Griff pulled my hand, but I shook him off. At his table, Will was aghast, plan and filming forgotten.

Mitzi whirled towards me. "Excuse me?"

What I had blurted out wasn't everything I wanted to say; it wasn't an articulation of the careless and ruthless way Mitzi had oppressed this school. But it was all I could think of because I was *dying*. I pictured my heart blowing out of my chest, bits of arteries and blood splattering on the painted white cinder blocks.

I stood up, but then my body abandoned me completely. The air in my lungs whooshed away, my muscles weakened. The only thing left was sheer terror and sweat.

Mitzi was incredulous. I don't know what surprised her more: that she would be challenged, or that it was me. Again.

It had to be me; I had already been identified as a target, and Mitzi didn't know the rest of the Nerd Net existed. She said she knew who we were, but she *had* to be bluffing. Otherwise we would have been toast by now.

Now everyone just had to get behind me.

But it was quiet. Too quiet.

I looked over to the honors kids on the side, the frozen students by the food line, who were clutching their trays. I waited for some support, for some affirmation, but no one was making eye contact with me. Why weren't they making eye contact with me?

Oh

shit.

The panic came in a wave then, starting with my hot face and exploding outward. I was the card player watching the dealer flip over a perfect twenty-one. I was the general who rushed into battle, only to turn around and find the field behind her was empty.

Across the room, Will and Heidi were locked in a stare, their fight forgotten. Will started to stand up, and Heidi looked like she was going to rush over to Peter, as if she could physically shield him from Mitzi.

No. They couldn't stick their heads out of the gopher hole, not now. That would blow their cover and be the end of the Nerd Net, of everything.

"They act like they own this school," I called. "Why are we letting them get away with it?"

As I hoped, Mitzi kept her attention on me and didn't notice Will or Heidi.

No one else moved.

What about all those people who had been in the flash mob? Who wore their orange and gray clothes? Who tried to breach the "A" lot during Operation Parking? The floaters, the drama geeks, the outcasts? Why weren't they outraged?

But no one was angry. No one could even look at us.

Griff's expression was worse than disappointment; it was resignation. Peter was still locked in his seat, his eyes wide. Will and Heidi were starting to get up again.

Oh no. Not now, not when the cavalry was never coming.

I had only one overwhelming instinct: save the revolution. This was my operation, this was my plan, and now that it was going horribly south, it was my responsibility to give cover so the others could regroup and come back another day. I had to become the bomb in the doorway, exploding so everyone could escape out the back.

I detonated.

"You couldn't hear me?" I said. "No one wants to sit next to you, not anymore."

I'd thought things were quiet before, but it was nothing compared to now. I could feel the flat eyes of a hundred cell phones, silently recording everything for posterity. But still no one moved. No one dared. I could only see the sea of cell phone cases, the round stickers with Mitzi's TikTok logo stuck to their backs.

Before we had started Operation Cafeteria, I had made a mental tally of the groups that might support us. Where had I gone wrong? Where had I miscalculated?

Then it hit me.

I assumed that people were defined by their groups. That the outcasts were primarily outcasts and would therefore support us. That all musicians were tormented and would revolt. I had done what the school itself had done; I had grouped people and made assumptions about who they were, how they would act.

But there were people like Waverly St. Claire, who was part of the arts crowd. I belatedly remembered she loved fashion and wanted to launch her own YouTube channel to raise funds for multiple sclerosis research. One endorsement from Mitzi would knock her channel to the stratosphere. There was Sheila Antol, cello player, whose older sister was in the upper echelon of the VIPs. Sheila was not part of the group, but she'd never publicly cross her sibling. There was Richard Gauthier, who did his philosophy project on ethical egoism and its focus on prioritizing the self above all else.

No one was the sum of their social category, not the drama kids, not the athletes, not the musicians. Not the VIPs. That's what Peter had been trying to tell me all along, what he had been trying to show me, at Castle. It was what I was starting to realize, only now it was absolutely clear that I hadn't understood a thing.

And now I had completely and utterly screwed us over.

Mitzi's glare was a hook, yanking her friends back into order. They huddled closer to her, flanking her sides.

"They said it was you." Mitzi's voice carried through the room. "I couldn't believe it. Why are you doing this to me?" I could almost see her calculations: if anyone dared to post a video from today, Mitzi's sponsorship deals could wither, since it would be clear that she was less than a queen. The only way for Mitzi to get her brand back was by making herself into a victim and getting public sympathy.

She strode over to me, then hissed, "I was waiting for proof. You have no idea what's about to happen."

"Aren't you fed up?" I said to the others and tried not to sound desperate. "Don't you want things to be different? We can do this, together."

They could still rally behind us. Indeed, I saw some of the

students glancing at the others, as if waiting for someone to step forward first. But no one did.

Peter looked horrified. Dawn made a desperate gesture at me to *sit down*. Griff tried to stand up, but I shoved down his shoulder, again.

"It's not too late," I said to the crowd. But I knew it was.

At the popular table, some VIPs were looking down, humiliated. But some of them were starting to become angry. Adeline was already furious, staring at me like she wanted to carve me into twelve pieces and roast me over a spit. This was her worst nightmare, being shoved off the cliff of popularity. And now she wanted to take me down with her.

Quiet support was not rebellion. And the way to inspire people was not through pain or embarrassment. That was Mitzi's approach, and it had only created resentment.

What had I done? Had I just created a common enemy for Adeline and the VIPs to rally against?

That was my second mistake. And it meant the end. Of everything.

There were students who seemed more hopeful in the halls—Jennifer Hamlish, Krisha Chaudhary—who now looked at me in despair, because they could see it, too, where this all would end. I didn't know what to tell them.

"Apologize, *now*. And I might consider changing my mind," Mitzi snarled.

My plane was plummeting, the vast, unforgiving ground rushing up and filling the horizon. I was strapped to my seat, my muscles spasming out a Morse code of fear and regret. But Mitzi was trying to humiliate me, *again*, so I did the only thing left for me to do: I spewed out bullets on my way down. I had dragged us into defeat, but maybe there would be someone better—wiser—who could rise from our ashes. Who could do what I wasn't able to.

"No." I didn't look at Mitzi. I spoke to the kids in the back, in the lunch line, the ones who dared to harbor a cinder of defiance, who wrapped it, unlit, until the day the fire would come. I threw them my flag as I hit the ground. "You think you have respect because people don't challenge you. But you don't."

Mitzi's face twisted. "You have no idea what you're talking about."

But I understood, finally. Mitzi, forever suffocated as the daughter of someone who used to be famous, clawing towards the shrine of fame. Burning the bridge to the life she truly wanted, one choice at a time. She was now stranded on the other side, and there was only one path for survival left.

She must have seen the pity on my face because for a second—a second only—I saw Mitzi cracked open, her persona broken enough to see the desperate girl thrashing inside.

I may have been the only one who saw it, but she knew it and I knew it. And I don't think it was something she could ever forgive. It wasn't just the challenge to her authority that pissed her off; no, it was that a *nobody* could have seen the terrible and soft part of her that she furiously tried to hide. And that, perhaps more than anything, made me someone that she wanted to annihilate.

Mitzi leaned towards me and said, with chilling precision, "Remember—*you* made me do this. I gave you a chance."

"I'm not making you do anything," I said.

But Mitzi pivoted and left, her promise hanging over my head.

Thirty-Four

THE EMPIRE STRIKES BACK

LOOKING BACK, I often think about the other choices I could have made. What if I had stuck to my iron-clad rule and stayed anonymous from the beginning? What if I had never sat next to Griff? Had never joined the Nerd Net?

The Nerd Net had emboldened me, made me sloppy. I believed Mitzi was vulnerable, capable of being challenged.

That was a serious, fatal error.

Less than twenty-four hours after Operation Cafeteria, my life as I knew it ended. I went to sleep as a perfectly normal teenager, and I woke up in a nightmare.

The next morning, the doorbell rang as I was finishing breakfast. Griff was in the doorway, grim. He didn't need to say a word.

I don't remember saying goodbye to my mom in a daze, and

I don't remember leaving my house. Somehow I was in his car, and we were roaring down the street.

"What is it?" My voice was faint, which I hated. But I was terrified.

Griff's knuckles were hard, bony peaks on his steering wheel. He took a tight turn away from the school.

"Where are we going?" I said.

"We're cutting class today."

He drove us down an unfamiliar street, waiting on the side until a familiar SUV pulled out of a far-off driveway. Was that his dad?

Griff still hadn't said a word, and I was drowning in dread.

"Griff? Tell me."

He gunned his engine and shot into the driveway. He threw his car into park and tugged me towards the front door. Was this his house? It was pristinely clean, but for the living room table, which was covered with stacks of papers, like mine. A large calendar covered with appointments was on the far wall. Not many pictures, family or otherwise.

Griff gripped my hand, hard, as he led me to the table. I could feel the hard calluses next to my palm, the slight tremor.

"What is it?" I whispered.

Griff's phone pinged, but he ignored it. He put his hands on my shoulders, his fingers curling tightly.

"Livvy. They've launched a social media attack against you."

I felt the ground dropping, or maybe it was just me, sinking to the floor.

Griff's phone pinged again, and he finally pulled it out. "Shit."

"Let me see it." I tried to remember the act of breathing, the in and out of oxygen.

"It won't help, Livvy," he said. "It'll only make it worse."

"Show me." My voice was steady. I pictured my mom, striding into the fire of trial, her head high.

Griff opened his laptop, and there they were, a compilation video of photos, set to music. They were worse than I could have imagined. One was of me in a tight qipao with an exaggerated hourglass figure. There was a huge cutout by the chest and a long slit by the legs, along with the caption, "Me love you long time." Another picture had my face stretched out with buck teeth and a bamboo hat, pulling a rickshaw. Yet another had me chewing on a bat, the blood dripping from my mouth. Around me were dim sum steamer baskets full of crickets and dogs.

As I stared at the webpage in shock, it suddenly blinked off and was replaced by an error message.

But it didn't make it any better. They tried to steal my sense of safety at the school; they tried to make me doubt myself, to isolate me, to humiliate me. But when that wasn't enough, when that failed, they flew the fighter jet and dropped the bomb right into the heart of me.

Mitzi and Adeline had known right where to hit, where to make it burn. I knew they always targeted the things that would be the most painful to their victims. And this was it for me, a long line of events through my life, tied with string that crossed states, cities, years. Generations. This was what always happened at my other schools whenever I tried to speak up, or to stick my head out of the gopher hole; that was always, *always*, the first target they went after. My Asianness.

These images, these monstrous, twisted pictures were now all over the internet. On people's phones. In people's social media accounts. Everywhere.

Oh, God.

So many copies. A fun house maze of horror, with distortions of me at every turn. Memes. Posts. Retweets. If each person forwarded it to three people, then there would be tens, then hundreds of copies. Would this humiliation be crystallized, everywhere, forever?

Oh, God.

I was running before I realized it, halfway down Griff's driveway, slicing myself on the cold air. But I couldn't run fast enough to escape the shell of my body, to escape my face.

Griff called out behind me, but I kept going. I had one rule— one rule—when it came to new schools. *Be invisible.* That was my iron mantra. I knew what could happen. I *knew* it.

Griff caught up to me. "Livvy. Hold on."

But I wasn't stopping. I wasn't stopping for him, for anyone, ever again.

"Livvy!" Griff shouted. *"Please."*

I kept running.

I focused on the sidewalk ahead of me: one step at a time, one minute at a time, one hour at a time. That is how a girl survives when her father has left her; that is how a girl gets through all the moments of cruelty that are forced upon her;

that is the only way through. Second by second. Minute by minute. Hour by hour. Step by step.

"Livvy." Griff's voice broke.

It overwhelmed me again, then: the images, everywhere, the degradation. *Did you dare think you could be like us? Did you dare believe we would ever accept you? You?*

Did you think that you could change . . . anything?

I whirled around. *"Leave me alone."*

His face collapsed.

I ran home. He didn't follow.

Thirty-Five

TRENTON

EVENTUALLY—SOMEHOW, MIRACULOUSLY—I finally made it home. I locked the door behind me, as if a plank of wood and glass could keep everything out.

It couldn't.

In all those years, in all the anxiety-filled days in strange school after strange school, in all those mortifying moments when you realize that everyone is talking about you, when your cell phone is silent, when every second of your day is just about surviving—through all this, there was always one small thing: hope. Hope that maybe the next move would come, or someone would see you and smile. Hope that today would be the day that would be different.

Heidi had been right. Peter had been right. They had been so, so right. I thought I was doing unto Mitzi what she had done to me. That it was fair. But there were VIPs sitting next

253

to Mitzi during Operation Cafeteria, and they had gone from cheerful to small, embarrassed. One of them had been the girl who had performed at Castle. A person with her own story, her own challenges.

I had been trying to rally the troops with pain, but that had only led to failure. Peter and Heidi had known it. Even Griff was skeptical when I had told him my plan. And now the road had led to this: the rocket, flipped and pointed at me.

I thought of Peter's and Heidi's faces as we left them, how they had turned away from me before Operation Cafeteria. I thought of Griff's face as I ran, the brokenness of it.

For a moment—foolish, foolish me—I had something lovely with the Nerd Net. Then I ruined it. But better to be the destroyer than the destroyed; better to be the rejecter than the rejected.

That was what I told myself, and I almost believed it.

Now they were gone. And I was gone, too. With that video, Mitzi had obliterated my identity, my personhood. I was stripped to a caricature. We had escalated into war, and I had just been defeated, in the most devastating way possible.

My mom's car sped into the driveway, then she ran towards our house. She froze when she saw my face, wet with tears.

"Olivia." She wrapped me in a hug. "Your school called me and told me what happened."

I leaned into her, as if she could protect me, like she did when I was a child. But she couldn't fix this. Any of it. I had seen how she had gotten her own disgusting catcalls when she walked through the mall, how her boss had asked her where she learned English. She knew and I knew that this was a part of living, of surviving, for people who looked like us.

I thought the video was bad, but it was infinitely worse to see Mom's expression. She never wanted me to understand these things, to see them. When I was little, she would always quickly turn us in the other direction or try to distract me. But she knew it was going to come. She had warned me. But now that it had, it broke something in her.

Mom held me close for a long time, her arms tight. "Tell me who did this. Who made it?"

I could only shake my head. "It doesn't matter. It won't make a difference." None of it had. The Nerd Net, the revolution. The hope.

"Olivia." Now her voice was commanding.

I pictured the video flying through the invisible ether, landing in people's phones, on their computer screens. I imagined people—some who walked next to me in the halls, some who took classes with me, some who might have worn our N^N symbol on their clothing. All of them laughing at me now, sharing it with their friends.

My mom was silent, and I knew she was thinking, her quick brain evaluating our options. She never hesitated—not when my dad had left her with a baby and no job, not when she had to borrow money from her awful, controlling in-laws so she could put herself through law school, not when she joined the military and the JAG Corps. Where had that steel gone? It certainly hadn't been passed down to me.

"We can homeschool," she said. "I'm getting you out of that

racist hellpit. Then I'm taking this to the top of the administration. Why haven't they found who did this yet?"

My phone buzzed; it was Heidi.

Livvy. We'll fix this. I promise you.

I clutched the phone. Heidi? She was still texting me?

"Who is it?" Mom said. "Is someone else harassing you?"

I mutely shook my head. "It's . . . Heidi."

"Heidi? Who's that?"

"She's . . . someone I know." Could I have called her my friend, before? Maybe. But not anymore.

I remembered Heidi and Will handing me my red pin. Peter on the volleyball court, staring across the net at me, willing me to hit the ball. Griff wrapping me in his sweatshirt.

It burned then, the acid of regret.

The doorbell rang. Griff, Peter, Will, and Heidi all rushed in. My mom stood by the door, her hand still on the doorknob.

What? They were here?

Griff pulled me towards him, his hand gently cradling the back of my head. "I know you said you wanted to be alone. But it's not happening."

"I told Mr. Veevers I had a stomachache, which was not exactly a lie, but I kind of never went back to school and Griff picked me up at the corner," Peter said.

My phone had one more message on it.

P.S. Griff came to get us. We're coming over.

"And you are . . . ?" Mom looked at all of them. "Shouldn't you be in school?"

"We're Livvy's friends," Heidi said.

I tried to suppress them, the emotions, but they came too quickly. There were too many, from too many years.

"Livvy, this is awful—I mean, I know people can be awful, but this is especially terrible even for our school, which is pretty horrible," Peter said.

I waited for him to tell me that he was right about Operation Cafeteria, but he was gracious enough to hold it in. He only reached over for a quick hug.

Will was lit like a flamethrower, blasting arcs of rage. "We'll get those assholes, Livvy."

Griff led me to one of the couches and sat next to me. He placed his thumbs on my cheeks, wiping away the tears.

I had seen Griff furious, determined, haunted. But now he looked exactly like how I felt: as if he had been shattered and the pieces were never going to fit back together again. In all of those years at all of those schools, I had always held my pain close, shoved it into an iron safe. But here was Griff, sharing it with me.

He had come back. They all had.

"First thing. Before anything else," I said. "I'm so, so sorry. You were right."

My mom was curious, but she didn't ask. I told her anyways, everything from the beginning.

Mea culpa: take responsibility for one's mistakes. Acknowledge the wrong. Sincerely apologize. Take action to do better.

Mom was quiet as I told her about Operation Cafeteria and what had happened.

"I thought it was the right thing to do," I said. "I thought it was justice."

Mom winced.

"I know." I couldn't look at her.

"Intentions matter, Olivia. There's an important difference between punishment and genuine reform. You were trying to do the first, weren't you?"

My mother, dropper of truth bombs.

To be absolutely honest, I had been enraged and humiliated after the volleyball game. I had wanted Mitzi to feel the same. Hadn't I?

I turned to Heidi and Peter. "I'm so sorry."

Heidi didn't immediately say it was okay, which I appreciated. She showed up, she came here, and that was enough.

For once, Peter wasn't smiling. "If this is how we're going to operate, it's not going to work."

"I know," I said.

He stared at Will and Griff. "This can't happen again."

Will looked surprised at his tone. "But we can't give up. Not after what she did to Livvy."

Heidi finally spoke. "Peter's right. We, as a group, have to figure out what we want to do. Who we are. But Will is also right. Mitzi retaliated in the most heinous way. That's also not okay. Nothing justifies what she did to you."

I wanted to hurt Mitzi like she'd hurt me. She had done the same, only without restraint. I had wanted to punish; she wanted to obliterate. She came from a binary world where there were only winners and losers. And she was not going to be a loser.

"Mitzi? The actress's daughter?" Mom asked.

My friends glanced at me.

"We're pretty sure," Heidi said. "Even if she didn't do the video itself, she's behind it somehow."

My mom flipped to Scary Trial Prep Mom. Even I, who was used to it, was slightly alarmed. Peter looked terrified.

"I need proof," Mom said. "Is there anyone who can testify that she did it? Or released the video?"

Peter clutched Will in alarm, but Heidi nodded. "We'll get it. There is always a trail, and we'll find it."

"Next—let's talk homeschooling," Mom said. "I'll teach you everything you need to know to finish up the year. You can test out early and then go to college next fall. It can all be over."

Over. The word was like a beacon. I could picture it now: studying at Georgetown, in the heart of the nation's government. A new life, a new existence in Washington, DC. A new me.

But then I saw Griff. I saw my friends. I knew what lay ahead for them: the silent, grim hallways, the coldness of social shunning, the despair of a movement that had fallen apart in their hands. Mitzi continuing her reign unchecked during the year and a half until graduation.

Yes, I would be free, but they would not be. And neither would the rest of the students at Plainstown. If I left, wouldn't it be abandoning the Nerd Net? Turning my back on what we had started? I suddenly thought of a moment during Operation Cafeteria, at the end: I had looked across the room into the lunch line, and one of the sophomores was glaring at Mitzi. And two of the freshmen along the wall had taken minuscule steps forward. It wasn't a large movement. But it was something.

And I remembered this, a tale my grandfather had told me, so long ago. In the winter of 1776, Washington had crossed the Delaware with a decimated army. The men had no shoes, but they had still marched towards battle, wrapping their blistered feet with rags. They had taken the fire of their pain and swallowed it, hardened it into the fuel that would drive them across New Jersey.

It was those men who had taken Trenton, who had irrevocably turned the war in favor of the Colonies.

We had started this revolution because we believed in the idea of freedom and a life at Plainstown free from Mitzi's hierarchies. We believed we could make a difference.

I had made a mistake, yes; I had yanked us in the wrong direction. But that didn't mean our purpose—our first, true purpose—was wrong.

An image popped into my mind: seeing my mom in the middle of the night at our kitchen table, working on a pro bono case. I knew she had already done long hours at work and was exhausted. But she was focused. Furious, in fact, scribbling notes, jumping up to pace as she practiced her arguments.

"What are you doing?" I remember asking.

Her face softened when she noticed me. "Getting justice. For someone who can't get it herself."

I imagined Mitzi, sitting smugly in the cafeteria, surveying her empire. Crossing the stage at graduation in triumph.

I thought of Griff's cousin, and Sarah, and me, and every other person who had been tormented, ruthlessly. Mitzi had taken my Asianness and weaponized it. If I left it unchallenged, was that like saying it was acceptable? That Mitzi could attack me in this most visceral way, and there would be no consequence?

I had to speak. I had to. Not only for me, but for all of those who had been shamed and ostracized. For people, like my grandpa, who had been mocked for how they talked or what they looked like. For every person who was made to choke on their differences: I needed to fight, for them.

I would make the bloody march to Trenton. Live or die, it was time to take a stand. Homer had been right the whole time: it was better to live or die, all at once, than to die by inches. I had spent my whole life trying to live while slowly dying by inches. I thought I was doing what it took to survive. But every time I didn't raise my hand when I knew the answer, every time I scuttled through the hallways like I didn't have a right to be there, every time I was made to feel *less* because of what I was, I was dying. I just hadn't realized it at the time.

"We have to finish this," I said. "I have to go back."

I thought I was doing good by being in isolation. That I was protecting myself. But I was also letting the systems around me continue.

"Are you sure?" Mom grabbed both of my hands. "If you return, you know what it'll mean for you."

Here was the thing about my mom: though she always let me make my own decisions, she also let me suffer all the consequences—the terrible bangs I had to grow out, the time I got sick because I refused to wear an ugly blue coat, the second ear piercing that I was still kind of regretting. But it was always my choice. For a woman who had precious few choices, who had no say in the poverty that wrapped around her childhood, or how her mother died when she was young, or how her husband had left her, this was the greatest gift she could give to her daughter. It was only now that I saw it clearly.

I hugged her. "I'm sure."

"I'm still contacting the school. I can't let this go unaddressed."

I nodded. Mom stared into my eyes, like she had after Dad left. It was a look that said, *We're in this together.*

"This is beyond; I am getting all of the feels. Livvy, are you sure? Because you know we'll stand by you no matter what," said Peter.

Griff wrapped his hand around mine. He was steady, unwavering, as he had been that long ago day in the cafeteria when my shirt had gotten ruined.

"You don't have to do this," he said.

I knew what it cost him to say it. He desperately wanted a coup d'état for every Brynn, every outsider, who had been crushed by the hierarchy. But Griff placed a hand on my cheek and said, "Livvy. We should drop this. Before she does worse to you."

"No. What's the alternative? We let her continue? When we could have stopped it? We have a duty. We have a *moral obligation*." I glanced at Mom, the person who had taught me the definition and power of *moral obligation*.

"If we continue, though, there will be no harm to others," said Peter.

"I agree."

Peter checked to see if I meant it. I did.

Griff nodded, then Will did, slowly.

Heidi said, "Let's do this."

"Are you sure?" Griff squeezed my hand.

At my other schools, I always felt like everything was conditional. I would be allowed to keep my life of invisible peace as long as I didn't make a fuss; I could have some semblance of awkward conversation with other kids occasionally as long as I was not too opinionated or too disagreeable.

But Griff was waiting patiently. Next to him, Will, Heidi, and Peter looked concerned. For the first time, I knew I would not be alone in the trenches. I could decide, just for me.

"I'm sure," I said.

Heidi, Will, and Peter burst into motion, much as they had in the school library when I had first met them.

"Olivia's mom," Will said. "Can we call you Ms. C? Do you mind if we set up a few things?"

Peter started clearing off the table. "You said we wouldn't need a whiteboard, Will, but look who is laughing now."

Will said, "Why don't you go to the car and get the computers *and the whiteboard*, Peter."

"It is always better to be gracious when we are wrong, William."

Griff and Will helped to clean up, while Heidi began to pull a bunch of cords from her bag.

Heidi said, "Can we use your outlets, Ms. C?" At her nod, Heidi grabbed a laptop from Peter as he was walking through the door; Griff took the other one. Peter began to set up the whiteboard.

Will snatched it from him and wrote, *Thank God we have this whiteboard//Where all of our ideas may be stored.*

"There is no shame in organization," Peter said.

Will wrote, *YES THERE IS, PETER.*

My mother was watching all of this with an expression that was very similar to the one I had when I first met the Nerd Net.

"We were tracking the original website when Griff came to get us." Heidi cackled. "Step back, amateurs!"

My mom whispered to me, "Are your new friends hackers?"

"Only that one," I whispered back, pointing at Heidi.

"And Griff?" Mom practically sang his name.

I shushed her, violently.

"Is he your *boyfriend*? Tell me everything."

"SNACKS," I bellowed. "MOM, WE NEED SNACKS."

"This does look like a snack situation," Mom said beatifically as I shoved her towards the door.

Griff looked oblivious, THANK GOD. He paced around the table. "We know the video came out last night, and it went viral by midnight. Heidi, do we know where they first showed up?"

There was a long pause. "Got it. Looks like changchong.com." Heidi winced. "Sorry, Livvy."

"Can you trace who owns it?"

Heidi said, "One . . . minute . . ."

"Could you please get some nacho chips, Ms. C?" Will called to Mom. "Heidi works better with processed cheese."

"You've got to be kidding me. They used Domains by Proxy!" Heidi swiped her mouse. "Okay, assholes, how about some IP address tracking."

"I could not be more attracted to you right now," Will said. "But does Mitzi even know how to do any of this stuff?"

Heidi scanned her screen. "They bounced through a VPN! Who does that?"

Griff shrugged. "Someone who knows something about programming."

"So not Mitzi, then?" I said. I knew she did a lot of video editing, but this seemed like another level.

"There's no way Mitzi would know how to do that kind of Photoshopping," Will said. "She's not the sharpest knife in the drawer."

Peter stopped wiping the whiteboard. "That's not true, Will. Or we wouldn't be here."

He was right. Everyone underestimated Mitzi because she was an influencer and seemed to focus on fashion and makeup. But look at what she had set up in Plainstown and how she held on to her power. That was no accident. It took savvy, and intelligence.

Heidi shook her head. "She definitely doesn't have the tech skills for this, though. It's too advanced—"

"Oh my God." Griff's words were quiet, but everyone

turned towards him. "I know exactly who did it. And so do you, Heidi."

Heidi's "no" was an exhale, a bubble floating up into the air.

Peter, Will, and I looked at each other in confusion.

"Can you think of anyone else? Anyone who could have done this?" Griff said.

"She would never have the nerve—" Red spots appeared on Heidi's cheeks and neck. "She knows I would crush her."

Griff stared at her. "She's the only one."

Will said, "And for the rest of us? What are you talking about?"

Heidi leaned towards the screen.

"Holy shit," she breathed. "You're right. Look."

Heidi had a window open to one of the pictures. Luckily, it was so enlarged that you couldn't see the worst parts. Well, that wasn't quite true—the pixels were so big that you could definitely see something. Two letters and a number.

"What the hell?" Will said.

"What's HD4?" I'd never heard of it. "Some kind of chemical?"

"A message." Heidi slumped back into her chair. "For me. I'm H."

"Who's D?" Will asked. "And why are there four of you?"

"D was an old friend." Heidi's voice was grim. "And now she is my enemy."

Peter looked confused. "What's going on?"

Heidi said, "I need to tell all of you a story." Will tried to put a hand on her arm, but she stopped him with a look of pure misery. "You need to hear this, Will. I probably should have told you a long time ago. It all started sophomore year, when I was friends with Dawn Thompson."

Dawn? The same Dawn who followed Mitzi around all the time?

Heidi began to speak.

Thirty-Six

H & D, FRIENDS 4 EVER

IN A WAY, you know this story. Two childhood friends, both ostracized for being ridiculously smart, make a pact to elevate their standing. This was before Heidi's own exile, in the beginning of her social ascent.

The two girls were computing geniuses, disciplined and methodical. They spent hours plotting their breach of the upper echelon. New wardrobes were purchased. Makeovers were had. They identified a girl on the fringes of the VIPs (a nervous freshman named Molly) and began to befriend her. This was in the beginning of Mitzi's empire, when she was an underclassman who had already amassed a lot of influence due to her famous mother. Everyone could see that she was heading for the pinnacle.

But where Heidi began to doubt Mitzi and her group once

she learned more about them, Dawn was the opposite. She wanted to belong at all costs.

Heidi glanced at Griff, who looked unsurprised. "By the end of our freshman year, we were finally in. We knew Mitzi could turn on anyone, even her friends, but we managed to stay under the radar until sophomore year. Then Sarah Sloane started her own business and became an influencer. After Mitzi lost a bunch of advertisers to her, that was it. She wanted us to ruin her."

Will made a small noise of surprise and so did Peter.

"No," Peter said. "No, you don't mean—?"

Heidi was only looking at Will. He reached for her hand and squeezed it tightly.

"Heidi never would have done that," he said.

"You're right. I know you didn't. Did you, Heidi?"

Her head was bent again, her hair covering her face. "I said no," she whispered. "But Dawn said yes."

Griff put a hand on her shoulder. "It's not your fault."

"I tried to stop it," she cried. "I knew Mitzi was freaking out because of her lost advertisers. I knew she was going to do *something* to retaliate. I told Sarah they were coming. I warned her! But neither of us could have guessed they would be so ruthless. And I never would have believed that Dawn could have been a part of that."

"That's why," Will said quietly. "That's why you became an outcast during sophomore year. Because you left their group. Because you refused to be a part of what they were going to do."

Heidi nodded.

"Why didn't you tell us?" Will said. Even though we were all in the room, somehow the conversation had turned into one between just the two of them. "Heidi. Why didn't you tell *me*?"

Heidi said, brokenly, "I told Griff. I thought he deserved to know before I joined the Nerd Net. But the rest of you . . . How could I? You want me to say that I'm a failure, Will? I am. I failed Sarah and now I've failed Livvy."

"You didn't—" I started to say, but Will had already pulled Heidi to her feet. He placed his hands on her face, then bent his head and tenderly kissed her.

Peter beamed.

"THAT'S HOW YOU DO IT," Griff said. "FINALLY."

But now it was starting to look like they were trying to devour each other, or conduct an extremely through experiment on the physics of suction. Time to leave, stat.

Griff wrapped his arm around my waist and led me towards the kitchen. "Aaaand this is where we let them express their months of frustrated romantic tension."

"That was quite exciting!" Peter sprinted out of the room. "Love is wonderful. I need to tell Carlie."

"The real question is—" Griff said.

"—how long are they going to make out?" I said.

Griff snickered. "The second question is: Now that we know it's Dawn, what are we going to do?"

"How could someone be so cruel? I just don't understand," Peter said.

The thing was, I could almost get it. At Porter, the school

where I had done set design in drama club, I had something that sort of resembled friends. By that I mean they weren't enemies, which was close enough for me. I peeked at their social media accounts and witnessed the muscular pull of the internet, the seductive excitement that can come from hearts and comments. As the months passed, I could see them hamming it up in photos, acting sillier to get more likes.

Imagine you have that but times a thousand. Imagine what it is like to rise. To have people listening to you, following you. At some point, do they stop becoming human beings? Wasn't this what Adeline was saying, at Castle?

As for Dawn, she was trying to endure. I knew all about the torture of the day-to-day. I knew the sick feeling of scuttling through the hallways, praying not to be seen. But Dawn had clawed her way up the bloodied spines of Sarah and me. She had exchanged her survival for ours. Had she thought about the consequences of what she had done? Had she done it anyways?

I felt sick. That video had appeared and exploded, but it was a thing, a poison. I now knew that there was a real human being who had made and released it, deliberately. That was infinitely worse.

Griff curled his arm around me. I closed my eyes and pressed my face against his shoulder, focusing on the subtle scent of his soap, as if it were a kite string that could lift me up into an empty stretch of sky. I cleared my mind until there was only warmth and light and the sound of Griff's heartbeat under my ear.

"What are we going to do?" Heidi said, from the doorway.

Her hair was disheveled, her lipstick was smeared, and she looked radiant. Behind her, Will was holding on to her hand tightly, looking happier than I had ever seen him.

"Oh?" Griff said. "Are you finished?"

"Shut it." Heidi couldn't stop smiling. "I think we should all go on a field trip. It's time to pay someone a visit."

Will said, "For the record, Peter, we figured all that out without using the whiteboard."

"You have lipstick on your face, buddy," Griff said, grinning.

"So I do." Will kissed Heidi again.

"Friends," Griff said. "It's time for us to stop making out—sorry—and go see Dawn."

Thirty-Seven

MEETING AN OLD FRIEND

IT WAS PROBABLY not the best idea to let Heidi drive. We had waited until school ended, then Heidi roared across town, her face grim. She did not hesitate as she flew around the tricky turns and narrow streets of east Plainstown; this was clearly a trip she had taken many, many times before.

Dawn lived in a small, nondescript house much like my own, only her lawn was shaggy and cluttered with a million plastic kiddie toys.

Heidi threw the car into park and strode towards the front door. She pounded on it, the rest of us circled behind her.

The door opened, and Dawn's little face peeked out. In the bright afternoon sunlight, she looked more ghostly than ever, especially when she spotted Heidi, then me.

"Yeah, that's right," Will said. "We figured it out." His fury had risen again, cutting. I knew the others were behind me and supported me. But Will *understood*.

Dawn looked at Heidi, and there was a whole conversation in that second, years of history compressed. "Heidi." Her voice was pleading.

"Tell me it wasn't you. Tell me you would not stoop to this." Heidi was magnificent in her rage.

"I . . ." Dawn stopped. She started to tremble, her hands shaking. "Will you—will you come in?"

Heidi didn't move. "Tell me, D. I swear to God, tell me the truth. You fucking did not do this, did you?"

There was a long pause, then Dawn said, "Listen. I can't even begin to imagine—"

"No," Griff said. "You can't."

Dawn was focused on Heidi. "You remember. You know what it was like for me."

Heidi gave a curt nod.

"And suddenly it stopped, all the torture. Because Mitzi was protecting me."

Heidi was still silent, but I saw something flash across her face, a quickly suppressed expression of sympathy.

"It was going to school every day and not feeling sick. It was having people finally accept me—*me*!" Color broke across Dawn's cheeks, a scarlet bloom.

"Until they didn't," Heidi said.

"Until she threatened to take it all away. It would have been a million times worse than before. You know, Heidi. She would have wrecked me."

"She did try to ruin me," Heidi snarled. "Yet I am still here."

"Don't you dare be judgmental. You're rich and beautiful. You have no idea."

"Is that what you tell yourself? That may be true, but you did this, Dawn. When you had to choose between you and Sarah, you picked yourself. And you did it again, in the most horrible, racist way."

Dawn looked away. "I didn't know what was going to happen the first time. With Sarah. That's the truth. Mitzi pulls you in—you know, Heidi."

Heidi's face was stone.

"She makes you feel special," Dawn said. "That's how she got me. She invited me over for a sleepover with her friends—without you—one evening, and we were talking. I thought we were becoming close."

Heidi shook her head. "You're a fool."

Dawn flinched. "I . . ." She stopped. "I am. I . . ." Her voice trailed off. When she started speaking again, I almost couldn't hear her. "I keep thinking back to that minute, before we spread the first rumor. You tell yourself all sorts of things in that minute, you know."

"I don't," Heidi said coldly.

"Like, it's only a little joke, right? Mitzi and I were laughing—oh my God, this is going to be so hilarious. But then it wasn't."

"God," Heidi said.

"But the fake reviews about Sarah's stuff?" Peter said. "You had to know what was going to happen to her business when you posted those things. You must have known."

"You have to understand," Dawn said. "At the time—I didn't think. I thought I would only do this one thing—this little thing—and then my life would return to normal—"

Heidi was shaking her head. "You did think . . . about yourself. And only yourself. You know that's even worse, right?"

"And me?" I said. "Were you so *sorry* that you couldn't wait to do it again to me?"

Dawn shook her head. "No! No. Since Sarah—" She looked like she could barely say her name. "Since her, I've been plotting how to extract myself. It's our junior year. I finally decided the best, most logical course was to wait it out. Graduate, move away, and never come back. But then Mitzi came to my house."

"What?" Will said. "Did she promise to buy you a pony?" There was something unimaginable and sharp in his anger; a fury, a resistance to being resigned. Racism did happen over and over again, and it was deceptively easy to let things pass. Turn the other way. But Will never did.

Dawn took a step back. "No. She said she would tell everyone what I had done to Sarah if I didn't make those photos and that video of Olivia. She would tell everyone it was all my idea. It would have meant expulsion. It would have cost me Princeton."

I had never seen Heidi look so disgusted. "You're pathetic. Let me make this clear: you think you were the victim. That may be true. But you've turned into something much, much worse. And you're going to have to live with that."

Dawn flushed. "Maybe I will. But isn't—" She swallowed. "Isn't that what everyone else at school does, every day? Do you see other people lining up against Mitzi? During your little cafeteria stunt? People do what they need to do to get by."

"Is that what this is?" I said. I didn't know which was worse: being sacrificed, or seeing, up close, how little it mattered to her. "Kill or be killed?"

Dawn mumbled, "It was only a few pictures. A little video."

Will took a single, slow step forward. "What you did was *offensive*. Call it what it is."

Dawn flinched.

A few pictures? Did she honestly believe that? It's what people always said. *No big deal. You're being too sensitive.*

"It's not just a couple of photos," I said. I wanted to say more, to say so much more, but the syllables and acid and the years—so many years of humiliation and powerlessness—suddenly coated my tongue. I wanted to speak. But I couldn't.

Griff stepped next to me, placed a hand on my back. I could feel him there, not holding me up but supporting me.

"Everyone does it," Dawn said desperately. "You don't think we're judged every second that we're in school? You think you don't do it? We *all* do."

"Don't put the blame on everyone else," Will snapped. "This is all on you. I want you to look at Livvy. I want you to see exactly who you did that to."

Dawn shook her head, staring at the sidewalk.

Peter said, "You really are the worst person I have ever met."

"I'm done," Heidi said. "Let's go." She walked away quickly, as if she could somehow shed what she had heard, what she had seen her old friend become.

Griff wrapped a warm hand around my arm and gently led me towards the car. I had feelings I couldn't roll into words, smeared fury and helplessness. At Lake View, the middle schoolers there had done the usual karate *ching chong* thing because we were twelve and they had hardly ever seen someone like me, except on television. And most of those characters were martial artists.

But the adults were even worse. They would always stare at me a little, or they would come up to me and say their son was dating a Chinese girl and "she was actually quite nice," like Chinese people aren't nice? Or they would always tell me about the one Chinese restaurant in town. Teachers would make me answer questions about China, or Japan or Korea or Vietnam, even though I didn't know more than any other student. They weren't being malicious, and that was almost more terrible. Because they clearly didn't think of me as one of them. I was always something else.

Ahead of us, Will looked like he was ready to palm a knife and swipe it in circles. Heidi tugged on his arm and his face instantly softened. She wrapped herself around him, leaning her head on his shoulder.

We were halfway down the sidewalk when Dawn unfroze.

"Wait," she said.

Heidi continued towards the car.

"Just . . . one second, *please.*" Dawn ran into her house.

Heidi stopped, her face shattered. As she stared through the open front door, I wondered if she was imagining all the times that she was here, all of those years. What do you do when your enemy is no longer a faceless evil? What do you do when your enemy used to be your friend? When she had twisted into something monstrous?

Dawn ran out, a flash drive clenched in her fist. She pushed it at me. "Take it. I—I wanted some insurance in case Mitzi came after me again."

"Why did you do it? Why leave a message for Heidi at all?" Griff said.

"Because there was a part of me that knew she could do what I couldn't."

I closed my hand around the drive. "What is—"

"Mitzi's using bots." Dawn's eyes were wet, but she refused to cry. "I heard her talking about it once, so I started digging around. You won't ever be able to prove that she asked me to make those photos and video, or to ruin Sarah. It is only my word against hers. But this is at least some evidence."

"What are bots?" Peter said.

"It's using fake accounts to boost your followers." Heidi had returned, holding tightly on to Will's hand. "It's the kiss of death for influencers."

"Why would she risk that?" I asked.

"Revenue depends on numbers," Dawn said. "She was having problems getting traffic in the beginning. Her mom's movie had just flopped, and they didn't have any money. And her brother had his accident. So she did it. She borrowed some money from Adeline, and she hired some company to boost her accounts."

It was something I could almost understand.

Griff looked at the drive in my hand. "Wouldn't this also implicate you?" he asked. "Won't Mitzi know where this came from?"

Dawn nodded, once.

Mutually assured destruction. Mitzi's accusations could wipe out Dawn, but Dawn had engineered the weapon that could decimate her in return. Both stood on opposite sides, pointing their missiles at each other. Self-interest would ensure that neither of them would fire.

Yet now Dawn had given that ammunition to us.

"What?" I said. "Why are you doing this?"

"I know you're the Nerd Net," Dawn said. "Mitzi doesn't know about the rest of you—none of them do, but I know. I've known this whole time."

I tried to keep my face straight, but Peter blanched and started to shake.

"Why now?" Griff said. I could tell he was rattled, though he was trying to hide it.

Dawn looked at Heidi. "Because I had a chance to leave, all those years ago. But I didn't."

Heidi grabbed the flash drive and strode away. Dawn turned to me, almost like she was going to say something. But she remained silent.

I looked back at Dawn as we climbed into Heidi's car. She had the expression of a person stranded on an island, watching the last boat sail away. She was the person beside the bloody and crumpled car, trying to rewind time. Dawn had been compressed in the pressure of Plainstown, and had, to her own horror, revealed the core of her character to be something small and rotten.

But as we left Dawn's house, I couldn't stop thinking about the choices she had made, how she had gotten to this point. Was the line between right and wrong so easily shifted? Once you were in, would you do anything to stay in? I remembered my time at Lake View, the harassment I endured every day. I knew what it was like to live each minute in fear. If someone had offered me an out, would I have taken it? Could I be certain that I wouldn't?

All it took for Dawn was one mistake. One brief lapse in judgment led her down a path she could not escape. I looked over at Heidi, grimly driving in silence. Actually, that wasn't true. Dawn could have escaped. She just chose not to.

The Nerd Net was betting that we could find a way to get the students at Plainstown to support us, even though Operation Cafeteria had been such a disaster. But what if we were wrong? What if Dawn was right, and people were only interested in protecting themselves? And if they were, what would we do then?

Thirty-Eight

REINFORCEMENTS

WE WERE DRIVING back to Heidi's when Peter said, "Detour—can we go to Carlie's?" We asked him questions, but he did not respond; he kept texting as we drove towards Napleville.

Griff reached over, fingertips light over the back of my hand. "Are you okay?"

I wasn't. I was far from it. My mind was pinned to what had happened at Dawn's. Was it so easy to strip someone of their personhood? To ignore their individuality?

But it kind of was. I had done it. Hadn't I?

I wanted to hold on to the burning star of my anger and righteousness, to incinerate my hands with it. But years at the kitchen table with my mom and her legal briefs had trained my mind to examine things, to flip my perspectives. It had become a reflex, one that I now could not suppress: *What are the other angles of this problem, Olivia? Give me opposing counsel's best arguments. Now give me yours.*

I was outraged because my humanity had been denied. Because I had been judged. But—to be absolutely, uncomfortably, and searingly honest—hadn't I done the same thing during Operation Cafeteria when I had grouped people and assumed they would act accordingly? Hadn't I done the same thing when I first got to Plainstown, dismissing Dawn as a groupie and everyone else as mindless followers? I had thought of them as less than a whole person, just like others had done to me.

When all this had started, I had been condescending to social media influencers. And snippy to the VIPs when I called them sheeple. But I wasn't really sorry. Not truly. I was more outraged about what Mitzi had done to *me*.

I had disregarded anyone who liked shoes or fashion or makeup, simply because I didn't value those things. I thought the handsome poet with the back brace wouldn't have a story because he was attractive. I pushed away anyone who seemed remotely popular, because popular people had hurt me at Lake View.

Dawn said that everyone classified people. She wasn't wrong. The truth was this: the easy thing to do was to make the snap judgment about a person, to put them in a box and brush them aside. When I first got here, I thought Heidi was a popular girl who would have roasted me alive. And Will was a terrifying loner who never would have talked to me. How much would I have missed out on if I hadn't dug deeper?

Dawn had done something horrible, unforgivable. But wasn't what she had done a twisted and extreme shade of what the school did every day, by putting people into social hierarchies? Isn't that what society did, what racism *was*: classifying people at a glance, saying they were an *other*, simply because of the way they looked?

Here was the unanswerable question: If it was so easy to label and discard each other, and if almost everyone did it, then what chance did the Nerd Net have of ever succeeding in this revolution? What do you do when the enemy is within all of us?

Griff reached over and lightly touched my hair, his fingers running through the strands. "What's going on?"

I leaned my head back against the seat. "I'm thinking I don't know how this is going to end."

Carlie hugged me when she opened the door—the real kind of enveloping everything-is-going-to-be-better kind of hug that I usually got from my mom. She dragged me into the living room, where five or six of the poets were hanging out.

They stopped talking when they saw us. One of them said, "We heard. Peter texted us."

Carlie said, "Who does that? That's so fucking wrong."

Ethan rushed up to us. "Evil, soulless people."

His boyfriend, Ryan, clutched my shoulders. "Are you all right?"

I thought I could endure anything. But I never realized the devastation of a simple question. The tears came then, shocking and quick. Griff put his arm around me.

"My friends in drama know that Mitzi is the one behind all this." Ethan handed me some tissues. "You have our support."

"Was it her?" one of the Napleville poets asked harshly. "Joanna Clarke's kid?"

Peter nodded.

A bomb of chatter exploded.

As the others were talking, Ethan leaned towards me and said under his breath, "I heard a rumor. Are you behind the Nerd Net?"

I didn't answer, but Ethan smiled. "You have more allies than you think."

Next to me, Heidi was already on the couch with her laptop and Dawn's flash drive. Will was next to her, his face cold.

"We want to help," Carlie said. "A lot of us know all about bullying, unfortunately. And racism."

I shook my head, still thinking about Dawn. "I don't . . . I don't know what we should do. What we can do."

Ethan led me to a sofa. "This is not the time to hide. Mitzi has attacked you, and now you need to strike back. For God's sake, haven't you seen *Star Wars*?"

"Everything can be solved by watching *Star Wars*," Ryan said.

"YES," Ethan said. "Absolutely."

"I'm only saying that to keep him happy," Ryan whispered to me. "I'm more of a documentary kinda guy, to be honest."

"So we're . . . the defeated rebel alliance?" I asked. I had a vague recollection of the film, but I wasn't sure what light sabers had to do with our current situation.

"My God. You have seen *Star Wars*, right?" Ethan looked appalled.

"By 'seen,' he means have you obsessively watched and memorized it?" Ryan said.

"Um," I said. "Not really?"

Ethan sighed. "You're interested in military strategy, right?"

"How did you—?"

"You did a presentation on Sun Tzu in government, and you said your mom's in the military. Simple logic."

"Well deduced, Holmes," said Ryan.

"Thank you, Watson." Ethan bowed. "What do past conflicts and wars suggest we do?"

"Defend, then counterattack." It was a basic military strategy—block the aggression, then immediately press forward, when the enemy least expects it.

"Exactly," Ethan said. "Start with social media, and hint very strongly that Mitzi's behind what happened. By hint, I mean outright accuse."

"You should talk to Brandi Richards at Grande," said the girl who had previously admired Mitzi's shoes. "She has almost as many followers as Mitzi, and she haaates bullying because of what happened to her little brother."

Ethan looked at the others. "We hit her where it hurts. Mitzi's all about her brand. So we wreck it. Blow up her image, and all of her deals dry up. Not that I've thought about this a lot, but . . ."

"Ethan is also not Mitzi's biggest fan," Ryan said.

"I am not."

An imagined future rolled before I could stop it: Mitzi pulled under. Me, with the helium of popularity lifting me up. We could wage a multi-front war, with a defense on social media followed by an offensive push. I could see it now: the strike of bullying accusations, the buildup of chatter on social media. Then the catapult of Dawn's files, exposing Mitzi for what she truly was, a fraud. For an empire fueled by public image and goodwill, it would be a slice across the knees. Then the topple of sponsorships, social standing, power. The military called it *debellatio*—the complete and utter destruction of one's enemy.

It was so tempting. But now I knew it was a trap.

Mom was right; there was a difference between retaliation and trying to inspire true change.

I thought of one of Mitzi's friends, her hands tight around her lunch tray during Operation Cafeteria. By making her my collateral damage, I had made her my enemy. After my video had come out, I looked up all the people who had forwarded it; she was one of them. But would she have done it if I hadn't dragged her into Operation Cafeteria? If I hadn't humiliated her in the name of justice? Perhaps. But perhaps not.

This wasn't the path to transformation. It was an arms race.

In the beginning, Mitzi had done wrong by stereotyping Asian Americans. But I had also publicly insulted her TikTok account. Adeline had been horribly racist, but Heidi had inadvertently escalated things by posting that video of her all over the internet. Each was a brick laid upon the other, until there was a wall.

How could we tear down a hierarchy if we were building barricades?

"Livvy, what do you think?" Ethan said. "We can start

tonight. Brandi and I do theater together. I can ask her to do a video against cyberbullying. We'll drop it all at once—messages on Napleville's and Grande's socials, then Brandi's video. Then boom! Smear campaign."

One of the poets was typing on her phone. "I know Mindy at the newspaper. I can get her to cover a story about racism and hint that Mitzi is behind that video."

"The Napleville drama club has a blog that is super popular," one of Carlie's friends said. "I can post on there, too."

Next to me, Heidi was typing on her laptop. She stared at the screen, then leaned into Will, heartbroken. "We've got it. Dawn was telling the truth."

"So what do we do with it?" Will asked.

Peter said, "Listen, I know there is no question Mitzi is the devil, but if we do this, are we any better than she is? Isn't that the ancient philosophical conundrum of becoming the enemy you hate?"

"I know we said no harm. But isn't it what she deserves?" Will's fury was cutting, lethal. "Mitzi did this to Livvy, so she should pay."

"Destruction is never justified."

"But look at what she did. Are we going to let her get away with it?" Will's voice was becoming louder, and he didn't seem to notice that the poets were staring at him.

"But this has never been about Mitzi, not really," Peter said. "It's about who we choose to be in this world. Isn't that what Gandhi said?"

"Dawn never realized that," Heidi said, slowly. "Peter has a point."

"But if we don't take down the system, won't everything keep happening?" Griff asked. "Then what was this all for?"

"I totally agree," Will said.

"I'm with Peter." Heidi was firm. "What does the end matter if we compromise ourselves to get there?"

It's about who we want to be in this world. I get a small feeling, a tingling, when there is a pattern I am missing. And my sensors were going haywire. Dawn. Putting people into boxes. The system keeping Mitzi in place. What could inspire a real reformation. Arms races.

These were all connected. But how?

Griff looked away, his face tight. He finally said, "The decision should be Livvy's. The video happened to her. I will stand by whatever she chooses."

It would be so easy; just a nod, and we would scatter. By tomorrow, Mitzi could be ruined.

Just one decision.

Was this what Dawn felt like? She'd nodded and, in that second, her life had split. It was only this one small thing, and all the suffering would stop.

I would be exonerated. The villain would be punished. People would see that evil did not triumph.

And we would be right back in the arms race.

I looked at Griff, Peter, Will, Heidi, and Carlie. At my *friends*. I was at the lowest point I had ever been, socially, but I also had something I'd never had before—the Nerd Net. What if Dawn had a group like mine? What if Griff's cousin had one? Would everything have turned out differently?

For all the people who'd had their lives ruined in the time it takes a photo or post to go viral, there was one common denominator: they were abandoned. They were bullied, then made into outcasts. Could it have made a difference if one person had stood by them?

Could it have made a difference if a whole network of people had stood by them?

I had friends when my bomb hit, and that changed everything.

What if what we had started was bigger than taking down Mitzi? What if it could be a true revolution?

Peter and Carlie believed in the power of transformation; they pinned their faith to a hopeful future, even if people—they, me, us, everyone—took the easy path of judging and categorizing others. Which one was correct?

Could everyone do better? Could everyone *be* better?

Even me?

Peter was right. This was about who we wanted to be in this world. Who we hoped everyone else could become.

The pattern clicked and the path forward, clear and bright, unfurled before me.

Last time, with Operation Cafeteria, I had ignored Heidi and Peter. I was so certain I knew what was best. But this time I was listening; I was really listening.

I stood up. Everyone stared at me, but I only focused on my friends. I let them hold me up.

"I have an idea, if you all agree." The poets were nodding before I was done explaining. I had hoped they would support it, because I had been inspired by what I had learned from them, in this very room.

"But how are you going to—?" Ethan asked.

I glanced at Heidi. "I think I know someone who can get the job done."

Griff still looked skeptical. But then he saw my face. "Okay."

"Yes," Heidi said. "Absolutely yes."

Will nodded, then Peter.

"You'll help?" I asked the poets.

"It's like it's what we were born to do," Carlie said.

We were ready to launch Phase Five.

Thirty-Nine

WAITING

THE ONE MAJOR flaw in my plan was that it required a little time. And time meant more torture.

At school, I pretended Mitzi had won. We planted a few posts calling out the video, but nothing too obvious. Occasional comments here and there. But nothing else.

I sat in silence during class as the whispers hissed around me. I pretended to be broken when Mitzi's friends passed. I ignored Mitzi's triumphant TikTok.

At home, Mom nodded when I had told her our plan, but still she worried, I could tell. She passed off her upcoming trial to another lawyer on her team and began coming home earlier. She started sitting by me while I was doing homework and calling every day after school. I loved her for it. She was driving me up a tree.

Since Operation Cafeteria, Mitzi had been in a frenzy of

social media activity, promoting her projects at all hours and uploading an elaborately produced video each day. She looked exhausted. She began a new feature on her accounts, an advertising partnership for products that students would need at school, like binders and backpacks. Each featured her logo and was paired with matching accessories. The items sold out in less than a day. Mitzi and Adeline made a bunch of ads featuring their friends using Mitzi's products at school, strolling through the halls, laughing. Everyone else stayed out of their way. All the progress that the Nerd Net had made was annihilated with my public shaming.

Heidi had removed most of my videos, but somehow a few kept getting forwarded. The comments kept coming.

I thought I knew unbearable. I had been ostracized, given cruel nicknames, whispered about. I had survived my earlier debacle. But this, more than the last time, felt like the whole world tormenting me.

But my friends created a protective bubble and gave me a small space to breathe. I got supportive texts from the poets and the Nerd Net on my tater phone. Ethan Earle and some drama kids began sitting with me and Griff during lunch. I noticed that one of them was always with me in the halls, so I would not have to be alone.

As time went on, though, Griff began to look exhausted. The Nerd Net had started to send out emails to other teens who had been bullied, asking if we could share their stories. We found an empty space for recording and gathered equipment and lighting. We rounded up the poets for this last, final stand.

It was a lot of work. But it didn't have to be done by only one person.

Finally, after school one day, I dusted off my guilt trip car and picked up Peter, Heidi, and Will. We drove to Castle, where I knew Griff had gone to meet some of the poets.

"Livvy?" he said when I walked in. "Peter? Heidi? What are you doing here?"

Heidi plugged in her computer without answering and Peter went to talk to the others. One of them started to walk in Griff's direction, but Will smoothly intercepted him and led him the other way.

"This is an intervention." I grabbed Griff and dragged him into a back hallway. "You look terrible."

"Et tu, Brute? I thought we were opposed to cruelty based on physical appearances."

"You are supposed to be taking the day off. You look exhausted."

He was silent.

"Griff. You can take a break. We're all a team."

He looked away. "I just want to do everything I can."

"We all do," I said. "But it doesn't mean you have to wear yourself out."

"You don't understand." He didn't explain further.

"Tell me."

"I'm not sure this is going to work, Livvy." If words were water, this would be ice cold and shocking.

"What is?" I said carefully. Neutrally.

"This. Your plan depends on people. On people becoming

294

more than they currently are. But it's one thing to support a movement when you are one of many, when the risk is low. It is another thing entirely to be brave when the stakes are higher. Mitzi has made resistance dangerous. I don't think everyone is going to rise to the occasion."

Griff was talking about my plan. The plan.

"At my old school, when push came to shove," he said, "not one person went against their own self-interest to support Brynn or me. The same thing happened during Operation Cafeteria. You're asking a lot with this operation, Livvy. You're putting a lot of faith in it, and I just don't know if it's going to work."

"So why are you doing so much?" I asked. I knew the answer. I didn't dare think of the answer. "If you don't think this is a good idea, why?" The last question came out like a plea, because it was. Last chance. If you don't mean this, for the love of *everything*, please . . . don't. Don't be kind and charming and make me hope. Just don't.

Griff pulled at the end of my scarf, toyed with it. "Because you believe in it. And I want to. But I'm worried."

"About me?"

He nodded.

I kissed him. I put my hands on his face and placed my mouth on his warm, surprised one, then his hand slid behind my neck and nothing could have prepared me for the detonation of *feeling*. His arm tightened around my back and I pressed against him. I couldn't have resisted him anymore, even if I wanted to. I didn't want to. For the first time in my life, I dove into the uncertainty and joy, into the possibility of pain and the equal possibility of transcendence.

I was surprised by how vulnerable Griff felt, how gentle his fingers were when they threaded through my hair. I was glad I had never kissed Henry-from-honors-history or Luke-from-the-bookstore. I was glad it was him and he meant something to me.

Griff's hand trailed down my back, holding me close even as he stopped kissing me, briefly. He tucked my hair behind my ear. Smiled. Kissed me again, his mouth warm and certain.

He kissed me, and I kissed him, and we were there for a long time until I heard Peter shout, "CARLIE! OH MY GOD, FINALLY!" Then Heidi and Will and Carlie and Peter all tumbled into the hallway and my face was flaming, but Griff held me close and we both bowed.

"Now get out," Griff said to them. "All of you leave so I can make out with Livvy some more."

They pretended to go back inside, but I could hear their giggles from behind the door.

"So I guess this might be a good time for a ride in my guilt trip car." I grabbed his hand and dragged him down the hall.

"Oh? The mythical vehicle emerges?"

"If you have any guilt, about anything, it'll soak it up like a sponge. Or so my father thinks."

My father had disappeared for years. He never returned calls, never wrote one letter. And in the time after Grandfather died, when Mom and I were choking and gasping with grief, he only sent one curt note. Then he had met someone, he had fallen in love, he saw the error of his ways. Or so he said, in the card accompanying the car. I would rather have had a visit. Maybe that's why I hated it so much.

"You know what this car is not?" I said.

"Your childhood?"

I nodded.

I had craved certainty, a concrete answer to how my dad could cut us out of his life. I longed for a talisman against hurt, the same way Griff wanted a guarantee about whether or not our next, and last, operation would succeed.

But maybe life is uncertainty. And we have to step forward anyways. Maybe the stepping was the important thing.

Griff squeezed my hand, and we walked outside, where the snow was coming down in fat, graceful flakes. He stopped when he saw the car parked by the sidewalk. "Wow. There's a lot of guilt poured into that car."

"Yup." Cherry-red BMW convertible, the latest and fanciest. It was hideous.

Griff said, "And did your dad think that you would like that car?"

"I think he didn't bother to find out."

"Ah," he said, and there was a shared understanding.

"Also, he sent that to Ohio. Where there is snow."

"Well, for my birthday, my father shipped me off to football camp."

I laughed. "And do you like football?"

"I was the first person in the history of camp to spend the entire time organizing the team equipment," Griff said. "When I left, they offered to hire me full-time."

"Nicely done."

"I try."

I walked to the driver's side. The car still smelled new, since this was only the second time I had driven it. Every time I saw it in the garage, with its shiny paint and the fancy dashboard, I was consumed—almost obliterated—by a cherry-red rage. This car was what my father would have wanted, not me. Once again, he had made it all about him. He had sent this thing instead of himself, as if I wouldn't notice the difference.

But the poets at Castle haunted me again; it made me wonder what my father's story was. He was terrible, but could he be terrible in a complex way?

Griff peeked through the car window. I had placed a box of donut holes on the passenger seat—jelly, his favorite. Until he met me, Griff had to cook a lot of his own dinners, had to be on his own a lot. He took care of everyone: his cousin, the Nerd Net, me. When was the last time someone had done something nice, just for him?

Griff stared at the box, his fingertips lightly pressed against the window. "Are those for me?"

"Only until someone hotter comes along," I said. "So you'd better eat quickly."

"Did I ever mention I think that you're perfect?"

"You might have. But you can tell me again."

He brushed the snow off my cheeks. Pressed his mouth to

298

mine. I closed my eyes and floated; every string that had been holding me down had been cut, and Griff was my anchor. He pulled away, for a second.

"Do I get to pick the music?" he said.

"Absolutely. Not."

Griff folded himself into the car, and, bemused, cradled his box of donut holes. The car, for me, had been this sore spot for so long, a red-and-black thing that I wanted to get rid of but couldn't. But now, with Griff here, it seemed less cold. Less heartbreaking.

Griff lightly dragged his fingertip across the back of my wrist.

"For the record," he said, "you were dreaming about your handsome French partner this whole time."

I shoved a jelly donut hole into his mouth. Then I shyly kissed the powdered sugar off.

We drove around in my guilt trip car that afternoon. We zoomed around town with the top down, blasting pop music and laughing in the cold. For a few precious hours, there was no Mitzi, no school, no pressure from our final plan. Griff wrapped my hands in his wool gloves and kissed me under a tree covered in snow. He did not mention his concerns again.

But that didn't stop me from worrying. Because he could be right.

Forty

LIGHTING CAMPFIRES

WE BIDED OUR time. We prepared. We witnessed.

It became more and more difficult as time went on. Mitzi's video had become a tacit call to arms. I became open season. People whispered about me in the halls. Those who used to nod at me hurriedly turned the other way when they saw me coming.

Mitzi and the VIPs became canny about their hits and switched to Click, posting anonymous rumors about why I had gone to so many schools. Most of them self-deleted, but I saw glimpses on Heidi's computer before she shut them down. They kept popping up, getting reposted on random accounts along with nasty comments.

The goal, obviously, was to decimate me as Mitzi's rival.

It worked.

It was almost too much. But every time I thought of

surrendering, I remembered what my grandfather had told me about George Washington. After Britain's loss at the Battle of Trenton, General Cornwallis led thousands of British troops towards Washington and his men, with the intent of defeating them, once and for all. Cornwallis was temporarily deterred by a wide creek that separated the Continental army from the British, and heavy rain. As night fell, Cornwallis saw campfires across the water and was convinced that his enemies were surrounded, and it was safe to take an evening to regroup and rest before the final battle.

Cornwallis was seeing a decoy.

Washington had left a few men to light fires along the edge of the creek. Meanwhile, the remainder of his troops slipped up north, to Princeton.

When Cornwallis awoke the next day, Washington's army had disappeared. By the time he realized what had happened, it was too late. Princeton would fall, the Revolutionaries would eventually win, and a new country would be born.

We needed to light our campfires and wait through the long night. We needed to give the troops time to claim victory.

After school one day, the doorbell rang. I had sent Griff home to take a break. My mom was still at work. Who was it?

I peeked through the peephole and was surprised to see Heidi on my porch. She pushed herself into my house and marched up the stairs towards my bedroom.

"Hi?" I trailed after her.

"You're welcome, in advance."

"What?"

Heidi paused, then took a swift left and pushed open my door. She stopped. "Where's your computer?"

"In the living room?"

"Why don't you use your desk?" she said. "By the way, nice llama sheets."

She went back downstairs, me close behind.

"They're alpacas," I called.

By the time I reached the living room, she was already typing on my laptop.

"Hey!" I said. "That's password protected!"

She snorted. "Please." She typed furiously, then grabbed my phone. After fiddling with it, she tossed it towards me.

"My work is done." She left and I scrambled to find a pair of shoes.

"What did you do?" I ran down the driveway. "Heidi? Heidi."

She swung into her car. Will waved at me from the passenger seat as they roared off.

I ran back to my computer. But as soon as I tried to log in to my socials, my screen turned blue and a parade of dancing alpacas sashayed across the monitor.

What the hell? I called Heidi.

"Heidi's cell phone," Will said.

"Will? Put her on."

"You know I would, but she is currently driving her vehicle at speeds way over the normal limit THUS ENDANGERING

HER PASSENGER'S PRECIOUS LIFE. Ow! Both hands on the wheel, Speed Racer!"

"Ask her what she did to my laptop. AND MY PHONE."

"I'm just keeping you safe from yourself, Livvy." Heidi's voice was slightly muffled. I heard a faint honk in the background. "Whoopsie."

"Whoopsie?" Will said. "Yellow does not mean speed up."

"Listen, Livvy." Heidi sounded distracted. "I know what you've been doing on your computer and it isn't healthy. You have to cut yourself off from all of that nonsense. So I'm giving you a little break. For a day. Or two."

"You blocked all my accounts! And my phone!"

"Texts or calls to the Nerd Net only." There was a small screech of tires. "Or your phone becomes a brick."

"Oh Lordy," Will said. "Listen, she should not talk and drive at the same time."

Heidi shouted, "LOVE YOU, LIVVY. YOU'LL THANK ME FOR IT LATER."

"If we make it home alive," Will said. "Hanging up now. You'll be fine. Me, not so much." He paused.

I had seen Will's face when he looked at that video. I knew he felt it as much as I had, that he had gotten the same treatment, or worse, over the years.

"Listen," he said. "No matter how this ends, you're doing the right thing."

The tears were coming again, and I nodded, even though he couldn't see me.

"Do you think so?" I said. It wasn't a throwaway question. It was the one I was terrified to ask. I had always been one of the few Asian Americans at all my prior schools. I had no guidebook, no signposts. But now I had an ally.

I never would have talked about this at any of my previous schools. I never talked about it with anyone else, period. But now I climbed on the thin branch and trusted that it wouldn't snap.

"I do." Will went quiet. "I know it's terrifying."

It wasn't just frightening; it was everything that I had tried to hide suddenly dragged out and thrown into the sunlight.

"I know it's not fair," Will said. "We never asked for it. But this shit always happens, Livvy. Maybe less in some places, maybe more in others. To you, me, our parents, our grand-parents."

I sniffled.

"The question is, are we going to let it pass?" Will said. "Or can we do something? Our grandparents weren't able to deal with it; they didn't know how to. But we do. We know the system, we understand the language, the culture. We can fight, for them."

I pictured my grandfather, carefully scooping out the best dumplings for me, always giving me a gentle pat on the head. I knew he understood when people were being condescending towards him, even if he didn't know the exact meaning of what was said. Once, when I was young, a man yelled at him as we were leaving a grocery store. After we reached our car, Grand-father wrapped his hands tightly around the steering wheel and bowed his head. I often thought about that afternoon years later, when I was old enough to understand. What thoughts were pressing against him in that moment? Regret for coming here? Helplessness? Frustration? He never said. He loved me too much to give me that weight.

And I loved him too much to translate what I had heard.

I remember staring at the man who had thrown such hate, wanting to hurl my own words back at him: *Do you know what he's gone through?* But I was a child, and my grandfather, in English, was defenseless. What if he could have shared his story, explained why he had come here? Could people hear that and still tell him to go back to his country?

"What did John Lewis say?" Will said. "'Freedom is . . . an act.'"

"An act."

"This is how it starts, Livvy. Hang in there."

There was a pause and a loud screech. "Hey! Why are you pulling over—" There was the unmistakable sound of smooching. A phone fumble. Then Will's hasty "Apparently, she really likes inspirational quotes!" before the call cut off.

The house was still when I put the phone down. Without my computer, without my phone, I felt deeply alone in a way that I hadn't in a long time. I couldn't help but think of those other kids around the country; they were strangers, but we were all siblings, suffering in different ways. For me it was racism, but for others it could be torment because of who they loved, who they were, what they looked like. Each of them had a moment like this, suffocated by the insidious coils of the internet, which wound through everything. Hate and shaming was in their phones, on their laptops and tablets, swelling up like a river behind every log-in page. One click to open your account and you were drenched in acid.

We had reached out to others and had gathered their stories. They burned within me. For those students who had been crucified for their differences, I had to be strong. For Griff's cousin, and Sarah, and my grandfather, and everyone, I would endure. I would light the fire of their stories and wait.

Forty-One

PHASE FIVE: OPERATION NERD NET

THAT NIGHT, PLAINSTOWN High School received a message:

COURAGE, DEAR REVOLUTIONARIES. ALL IS NOT LOST.

Forty-Two

CLICKCOMM STORIES

ON MONDAY, THE ClickComm stories started. One every hour, starting at 8:00 a.m., for seven hours. Each released as the bell rang at the end of the period.

Each one was the same: a video of a person wearing white. Next to them was a poet,

who started to speak

of

the girl whose handmade scarf was the target she wore around her neck. Her grandma had knitted it from the yarn of her own wrap, and her daughter's//she had undone the loops and knots (trying to make each generation better, let's make each generation better), had smoothed it and blessed it with grit and remembrance. That is what they wanted to take away? They wouldn't dare.

The siblings who were mocked for their dad picking them up every day in a beat-up, taped-together van. No one could see (how could they not see?) it was the stallion that had blazed across vast countries they couldn't imagine; it had taken them to places full of empty, screaming air and cold waterfalls pricking your back, to dusty granite cliffs so sheer that they seemed impossible, until you jammed your fingers in and started to climb, to forests so still that you could almost hear the hum of *possibility*. They could not see, their vision was so blurry, they couldn't look beyond the flat earth under their feet

The boy who had been tormented for his poor hearing. His mother had stayed up for nights, terrified, as the fever raged. She had begged the doctor for something, anything, to save her child. He was saved. His hearing was not.

In the beginning, as the stories spread, there were whispers, mocking laughs. But as the day went on, as each bell rang, the school got quiet, then quieter still.

As the kids headed to classes, more than one of them looked at Mitzi and Adeline.

Then the final ClickComm story hit, at 3:00 p.m. Mine.

I knew this could be a mistake. That I was doubling down on putting my head out of my gopher hole. I was practically begging to be annihilated.

But the gift that the Nerd Net had given to me was this: the realization that there were some things worth dying to defend. They had been my net, catching and holding me up. But now they could be my springboard, launching me into the air.

I refused to let that video stand.

I refused to let people think that what was done to me was harmless.

I wanted every person to know that every one of those photos in that video were wrapped in the thorns of history and the blood was fresh and raw.

So we recorded my story. And I released it.

Ethan spoke of

my grandparents, who had borrowed the wrinkled bills that would take them to America. They had carefully wrapped the hopes of their family and neighborhood, tucking them in between their sweaters and shirts, and had carried them across the sea. And when the graffiti and hostility and scorn came, they tried to hide it *(kiss goodnight, don't worry) (it's just paint, it'll come off) (Baba's arm will heal quick, you will see)*. They held a faith so fierce that it lit the generations down the line, the belief that things would be better.

Ethan told the story of

my mother, who had clawed through poverty to go to law school, who had immersed herself in the thorny pockets of constitutional law, who traced the evolution of civil rights that had been pulled, thread by bloodied thread, from the quilt of cold amendments. But what she learned, as well

(Peter and Carlie stepped forward)

was a history

    that made it against the law for people like us to come

    to America

    that put American-born citizens into internment

    camps

because

    with or without the passport of an American accent

        they

                mocked our eyes

                and skin

        they

                made us the Other

                because of our faces

        they

                killed people that looked like us

(The poets, off to the side:)

Chingchong   It's just a joke

Waaah karate   *Come on it's funny*

Oh no speak Engrish   **why don't you fucking**

                    learn English

Me so horny   I am not an object

   Aren't you all related?   I have a name

Asian Girl   I am a person

(Me, in the background. The poets:)

  Go back to your country   But this is my country

You don't belong here   *I was born here*

We don't want you here

I don't belong

anywhere.

I left school that afternoon with Griff next to me. A few people took small steps towards me, but I had to keep moving. It was the only thing I could do and keep myself together. There was only one place I could go, only four people I could speak to.

When Griff and I got to Heidi's basement, she hugged me tight, for a long time. Will put a hand on my shoulder, and a raging river of understanding flowed between us.

Peter was practically bursting. "I think it went well! I mean, we did a pretty good job, don't you think?"

I had to laugh. "You were perfect."

Griff kissed my temple, but he looked worried. "Are you all right?"

I nodded. I knew the poets would come soon, and Carlie and Ethan. I knew my story—and the others'—were there, in the ether, and there was no telling how or where they would land. I could be getting sliced in the clouds right now. But I hadn't run; I had done it anyways.

People in our school had forwarded messages, left cruel comments on the internet, laughed at my pictures. They could be doing the same now. I thought Operation Cafeteria would force things to be different. But people can't change without first acknowledging the wrong. *Mea culpa.* And the wrong was this: ignoring the fact that each person carries their own burdens, ones we are not aware of.

Yes, there were those who were truly horrible, who were not capable of remorse. But I wanted to believe that there was a greater number of people who, when confronted with the impact of their actions, would pause, and think. Maybe atone.

I had to believe it. I was banking on it. Or this last operation would be a disaster.

Forty-Three

THE FINAL BATTLE

THE NEXT MORNING, the Nerd Net met in the library before the pre-homeroom laps started.

Heidi held up her phone.

"Ready?" she said.

Griff gripped my hand. "Are you sure, Livvy?"

I nodded.

She hit send.

We scattered.

Forty-Four

FINISHING THE REVOLUTION

OUR CLICKCOMM, SENT at 7:35 a.m.:

BE THE PERSON YOU'VE ALWAYS WANTED TO BE.
TODAY, DEFEND PEOPLE WHO CANNOT DEFEND THEMSELVES.

Forty-Five

HOW YOU DISAPPEAR

THE PRE-HOMEROOM LAPS began as usual. The stratification had come back full force after my video, with Mitzi and her friends in the inner lap, the freshmen in the outer lap, and the rest in between.

Griff had picked me up that morning. As we drove to school, I held my ClickComm story close, wrapping my hands around its warmth. We visited my grandparents' graves every week, but telling the poets their stories made me deeply think about the sacrifices they had made.

I had spent so many years translating for my grandfather, in stores and libraries and pharmacies. In all that time, he always held in the tales of his life, dammed behind a wall of American language and customs he didn't quite understand.

I lit the torch of his story, for him. No one ever had before.

None of us knew if the ClickComm stories were a call to arms or the last feeble cry of a dying movement. But I had seen everyone reading the stories yesterday. I had seen their faces, had heard the muted chatter. It must have had an effect? Right?

But as we entered the school and walked down the hall, it was dead silent.

Griff tugged me closer as we heard the whispers behind us.

"Damn right you don't belong anywhere," one of the guys called out to me. He elbowed his friend, and they accidentally stumbled into a freshman, who hit his arm on a locker. No one moved to help him. No one even tried.

The loners were still by themselves, hurriedly ducking into homeroom before the crowds could descend. The VIPs still took their laps in the center of the hall, and everyone still moved out of the way. And though some of the others looked our way, no one approached us or moved to help anyone else.

Everything was the same.

The first time I had gone to Castle, I was transformed by the stories I heard. I thought—a part of me had foolishly wished—that the ClickComm stories would be the flint that could spark a true revolution.

But the things keeping the system in place had not changed.

I should have known better. I did know better, but I had dared to hope, and that was the gutting part.

Griff put an arm around me; he didn't have to speak. Wasn't this what he had been worried about all along? What he had seen for himself?

They say the human mind has a remarkable ability to acclimate to things, to take the unusual—traffic noise, heavy perfume smells—and normalize it.

That was a lie. Because I had been dealing with this for years, and It. Never. Got. Better.

Down the hall, Heidi scanned the corridor with a terrible disappointment. Close to her, Ethan huddled with his friends. I could read his face perfectly: *Press forward? Or retreat?*

What had I been thinking? That the few of us could take down a whole system? That people would see a few performances and dare to do the hard thing, which was to take the extra moment to imagine someone else's perspective, the context of their actions? That people would step forward and shield those who needed protection?

"What do you want to do?" Griff asked me quietly.

This was the empty field, our tattered flag flapping in the wind. The enemy troops—fear, self-interest, blindness—flanked the horizon.

We could surrender. No one knew we were the Nerd Net. We could let our revolution die a quiet death; we could cradle our disappointment, entombed in our bitter hearts. I could retreat and continue my evasive maneuvers.

Because there was no question that we were going to lose, badly.

I remembered—it seemed so long ago—sitting in Heidi's basement, dreaming of the overthrow of the regime. Imagining a what? A dramatic repudiation of Mitzi's empire? A place where equality and compassion existed?

At the other end of the hall, Will's face hardened into the mask he usually wore at school. The one he needed to survive. But there was something more rigid about it now; it was the stiffness that comes from cold experience. Heidi put a gentle hand on his shoulder, but he just shook his head.

I remembered the warmth of my ClickComm story, how it felt to finally show what those photos, that video, had done to me. How it felt to be seen. Was that wrong?

"Livvy?" Griff said.

I had looked up the quote Will had mentioned, from John Lewis. He was slightly incorrect; the full quote was, "Freedom is not a state; it is an act." Freedom wasn't a skirmish. It was present, ongoing, relentless battle.

It wasn't wrong to want a revolution.

No.

What was wrong was that I had thought it was going to be easy. But when had change ever been easy?

My grandparents had done the hard thing. They had done it every day. They had willingly lived in the discomfort—the different language, the different food, the different values—they had stood in it and refused to move. The only fuel they needed was the hope that the future—for their children, their grandchildren—would be better.

How do you cup the flame of grace in a tornado of hostility? What do you do when it swirls all around you: in your school, your neighborhood, your country? When it is all shades of the same, unsolvable problem?

There's only one option: you shield that flame with

everything that you have. You keep fighting, because today you can.

Down the hall, Peter crouched next to his locker. He had already gotten pelted with scorn when he came to school. But I also saw two boys speaking softly with him about the Click-Comm stories, and Castle.

I thought of Washington's campfires along the bank, how perhaps they were not just a decoy. They could also be a beacon. The fire—the stories we told, the actions we took—could be the small points of light against the huge, dark sky.

What did I want to do?

I locked eyes with Peter. *This is about who we want to be in this world.*

The word I wanted to carry in my heart was not *defeat.*

It was *resist.*

I tugged Griff's hand and crossed the hall towards Lorna Moore. Her usual friend group had distanced themselves because Lorna's parents didn't allow her to go to any sleepovers or parties. I had seen her over the past year, first trying to fake smile as her friends laughed at inside jokes, then getting quieter and quieter. Then standing on the outer edges of the hallway, alone. Lorna was a stranger, and I didn't talk to strangers, but today I was going to do the hard thing.

"Can we walk with you to class?" I asked. Lorna looked surprised, then relieved.

She nodded.

Ethan gathered his drama club friends and they made a quick huddle. Then they scattered.

We were badly outnumbered. Some boys covered lockers with a crossed-out N^N logo. Some of Mitzi's friends started bombarding social media with false posts about how the N^N was a cult that encouraged people to bully each other. Some people started a rival ClickComm account, encouraging total anarchy.

But the thing about change is that it doesn't take everyone for it to happen; it only takes a few. The thing about friends is that you don't need everyone. Sometimes it only takes one.

Revolution doesn't always start with bullets or gunfire. It can start small, with a march or a meeting that flares into protest. It can begin with the poet VIP, silently walking down the hall with a freshman, after someone called out rude remarks about her religion. It can begin with a chilly silence that meets cruel jokes, an absolute refusal to grant the polite laugh.

It can start in the lunch line, where Griff and I talked to a girl who normally would have terrified me. She was elaborately dressed, in high heels and a sparkly skirt, and had pencils stuck in her updo. I noticed she was almost always alone.

She told us how her shoes were a form of art, as much of a statement as a speech or a song; they could be armor or a status symbol or a tool for strength. She wore them to shine a light on León, Guanajuato, where she had studied over the summer.

The revolution could start with me, owning the fact that I had done my own judging of others who might love clothes or shoes or things I didn't prioritize. Or popular people who reminded me of the ones at Lake View.

It could begin with my study of the drama kids, watching

how they courageously threw out the lines of friendship to others. At another cafeteria, at another school, I had once been one of the drama crew, hanging out on the fringes. I had joined because they were doing a production of *1776,* but soon I was around enough that people started to invite me to cast parties and other events. I always said no. It wasn't even a thought; it was more of a reflex. My memories of being burned at Lake View were too vivid.

I was disappointed when the invitations stopped, but I understood why. Or I thought I did.

The truth was this: there had been times when I had been too terrified to accept the branch of friendship. But that very acceptance—that vulnerability—was the necessary thing to forge a true connection with others.

I had said yes to the Nerd Net, and that made all the difference.

Mitzi was standing at the end of the cafeteria, looking puzzled. Her friends huddled nearby, but there was no threat to protect against. This revolution was not about her; it had moved beyond all of them.

Griff was quiet as we sat at our usual seats. He took our fries and jumbled them together in a paper tray, absently sprinkling Parmesan cheese and a small container of dried parsley on top.

I tossed a bit of pepper on the fries and he finally looked up.

"You don't have truffle oil in your backpack, do you?" he said.

"Alas. Only whole truffles."

He finally smiled. "So, your dream reincarnation is which of the following: truffle hog, dumbo octopus—"

"That's not a thing."

"It's absolutely a thing. I'll wait."

I checked my phone. He was right.

"Or," he said, "tufted deer."

"Specifically the ones with tufts?"

"Only the ones with tufts."

"Are we going to talk about this?" I asked.

"About what?" he said. "About how you're totally going to pick the truffle hog? Admit it."

"Griff."

He had been betrayed so badly; he had never really believed that people could do better. But he supported me anyways. Did he think it was worth it?

Griff picked up my hand. This was still new and shocking to me, how easily and wonderfully someone else could enter your space. He traced my vein with his fingertip, as if it were a map.

"Almost everything is the same," he said. "They're not going to change."

"Some will."

Griff gazed over the cafeteria. Salma Hanif usually sat with her BFF, Jaime Tucker, but he was absent today; when some marching band players noticed she was alone, they came over to her table. Salma wasn't into music, but she was soon laughing at their stories. Next to them, a small group of manga fans were talking to some yearbook editors about graphics and layouts. Mitzi's friends would have normally tossed over a scornful look or comment. But today, they didn't.

"But how many?" Griff said.

"Why did you start the Nerd Net?" I asked. "In the beginning?"

"For the pins?"

"And?"

He sighed. "Fine. But is it really enough?"

Ethan slid next to us and grabbed some fries. "What is?"

"The small victories," Griff said.

Ethan chewed. "Don't those lead to the larger ones?"

Griff slowly nodded.

"And isn't the most important thing that we don't give in?" Ethan said.

"Is that a *Star Wars* thing?" I asked.

"It's a rebel thing," he said. "What matters is that we stand when everyone else does not."

Griff looked surprised, and I wondered if he was thinking about his other school. I knew he had been bitterly disappointed that his friends hadn't supported him and his cousin. He had wanted a repudiation of the system here, the coup he hadn't been able to get for Brynn. But forgiveness doesn't always need a dramatic overthrow, or a cherry-red car. Sometimes, the best and only thing to do is to show up. To right the wrong by doing things differently.

Maybe this is how a new beginning starts. For all of us.

I could tell Griff was turning this over, that the idea was catching and snagging on what he had tightly held to be true.

I thought of a story my grandfather had told me, about how boulders in the ocean get so round. Their shape can't be created with tools or force; the water must flow around them and wear them away, layer by layer.

If we wanted an honest transformation, we needed to walk next to someone along their path, to listen and truly understand where they were coming from. Only then could the water begin to, incrementally, wash away the jagged edges. I had thought that Mitzi's friends were mindless groupies, and it didn't matter to me why they were doing what they were doing. But the *why* was the most important thing.

If we could truly shift a person's perspective, we could change . . . everything. One person at a time.

Ethan pointed a french fry at Mitzi. "Anyhoo. Not that it matters, but I imagine she probably has bigger things to worry about."

"Oh?" I looked at Mitzi, but she seemed careless, as usual.

"Adeline's pissed at her."

I had seen Adeline drift into school today, alone. She didn't speak to anyone and turned the other way when Mitzi came down the hall.

"Why?" Griff said.

"Rumor has it that Adeline finally got Mitzi into the biology internship," Ethan said. "She talked to everyone over there and vouched for her."

"So?"

"So Mitzi was super excited about it and posted about it on her account." Ethan sprinkled more Parmesan cheese on his fries. "These are so good!"

Griff gave a little bow.

"But all of these people gave her shit about it in the comments," Ethan said. "So she bailed. Never showed up."

"No." Even I was surprised by this, given how hard she had worked to get in. "Did her mom make her quit or something?"

"I don't think her mom is even in the country," Ethan said. "She did that all on her own. And now Adeline is on the verge of losing her internship since Mitzi quit without any notice. They got into a huge fight about it. Anyways, Mitzi's screwed. She also failed another bio test. I think she went to some gala instead of studying. I don't know if she can make it to senior year."

I saw the split clearly now, the divide of Mitzi's life and mine. I thought the difference between us was that she was popular and I wasn't. But I now knew the truth. I could see the path of her future, one seemingly small choice leading to another, until, somehow, she derailed.

Ethan plucked another fry from the tray. "I think she really wants to go into bio and medicine, is the thing. God knows I don't like Mitzi, but that's kind of pathetic."

"What's pathetic?"

I whirled around. Mitzi was behind us.

The cafeteria hushed as I sprang to my feet. Griff stood up next to me.

Mitzi didn't look nervous or remorseful. I pictured what she could have been in another life: a confident leader, an unstoppable force. But then her eyes scanned the room and calculated the temperature of her popularity. Mitzi had always been a wisp, a ruthless chameleon at the mercy of the social winds that blew through our school. She had used all her formidable will to triumph within the system, but she'd never once questioned if the system itself was flawed.

I finally understood everything that had led her here. But what she had done to me was heinous. As Peter had said, both things could be true.

My grandfather verbally sparred with his attackers, but sometimes that anger was oil, making the heat of conflict hotter. My mother, when I was little, curled her arm around me and walked quickly away from our tormentors. I had hidden myself, ducking out of sight, as if the ugliness would disappear if I did.

Not every boulder could be smoothed over. Maybe there were some that were too spiky, too broken. But you couldn't know which stone was which until you placed it into the river.

"I know you were behind those photos," I said. "I know you think you had to do it. But you didn't. And especially not in that way."

Mitzi spat, "Don't you dare lecture me."

Life to her was a zero-sum game; she thought loosening her sweaty grip on power meant she would lose everything. But acknowledging a wrong wasn't a weakness. It was the first step towards making the broken thing stronger.

Mitzi said, "You can tell people I was behind everything, but no one will believe you." She pushed my shoulder. "Plus? No one cares."

Heidi jumped to her feet. "Wrong. I do."

Will and Peter stood up. Griff wrapped his hand around mine.

Mitzi stared at Heidi, then the others. "Who do you think you are?"

After the ClickComm stories, I had seen a few people—some of the VIPs, even—whispering with each other. Holding their phones tightly in their hands. And now, those people were not looking at her. They weren't standing up, but they weren't supporting her, either. In the corner, sitting alone, Dawn was still, waiting.

Griff was right that the system might not change. Clearly, Mitzi wasn't going to. But we could. And we could, perhaps, light a few cinders along the way.

My mom had once told me the two most beautiful words in law: *I dissent*.

"Who are we?" I said. "We're the fucking Nerd Net." I quickly typed a message and pushed the send button. The cafeteria vibrated with the buzz of a hundred phones, receiving one final ClickComm:

TODAY, STAND UP FOR YOURSELVES.

"It's time to stop," I said, and I was not talking to the girl in front of me, but to the Mitzi who would give up a subject that she loved rather than lose social capital, the Mitzi who would scrub her eyebrows off to look perfect, the Mitzi who allowed thousands of strangers to control what she wore and what she liked and even, I knew, how much she valued herself.

Mitzi hissed, "Fuck you." She whirled around. "Is this you, Heidi? Some sort of petty revenge?"

"No," Griff said. "This is all what you made."

Heidi took a step towards Mitzi and said quietly, "We know all about your bots."

Mitzi flung a glare at Dawn, pinning her in her seat. Dawn had the still dignity of a person taking the last walk to the gallows, head up, steps deliberate. She had the hard gaze of someone who no longer had anything to lose. Mitzi froze.

Heidi leaned in. "We have numbers, screenshots. *Everything.*" Heidi's voice was low, but I knew Mitzi heard her perfectly. "All relating to the inexplicable spike in your follower numbers, about two years ago. You might have done it for survival. But that's not the only reason why you're doing it now. You'd better delete all your social media accounts or I'm plastering the internet with details about how you got so popular. These people may not know what it means to use bots to fake your popularity, but they soon will. I'll make sure everyone knows. Including your sponsors."

Will coughed. "My girl gets scary when she's pissed."

Mitzi's glance skittered between Peter, Will, Heidi, Griff, then landed on me. But I was no longer fooled. I had seen straight into the weak, frightened heart of her, and that was why she loathed me so much. That was the unforgivable act.

She spat, "Don't you dare pity me."

But I did. Despite all she had done to me, despite all the suffering she had caused, I couldn't help but think of what she had done and why. I had seen a picture of her and her brother on her

329

Instagram; he looked like her but tiny, messy haired. He was gazing at her adoringly, and her arms were tight around him.

I didn't have to forgive her. I didn't even have to like her. But I would do this one thing, today: I would grant her the grace that she had never given to me.

"You can be more than your accounts," I said. "That's not all you have."

"Yes." Her voice broke. "It is."

I knew she believed it. Maybe that was the sum of all the lessons her mother and society had taught her. The lie she would tell herself when things went wrong. She would believe that it wasn't her fault; she hadn't gotten the grades she wanted because other students had somehow taken it, not because she had chosen not to study. She had done terrible things but for a good reason, so she wasn't a bad person. But the concrete of her choices was hardening around her feet the whole time, whether she realized it or not. That's why she couldn't move her path even as everything burned around her. *Mea culpa:* acknowledge the wrong.

Mitzi pivoted and left the cafeteria. I could almost see her walking through the years, at each key moment choosing to yield to peer pressure, being blown off course until she could no longer be seen. She had vanished.

Epilogue

BY THE END of the afternoon, all of Mitzi's social media accounts were down. But she immediately started a rebranding campaign and set up new ones. The last time I checked, a majority of her followers had happily trotted over to her new sites. Since these were clean and did not involve bots, there was little that we could do.

But Dawn left. And some of the VIPs did as well.

Mitzi's sponsors somehow found out about my pictures. When Mitzi got accused of racism, she laid all the blame, like a thick carpet, at Adeline's feet. Adeline was shell-shocked. She started getting huge waves of hate in her accounts, almost the same as the amount she used to dish out. After all her advertisers fled, she shut everything down.

I saw her, days later, crying. She never apologized to me.

Instead, she started a vicious campaign against Mitzi's new accounts. It was the last, feeble swipe against the untouchable monarch. But Adeline's reputation was already in tatters. It was, sadly, too easy for Mitzi to obliterate the rest of it. She made and posted interviews with Adeline's old victims, all discussing the dangers of cyberbullying. She made a new logo, a teal-colored M, which was supposed to symbolize kindness in social media.

Adeline went from isolated to completely shunned. But Peter came up to her one day and invited her to perform at Castle. I saw her one night, sitting at a table by the stage. She was lit by the edge of the spotlight, engrossed. Listening to what applause sounds like when it's not at someone's expense.

Mitzi's social media numbers continued to climb. No one seemed to notice that she had no close friends in any of her pictures. It was always only Mitzi and her followers. Just like she wanted.

I got an anonymous note slipped into my locker, a small slip of paper with two words on it: *I'm sorry.* I didn't know who it was from. Someone. Everyone.

I also saw this: Salma Hanif and Lorna Moore shyly eating lunch together. Ethan pulling a freshman into the gentle protection of the drama club after he was bullied in the locker room.

And one of Mitzi's former friends, the poet VIP, quietly asking a girl why she was crying. And listening to the answer.

I don't know how many other people chose to push past their reflexive judgment and to dig for golden complexity, even if it was sometimes difficult or messy. How many people would dash across the field and shield those under fire. Maybe only those few.

I knew that not everyone deserved forgiveness. But you can seek understanding without granting agreement or absolution. You can keep protesting. And on the days when you are too tired, when it seems unfair that it has to be you, again—on those days, perhaps there will be someone who will gently lift you up from your shredded knees, who will take the flag from your curled hands and hoist it for you. They will pull it across the cold air until you can see it, bright and unyielding, along the horizon.

Around us, the system churned. But I had hope.

And maybe that was enough.

A week after our final ClickComm, Griff, Peter, Will, Heidi, and I were in the cafeteria, eating our lunches together.

"So, our next project," Heidi said, "has got to be changing these school lunches."

"I don't know." Griff kissed my cheek and slid his tray in front of me. "I kind of have an affection for these fries."

"That's it?" Will called from across the table. "You're trying to charm her with fried potatoes?"

"Have I taught you nothing?" Heidi said. "You're going to have to do more than that."

"Is that right?" Griff was gazing at me.

I said, "Damn straight. There had better be some donuts involved, too."

He smiled and I tried to figure out why he looked so

different. Then I realized the slight tension that Griff normally had—the one he sometimes buried in snark or detachment—was gone.

"What?" he said.

I shook my head. "You just look—" *at peace*, I almost said, but then he leaned over and gently pressed his mouth to mine.

I finally let it loose, then, the balloon of happiness. I let it fill up and float over me. Griff and I clinked our cartons of milk together like champagne glasses.

"What a glorious day in the Republic of Plainstown, Mr. Griffin."

"Indeed, Ms. Chang," he said. "Indeed."

"You know, I think we should start thinking of bigger projects for the Nerd Net. Carlie tells me we can make a real impact on global warming—" Peter said.

"Us?" Will said. "Us personally? How? By farting less?"

"This is serious, William. We should be thinking of the world beyond ourselves and trying to make a larger impact. Maybe we could start something viral, but for the environment?"

Heidi shook her head, laughing. "Challenge accepted, Petey."

Will looked at her affectionately, then kissed her. "Fine. So we'll try to tackle climate change. Which is impossible, for the record. Listen, when the world ends because everything is now one hundred degrees and we are forced to live in little hot bubble colonies in Northern Canada, Livvy will write a history book about how things once were, right? You'll write about the good old days and the Nerd Net and how we tried to change the world?"

I nodded. On my backpack was my most treasured posses-
sion: a small red pin. I wondered if, somewhere, my grandfather
saw it. If he was proud.

I pictured small pockets of light, rebels shooting flares into
the sky, the country crisscrossed with a network of resistance.
Of people, who choose, every day, to take the hard path.

I looked at my friends, at the school.

And it would start

here.

Acknowledgments

TO MY BRILLIANT editor, Jen Ung: I am constantly in awe of you. I am so deeply grateful for what you saw in my book and what you helped it to become. Years ago, I read *American Panda* and it was the first time I had seen a Taiwanese American main character in fiction. Little did I know that, years later, I would have the honor of working with you. So many readers feel seen because of what you do every day. Thank you!

To my agent, Alex Slater, who has championed this book from the beginning: I knew from our first conversation that you understood the heart of this book and would be its most incredible advocate. Your unwavering support has meant so much to me. Thanks for being the Best Agent Ever™!

The writing journey is a long (and often solitary) one. But I was never alone thanks to my mom, dad, and brother; George's wonderful parents; Ariana, Camillia, Chris, Keralena, Kienan, Ivan, Phoebe, Rachel, and Sophia. Mom and Dad, you sacrificed so much so that I could have the opportunities that I have today. I love you so much! And to my brother: I truly won the sibling lottery with you. Thanks for always being the milk to my OJ.

To my ride-or-die CPs, C. H. Huang and P. J. Park: I absolutely could not have made it without you both. You were there for every one of my bazillion drafts, messy queries, and random, panicked questions about fried potatoes. Allison Singh, your incredible notes always make my writing better. Thank you as well to the following people who provided invaluable guidance, support, and feedback on this book and its path to publication: Susan Upton Douglass; Sher Lee; Yasmin Moorman; Sharon Song (thank you for the translations!); Carolyn Wang; Kathryn Williams; Reina M. Williams; CAPT S. W. Wong, JAGC, USN; and Lee Ming Yeh. Special thanks to Nicola DeRobertis-Theye and Salvatore Scibona, who held my hand through the whole harrowing querying, submission, and publishing process; and Daniel Sorbello (who is my unerring guide for selecting quality entertainment that we will both unironically love).

To my Nerd Net: Yuli Hsu, Matthew Kovach, Dr. Anne (Schmanne) Lyman, Captain Jason McLaughlin, Susan (Schmue) Murphy, Leslie Sullivan, and Salvatore and Daniel (yes, y'all are in here twice). And to 30J: Lisa C, Jenny B, Mike D (honorary member of 30J, forever), Chris H, and Amy S.

Eternal thanks to Mark Hickman, who made this debater

compete in poetry and changed her life. And to the other invaluable teachers who helped me to love and craft the written word, especially David and Linda Lackey, Josh Henkin, and Steve Schmidt.

Thank you to the incredible individuals at Quill Tree and HarperCollins, who all worked tirelessly to bring this book to life: Rosemary Brosnan, Lisa Calcasola, Tara Feehan, Jon Howard, Monique Vescia, Jean McGinley, Trish McGinley, Laura Mock, Suzanne Murphy, Andrea Pappenheimer and the Harper sales team, Laura Raps, Patty Rosati, Celina Sun, and Steffi Walthall.

And with infinite, shout-from-the-mountaintops love to my husband, George: you bought me gloves when my fingers got cold, built me a desk when I needed space to write, and made sure my dinners were more nutritious than cereal and milk. I share every word here with you, now and always

and

to my two fierce daughters—it has been a privilege watching you both grow up. You are in every part of my heart, which you make bigger every day. I know I had to spend many hours writing this book, but I hope that someday you will read this and know why. It was always for the both of you, all of it.